D1825014

Storm Portal

Storm Portal

Quantum Touch Book 1

Michael R. Stern

Copyright (C) 2017 Michael R. Stern
Layout design and Copyright (C) 2018 Creativia
Published 2018 by Creativia
Cover art by Cover Mint
This book is a work of fiction. Names, characters, places, and incidents
are the product of the author's imagination or are used fictitiously.
Any resemblance to actual events, locales, or persons, living or dead,
is purely coincidental.
All rights reserved. No part of this book may be reproduced or trans-
mitted in any form or by any means, electronic or mechanical, in-
cluding photocopying, recording, or by any information storage and
retrieval system, without the author's permission.

This book is dedicated to my wife, Linda,
whose generous spirit has allowed me to pursue
the truly enjoyable process of writing a story
that has bounced around my brain for a very long time.

Acknowledgements

Every writer relies on others. Most readers are happily unaware of all the steps that create the story they read. But there are people to thank for what you are about to read. First, to my family members who were my first critics, whose suggestions I hope have made me a better writer and the story more fun.

To my designer, Jack Parry, who has once again, created the cover which caught your eye.

To my editor, Amy Davis of Riverfog Writers Group, who has patiently showed me the world of words, and how they blend to show the story as I tell it.

I want to mention that for a writer to create dialogue from different generations, having the ear from another generation is critical for accuracy. I want to thank Sean Patrick Geraghty for lending me his.

I would like to give a shout-out and a special thanks to David Rosica, who at fifteen, read the first manuscript (in a day), and used a word no one likes to hear, "but." His intuition told him that if I changed the ending, I could keep the story going. I took his advice.

Another book you might like is:

Reflections on a Generous Generation, a story about a generation of Americans, born in the early twentieth century, who through the trials of deprivation and war, built the foundation of the greatest country in history.

Chapter One

ONCE I'D FOUGHT through the crowd inside the door, I saw why my students had frozen in a cluster. The desks had disappeared, and so had the walls and windows. All I could do was gape along with them. A massive forest of ancient trees surrounded us. Oaks and pines towered overhead, along with other trees I did and didn't recognize. Just beyond was a wide field pockmarked with muddy indentations. The blue-green linoleum floor had become earthen, soft. Bearded loblollies were crowned in morning mist. The sun trickled through the high canopy, our new window. The lingering pungency of sulphur invaded my nostrils in strange combination with the honey nectar of a clump of battered hyacinths. Gunpowder sweet.

We stood on a battleground. At the edge of the woods, a man with a neatly-trimmed gray beard, erect as the timber around him, looked out over the valley. He wore a Civil War uniform. A dress uniform. Confederate.

"Stay here, all of you. And be quiet." Slowly, I approached the man. My curiosity overcame my caution. The kids, surprised and a little scared, ignored my instruction and followed as a unit, marching about five feet behind. Carefully avoiding the twisted roots, I looked at the trees, their chipped bark, and the bullet holes. Water dripped onto my hair and face. *Tears,* I thought, *the universe mourning.* Movement in the valley below caught my eye. Next to tents, soldiers filled wagons. Each step through the misty damp brought me closer to the man. The snap of a branch diverted his attention. He turned his head, first to me, then beyond to the assemblage of young people at my rear. Not startled, he calmly matched me, step for step, coming closer, past the splintered, shattered tree trunks that encircled the clearing. Upturned roots reached out like tentacles.

Near enough now to count his embossed buttons, I realized I was facing General Robert E. Lee. I extended my hand, slowly so as not to alarm him, and said, "Pardon the intrusion, General. My name is Fritz Russell. These," gesturing behind me, "are my students." Lee looked harder, almost as if he hadn't really seen them there until that moment. "General, I'm not sure how we came to be here, and I hope we're not lost. Could you tell me where we are?"

The general took his time answering. He looked at the strangely dressed group of young men and women, not sure what to make of them. "Mr., uh, Russell? you said? Well Mr. Russell, this is the Appomattox Court House." His voice, commanding yet lilting, spoke from a time I thought I knew only from books and imagination.

Understanding becoming consciousness, I asked, "General Lee, what day is today?"

The wary general responded, "April tenth."

"1865?" I asked.

"Of course," said Lee, growing more puzzled, becoming impatient. My studies had told me that General Lee was not known to make rash decisions or to anger quickly, but we had surprised him, and I could see caution in his eyes. He was, after all, alone, unarmed, and unprotected. Yet he appeared to sense no danger.

"General, I am aware of what has happened here, and please forgive our disturbing your quiet time. You haven't had much lately, I know." General Lee nodded his appreciation. I gave him a nod and signaled the class to turn around and head back to the still visible classroom door, an outline seemingly imprinted against the scenic backdrop. Once the students had turned back, I turned toward Lee, planning to wave farewell, when he called out, "Mr. Russell, may I ask you a question?"

"Of course, General." I took a few steps back in his direction.

"You are all strangely attired. There are some young men among your students who should by rights be in uniform." He pointed to the kids. "Where is your school?"

"Sir, you studied engineering and scientific theories at West Point. I say that because I presume new discoveries would interest you." I paused, not sure if I should tell him, but how could I stop at that point? Tempting him, or maybe me, I answered, "General, my school is in New Jersey. But General, more important is that when we began our class today, the date was over 150 years in your future."

"You are of course trying to hoodwink me," said the general, his voice soft, but sharp. "I have important things to accomplish today, and I do not appreciate your wasting my time." He turned to leave, stepping carefully on the soft ground.

"It is difficult for me to accept, too, General Lee. It appears that, at least for the moment, the door to my classroom opens a pathway that allowed us to travel to the past."

Reversing his motion, he stared at me, silent except for the piercing blaze in his eyes as he considered this outlandish possibility. "Mr. Russell, after what I have seen for the past four years, I did not believe anything would ever again surprise me, but your presence and your proclamation are most certainly proving I can still be surprised. Astounded, even."

Chapter Two

A FEW DAYS EARLIER, we'd hit the court. Ashley wore his Edgar Allen Poe tee, one of the great-authors shirts he had accumulated. I had worn whatever was at the top of the drawer. Ash had on his expensive hightops; I wore my cut-the-grass best. Rain had been falling for the previous few days. We expected more; it was April.

We have our own rules, and we play for a buck a point. We play GIRAFFE—HORSE with two extra shots. I always need to be ahead by the time I get to the first F because Ashley's a sharpshooter from outside the three point line. He's also four inches taller. We both missed the second F, so he was shooting again.

"I want your money," he hissed at me as I badgered him to "shoot the ball, not the wise cracks." He smiled at me, shot, and missed again.

"You're getting old," I said. "Not to mention grumpy." Ashley, wise guy that he is, had once told me that RSVP meant *repartee, s'il vous plait* and that *reparte* is French for trash talk. I missed.

"Speaking of old, we should quit soon. I have too many papers to grade even to be here," he groused. I told him a war could end in the amount of time he talked between shots. I had white flags on my mind. His and the Confederacy's. I'd done one of my exercises in kid-shock earlier that day when I pointed out to my class that the Civil War continued for seven months after Lee surrendered. He missed again.

Ash can talk history with me, discuss Ulysses with anyone, and opine about baseball and football like a sports radio host. That is, he's right about what happens on the field no more often than he's ridiculous. He teaches creative writing, recites Shakespeare to his English classes, and doesn't bother to discard his slight New England accent when he says, "Wherefore art thou, Romeo." My shot rolled around the rim and out.

I had been here a year when I met Ash, who'd been assigned a room down my hallway. When I stopped in to welcome him, I should never have asked why he'd come to Riverboro. "To suffer the slings and arrows of outrageous fortune," he glared, "why else?" And then he laughed. We talked a lot in the few minutes between classes. I told him I had once planned to go to law school. "Me too," he said. But, he added, he had decided to work in the Teach for America program first. "Me too," I said.

"You should have seen my kids, Fritz. We put on a Shakespeare recital for the whole community. It sold out, even the SRO tickets." His poetic soul, I have learned, is hidden in a dense fabric of wisecrackery. I told him I had been assigned to New York City, which had come with one benefit. I met Linda there. When I finished my two years, I took the job in Riverboro because it felt comfortable. I wanted out of the big city but not to be too far away.

Riverboro's near Philadelphia and dates to the American Revolution. A volunteer tree commission keeps the old trees on every street healthy and safe and guarantees the perpetuation of summer shade and fall colors. Everyone tracks the fortunes of the high school teams. The town puts on a Halloween pageant, and Santa visits every Christmas on a fire truck. Last year, Ashley delivered the Declaration of Independence, in costume, to a Fourth of July crowd that was probably as large as the first one in 1776.

One of the things I like about Ashley is his quick grasp of so many ideas. He's especially good to have around in difficult situations. Hidden behind his humor and sarcasm is a very intelligent, analytic man. And he can tell a joke. Even playing basketball, we laugh a lot. Linda likes Ashley too. They talk about books and movies, politics and government policy, and cooking. Sometimes I just listen. She says he's "movie-star handsome."

He hit F; I missed again. He made his shot for E, a flowing jump shot that sailed through the hoop without a sound. GIRAFFE was done. I was down $2.00, and we began the sweat session. He's good, but I'm no pushover. Actually, he taught me. When we first started this ritual, he coached my footwork, showing me how to slide step, and he also taught me where to focus. This time he got the ball first. He faked right, took two steps to my left, spun, and took a sharpshooter jumper, his long hair flying. One to nothing. His second try was a left-handed layup, two slapping steps on the asphalt between bounces that splattered in small puddles, a sharp elbow to my shoulder, and it was two-zip.

He held the ball out to me, daring me to grab it. His brown eyes watched to see if I committed to his moves. My weight on my toes, I watched his chest, and as he slid left, I poked the ball away. Most of the time, I shoot long shots to keep him from blocking me. I lose money in the winter but make it back when we play golf. Before my turn, I gazed out over the athletic fields, their new green already muddy. The distinctive harmony of bat on ball turned my head. Batting practice. The boys' and girls' lacrosse teams ran up and down splattering watery dirt on their respective fields and shins. The track teams loosened up for their afternoon drills.

"Come on. Stop wasting time," said Ash. He had bent over to catch his breath, sweat already dripping from his face, his shirt sweat-soaked at the neck.

I searched the sky to see how much time we had left. Gathering clouds had turned black and looked ready to unload. The gusty wind whipped our sweaty shirts. "What's the hurry? You have a date?"

"Yeah. With twenty-seven hot … tenth grade essays." When he laughed, I slid by him and tossed a layup that went in. 2-1.

"Okay. Lucky shot. I wasn't paying attention."

Before my next shot, I glanced through the chain link and nodded to Ash. We had drawn a crowd of teachers and students. I hadn't heard them, but they were cheering. And laughing. When he was paying attention again, I dribbled the ball around, looking for an opening. When he put his hands down to block my fake, I shot a jumper that banged off the backboard and went in. 2-2. Still my shot. Not wasting time, I took one step forward. And the rain came. I put the ball down and headed for the door. Ash picked it up and shot. Swish. And he ran toward me. I held the door. Our shirts dripped as if we had been playing in a sauna.

Ash told me later lightning reached down, hit the school, and sent me flying. He said I floated about five feet through the air before I landed on my back like a slab of sidewalk. I hit my head. Hard. He said he tried to catch me, but he was too far, and I hit full force. "Splat," he told me later. He called 9-1-1. Our remaining spectators climbed the fence, but Ash was already at work. When he realized my heart had stopped, he pumped it for me. The EMTs arrived in about seven minutes, he said, and took over. One unpacked a defibrillator; the other gave me a shot of epinephrine in the chest. When they had me breathing on my own, Ash called Linda to tell her what had happened and that he'd meet her at the hospital.

Chapter Three

ABOUT A WEEK LATER, I felt well enough to return to work. But I wasn't sure I wanted to go back. "Lin at this point, I know this stuff blindfolded. I'm bored. I'm stale as two-day-old French bread. It's a treadmill."

"Do something about it," she counseled. "Stale bread can still become bread crumbs. Go back to school. Go to law school. You've always wanted to. Or write a book. You always say that the text misses the essence of history. Write one that captures it. I'll help."

I entered my classroom prepared to compete for a corner of my students' brains with my hand still bandaged and the aftermath of my hard landing still with me. The bruise on my chest reminded me that I was glad I was unconscious when the needle entered.

I love the elective course I teach twelfth graders; it's on the history of Americans at work. It lets me go over some basic economics and sociology and a lot of current events. The seniors are bright and ready to do battle. I never know what they'll come up with, and they keep me on my toes. *That's why I teach,* I thought that morning, overcoming my frustration-laced boredom. Still, I was tired and anxious. I reminded myself it was already Thursday. *Just get through today and tomorrow, and I'll have a chance to get things in order,* I remember thinking.

As I'd guessed, the students were both concerned and ready to distract me from the task at hand. Some looked sleepy; some like they had just been dry cleaned.

"Mr. Russell, what did it feel like?"

"Is your hand completely OK?"

"Are you ever going to play basketball again?"

I answered all the questions honestly, knowing that anything less would just lead to more questions. It was also the right thing to do. I asked how far they had gotten with the substitute teacher. Not far. To get to where they should be, I laid out the plan for the coming week. "Stop complaining," I said. "You could have avoided this if you had been more helpful with the subs. Also, you'll be having pop quizzes on the reading. So do it."

When the bell rang, clatter and chatter began as the class started to leave. Ashley checked on how I was doing. I told him I felt better, but I'd have a lot of grading to do given the extra homework. At least I knew what Day One Back would be like.

The only class that was less than sympathetic was my last—ninth graders tired and irritable at the end of the afternoon. They had made life miserable for the substitutes. More than most classes, this one tested constantly, always trying to see what they could get away with. Even with me, even this late in the school year. They are especially good at hiding their phones, which they are supposed to leave in their lockers. I told the class they would have quizzes if they didn't do the work and get caught up, and the grades would count. "You know what they say about payback time," I grinned when they moaned. As the day ended, and the much quieter ninth graders filed out, Ashley stopped in again to give me a ride home.

"Just about ready. Want to come for dinner?" I asked.

"You know I'd never turn down Linda's magic masterpiece, whatever it is, and besides, I'm starved." I phoned Linda to tell her. She told me she needed some stuff at the store, and I wrote down her list. At the supermarket, Ashley bought a chocolate cream pie for dessert.

"Funny, you don't look hungry," I said. Ashley loves to eat but never gains a pound. He doesn't cook much when he's by himself; he reads and munches. As we left the store, I called Linda to tell her we were on the way. She told me to hurry.

"Hi Ash. Put those things on the counter."

Depositing the bags on the no-longer-new granite, he asked what we were having that went with chocolate pie.

"Everything. Now set the table." She stirred in some of what we'd brought. "It needs to simmer."

Dinner was a treat for both of us, especially Ashley. It always is. Linda had made spicy chicken and pasta. She added garlic bread, and we left only the crumbs. We ate in the kitchen at our oversized hardwood table, the site of lots of conversation over the years. We've watched the seasons change in our garden from the large bay window and window seat. Linda asked how the day had gone. I told her I was a little tired. "And I have a little headache," I added, eliciting a glance. I never have headaches.

Ashley said, "Probably a storm coming."

After Ashley's chocolate cream pie and coffee, conversation turned to the school day. I told them that the kids had been predictable for once. They wanted to know what it was like to be hit by lightning. But I couldn't really answer. "It happened so fast, and I was out cold. All I really remember was holding the door for you."

"Then you don't remember that I was beating you," Ashley said. "Too bad." Then he told me I owed him three bucks. "My last shot was swish."

"Yeah, but I was standing by the door," I argued. "What do you mean, 'Too bad'?" We'd been tied when the lightning hit.

As we began to clean up, I noticed a package on the counter. Linda had gotten a new book to edit from the publisher she works for. There was also a pile for a project for her marketing class at Wharton. She was analyzing the bicycle industry and opportunities she could explore when she finished her MBA. Linda has always loved bikes: riding them, fixing them, and writing about them. Her time in Manhattan created her hatred for commuting, although she loved her part-time job at Bicycle Habitat. She likes being her own boss. Bikes and books. I call her a vocabularian. Masterful at choosing the exact word to fit a treasured phrase. She doesn't edit; she nurtures.

The first time she met Ashley, we'd gone to a Knicks-76ers game at Madison Square Garden. She cheered as loudly as he did. She'd gone to the gym to watch her brother play ball when they were in high school, and she knew her stuff. She, though, was a bike racer. Early on, she and I would go riding. But it wasn't the same for her with me trailing along.

Ashley began our ritual after-dinner discussion of the world. He'd read a story about oil companies trying to undermine negotiations in the Middle East. He also asked for Linda's recipe, 'though he rarely cooks. I think he takes the directions home, hoping someday he'll try them out on someone. Evening was passing, and after a few laugh-filled stories, Linda told Ash it was time for him leave. "I'll pick you up in the a.m.," he said.

"Sure, thanks, see you then," I yawned.

Linda stared at the door Ash had just closed. "I'm worried about him."

PERFECTLY FITTED white dinner jacket, red carnation bouton-niere, his prom night had begun perfectly. Pulling the wrist corsage from the fridge ... how could she leave with another guy ... who was that guy ... didn't know she was leaving, but she didn't come back with the gaggle gone to the girls' room ... Mom said, "There's more than one fish in the sea." ... But she wasn't a fish.

Ashley laid the book down, glanced at his watch, and went to bed. He had to be at work in four hours.

Chapter Four

I WAS WORRYING about how Friday would unfold when I heard Ash honk. I felt wobbly as I walked under the ancient maple, which was still dripping from overnight rain. It must have shown because when I got in the car, Ashley had ruts between his eyebrows, his concerned look. I told him I still had a headache.

"You could take the day off, you know."

"No. It's Friday, so I'll have the weekend to gather steam." I closed the door gently because Ash babies his car. "I'll be ready by Monday."

Twigs rocked like a miniature armada in the parking lot's puddles, reflecting the turbulence above. A gust of wind overturned a trash can and sent its contents our way. We hurried inside. Ashley went to his class; I went to the principal's office. When George McAllister came out to the anteroom, he asked, "How are you feeling, Fritz?"

"Not as good as I'd like, still have a slight headache. George, I just wanted to talk about half-days. Is that possible until I get up to speed?"

"Today?" George asked. I think *irritated* is his middle name.

"I don't know. I'll try to get through today. I was just checking if you had been serious yesterday, in case I'm still shaky on Monday."

"Well, let me know as soon as you can." He has a quiet bark.

"Okay. Thanks." I headed for my classroom. On the way, I passed Walt Houston, who said, "Fritz, you don't look too good" and Helen Green, who asked, "Are you feeling okay?"

Do I look that bad? I wondered. I stopped in the boys' bathroom and looked in the mirror to see if I could see what they were seeing. What I saw looked pretty normal to me, but with hairs beginning to cover my ears, I knew it was time to visit the barber.

"When you're that good-looking, anything less is bound to be bad" came from the corner. Joe Rosenberg, the chem teacher, had a paper towel crumpled in his hand.

"Thanks Joe," I said. "Glad you've learned to read minds. Seriously, do I look sick to you?"

"You look tired, but that's chronic with teachers." He tossed the towel in the trash. "I've been tired for ten years." Checking his watch, he headed out the door, and I followed.

As first period began, it was raining again, with thunder and lightning as complements. "Settle down, everyone." I knew I wasn't on top of my game. At the crack of thunder, I looked at the drops tapping on the window and said softly, "April showers."

Voices through the class responded, "bring May flowers."

I turned to them and asked, "And what do May flowers bring?"

"Pilgrims!"

I thought, *Pavlov was right.* Smiling at them, I knew they were on top of theirs.

"Let's talk about your homework. Who didn't do the reading?" Bill Carlson's hand went up. "Any excuses?" I asked.

"No," said Bill, shaking his head.

"Not even a little one?"

"Nope."

Before my accident, we had been talking about the changes taking place in Europe, especially Germany, in the 1870s. I asked the class how far they had gotten. The First World War, someone said. So I asked how the war started. No hands, dead silence. "Okay, choose sides. World War I baseball. Bill, pitch. Janet, you're one captain and," looking for the least enthusiastic face, "Louise, you're the other one. I'm the umpire."

As the class split up, the kids moved the desks to create our diamond, and I extracted a paper-clipped, dog-eared sheaf of questions from my desk. Bill took the list. I sat just behind him. "Batter up," I announced.

Up stepped Janet. Teachers aren't supposed to have favorites, but she's special: attentive, inquisitive, and kind to everyone. And polite. "May I have a single, please?"

"Whose assassination started the war?" Bill asked.

"Archduke ... I know it starts with an *F*. Freddy?"

"I'm calling that a foul ball," I said. I asked myself later if I'd been playing favorites. "Give her a new question, Bill."

"OK, Mr. R. Which general commanded the U.S. Army?"

"General Pershing."

"Take first base," I said. I'm a great umpire. She went to the first-base desk.

"Next batter." Up stepped Dana Goldsense. "Double, please."

Bill asked, "What was the American military force in France called?"

"The army?" Dana offered.

I said, "Wrong. American Expeditionary Force. You're out. Next batter." Louise's team cheered.

The next batter was Steven Chew. "Single, please."

Bill asked, "Who was the president of the United States during WWI?"

"Franklin D. Roosevelt," said Steven.

"Are you all reading ahead?" I asked, shaking my head. "Wrong war. Woodrow Wilson. You're out. Two down. Next batter." Steven frowned.

Harry James was next up. "Triple please."

"Trying to drive in a run, Mr. James?" When we play baseball, I also offer both play-by-play and color commentary.

Bill found the list of triples and asked, "What future U.S. president was an artillery officer in WWI?"

"Eisenhower?"

"Nope, he was in charge of training the army's tank corps. Never left the country. The answer is Harry Truman. You're out. That's three outs. Louise's team is up."

The first batter for Louise's team was Dylan Lake. "Home run." Dylan is a sponge. I think he hears every word I say and remembers them all.

"Swinging for the fences," I said. Dylan took a fake swing.

Bill's next pitch, "Who were the primary signers of the Treaty of Versailles?"

"England, France, Germany, and the United States," said Dylan without a hesitation.

Bill looked back at me. "Hmm, that's technically right, but we were looking for Lloyd George, Clemenceau, Woodrow Wilson, and the German, Mueller. Umpire huddle."

I leaned over to Bill. "Home run?"

"I think so, Mr. R," said Bill.

"Home run." His team cheered as Dylan touched each of the desks, his other arm raised above his head in celebration.

Next was Vicki Ann Brothers. "Single, please."

"When the war was over, what did people call the last day?"

"Susan," shouted Harry James. We all laughed.

"Wrong." Harry was still laughing. "Besides your team's not up. So you guys only get two outs next at bat." Dana punched Harry on the arm.

"Ouch," he grumbled.

"Your answer, Vicki Ann?"

"Decoration Day?"

"You are all warriors," I said, "but for the wrong wars. Armistice Day. You're out. Next batter."

Sherry Steinberg asked for a double.

"What country quit fighting WWI?"

Sherry hesitated. "All of them?"

"Good answer but wrong. The Russians actually left the war in 1916 at the beginning of the Russian Revolution. The rest didn't quit but surrendered. Or won. You're out, Sherry, but like I said, smart answer." Sherry went to the back of the line, but smiling.

"Thanks, Mr. R," she said.

The next batter was Johnny Autumn.

"Single," Johnny said.

"What rank was Adolf Hitler in the German army during WWI?" asked Bill.

"He was a private."

"That's three outs. He was a corporal."

The game continued through a couple more at bats for both teams. When the bell rang, the score remained 1-0. Louise's team won. The kids put the desks back.

With a bright flash of lightning and a sharp crack overhead, the classroom briefly looked like a Phillies night game. I walked out and let the door close. Ashley was outside his classroom, two doors down on the opposite side of the hall. I waved and opened up for the next class.

"How's it going," Ashley called.

"Easy, played baseball," I answered.

Ashley said, "Isn't it great to have a trick up your sleeve for those bad days?"

"Yup. Wanna come for dinner? I'll call home."

"Sure," he said.

As my next class started to enter, I waved to Ash. Going through the door, I thought about how the room exuded boredom. Straight rows of desks, walls painted what you might call *institutional blah*. Sometimes that's how I feel. I keep two maps hanging on the front wall: the U.S. and the world. And I still use the blackboard and chalk, which helps keep everyone awake. Four large windows look out onto the school's semi-circular driveway and main entrance. The kids watch the cars and the weather. I watch the sky.

My second period class is Twentieth-Century World History, all seniors. *Good,* I thought, *the Sixties.* The class entered with more than the usual chatter. They had spring fever and senioritis.

"OK, class. We didn't do anything yesterday. Let's get caught up, okay? Where did the substitute leave off?"

Melissa Nicholas raised her hand and said, "Kennedy's assassination" before I could call on her.

"And did you all do the reading?" Heads shook yes, and hands went up. "Everyone? You suddenly start to do your homework while I'm out?"

"The sub scared us," said Marjorie Cousins.

"I'll have to try that," I grinned. "Okay, let's back up a bit. What about 1963 was most important beyond the president's assassination?"

The first hand up was Susan Adams's. "Mr. R, I don't think there was only one thing. The Civil Rights Movement was very active, but there were a lot of events that mattered."

"Which ones did you have in mind, Susan?"

"Well, President Kennedy signed the Equal Pay Act, you know equal pay for equal work, but that's still an issue, Mr. R. Why do women still get paid less if there's a law?"

"Susan, that's a good question. I don't know the answer. But here are some of the pieces. For one thing, many jobs aren't covered by federal law. Also, most employers don't post their pay scales publically. They offer a job and wage, and if someone accepts it, that's what it is for that person. But studies show that women don't bargain as hard. Maybe they expect to be shot down, and bosses prefer to save a dollar rather than offer them as much as the men. But we all know that pay discrimination is still with us. Even today, women make only seventy-five percent of what men are paid for the same job." Three girls and two boys booed. "That's a government statistic. Thanks for asking, Susan. Maybe we'll have a chance to discuss it more. Back to 1963. What happened in the Civil Rights Movement?"

Walt Bridges raised his hand. "March on Washington, Mr. R."

"What about it, Walt?"

"Every year there's something about it on the news. Thousands of people went to Washington to protest discrimination. And Martin Luther King gave his big speech at the Lincoln Memorial."

"Have you all heard Dr. King's 'I Have a Dream' speech?" I looked around at mostly blank faces. "No one?"

Peter Panzoni raised his hand. "I've heard parts of it, Mr. R. Lots of us have. But it happened more than fifty years ago. Why does it matter today?"

"Does anyone want to answer Peter's question?" I looked around for volunteers, and some kids looked almost ready. I waited.

Dick Powers spoke up. "Mr. R, first of all, I read somewhere that it was one of the greatest speeches in American history. And it affected lots of people. But I think it matters now because there's still discrimination. Maybe not like the fire hoses and police dogs in Alabama back then, but what about with Hispanics and most immigrants. And gay people. And Native Americans. That speech was about all men are created equal, including women."

"Good, Dick. Did you forget African Americans? The issue is still with us, isn't it?"

"Sorry, Mr. R. I didn't forget. African Americans too."

"Can someone tell me how we know that we are still waiting for Dr. King's dream to come true?" I could tell this was a difficult discussion for these mostly middle-class kids, almost all of whom were white.

Susan raised her hand. I nodded to her to go ahead. "Mr. R, African Americans make less money than white people. They have higher unemployment rates. Fewer of them finish high school. It seems every time there's a bad statistic, minorities lead the bad things."

"Good answer, Susan. Class, we don't have enough time today to discuss all the issues you've brought up. But I want you to think about what makes your freedom so special and which of YOUR freedoms other people shouldn't have." There was a murmur, an undercurrent at my loaded question. "In 1963, President Kennedy also gave a speech on civil rights. He said we should all want the equality for everyone that we want for ourselves. His speech was two months before Dr. King's. In 1963, another speech, by Governor George Wallace…"

Susan interrupted. "He's the one who stood in the doorway to keep students from entering the college, wasn't he, Mr. R?"

"He was, and in his inauguration speech, he said, 'Segregation now, segregation tomorrow, segregation forever.' That was the world then, and that was the context when President Kennedy proposed a federal law to end discrimination in public accommodations, like hotels and restaurants. The Justice Department began to play a bigger role in lawsuits to make sure it happened. He also talked about desegregating public schools and protecting voting rights. Does any of this sound familiar? Class, I'm not going to preach about this. But for homework, I want you all to read President Kennedy's Civil Rights address and Dr. King's 'I Have a Dream' speech. There's video of both on the class website. Watch them. Pay attention to how they frame the issues and the rhetoric. We'll talk more about all this next week."

Josh Martin raised his hand. "Mr. Russell, the civil rights stuff was a big part of 1963, but it wasn't the most important thing." He was up to something. I watched as heads turned toward him. He had rascal all over his face. "The most important thing was the Beatles." Some of the class laughed, but Susan said, "Don't be ridiculous, Josh."

Josh pressed his point, that the Beatles initiated social change for a generation, and I let him go. When I want the class engaged, I call on him. The fun part is that he doesn't always believe what he says. You can imagine what that can start. I had a feeling today was one of those times. Josh argued that not only music changed but that the Beatles started a youth revolution in hair styles, clothing, even morality.

"The Beatles might have been important, Josh. But no one was shot because their hair was too long," Susan retorted. "The Beatles were fun for middle-class teenagers. The Civil Rights Movement brought discrimination against African Americans to the whole country's attention. It changed the way we all live."

He laughed at her. "And the Civil Rights Movement is still trying to get civil rights. The Beatles are still popular forty years after they stopped making music. So which was more successful?"

"Oh, Josh, be serious."

"Why?"

"Okay, okay, thank you both. Is there anything else?"

"Mr. Russell," said Susan, while Josh's antenna were raised, "my grandmother told me about Kennedy's assassination and said that it changed her generation's view of government. She said that before he was killed, there was a lot of hope in the country, but it was like when he died, the country started to wonder about all the things government did wrong. Like the Viet Nam war."

Susan plays counterpoint to Josh regardless of the topic. I think they like each other. Before class time ran out, I thanked them for their thinking and then reminded everyone that 1963 had been a very important year. I listed a few other events for them to think about. I asked them to consider the aftermath of Kennedy's assassination. "Do you think the Civil Rights Act would have passed if Kennedy hadn't been killed?"

I mentioned the murder of Medgar Evers, the church bombing and protests in Birmingham, and Dr. King's *Letter from a Birmingham Jail.* I reminded them that in eleventh grade, they had studied civil disobedience and Henry David Thoreau, who inspired Dr. King and Gandhi. I also mentioned the introduction of zip codes and instant replay. There was the Nuclear Test Ban Treaty, which ended above-ground nuclear testing, the Supreme Court's forbidding prayer in public schools, and the Court's ruling in *Gideon v. Wainwright* that anyone charged with a crime who couldn't afford a lawyer had to be given one. And finally, I reminded them that we were at war in Vietnam.

"Hey Mr. R," Josh said. "You should teach a course about just 1963."

An extended lightning flash lit the room, and the thunder boomed as class ended. "You have your homework assignment. Take notes." Lightning flashed again, and a sharp pain coursed through my head. When the bell sounded, I walked to the door to let the kids go. Grabbing the knob on the outside to hold the door open, I got a shock and let go. Standing in front of the door, I rubbed my head. Ashley came down to see if I was all right.

"Yeah, but that last flash felt as if I'd put my brain in a socket." I shook my head like a dog shaking off the rain. "I'm fine," I said looking up at Ashley.

"I'm not so sure about that." His ruts were back. The next period was about to start, though, and he just said, "See you later."

My next class was waiting in the hall because I was blocking the way. I apologized and then got another shock when I touched the knob. I opened the door, propped it open with my right foot, and stared at my hand. The bell rang, and I headed inside.

Chapter Five

THIS IS CRAZY, or is it me? Time travel is real. I, we, did it. His eyes are brown, not blue. How did it happen? Look at these kids, as comfortable with General Lee as they are with each other. If we get back, can we go again, somewhere else? I've seen black and white pictures, but to see him as he really looked. Looks. Wow. His uniform more light blue than gray. So that's what cadet gray looks like. Even the braid is gold, woven to the sleeves, not like Hollywood yellow.

But his eyes more than everything, not the blue I had read some-where, but brown. Sharp, yet sad. Piercing and aware. He's a little taller than me. And he seems at ease with us, even glad to talk to the kids. I can't believe this. I'm talking to Robert E. Lee. This is amazing. I'd really like to spend some time with him, but is it safe here for the kids? Can we get back? He looks tired, but maybe willing to talk? I can hope. Those thoughts ran through my head when I'd first realized who the man on the hilltop was. I wanted a chance to think about the rest of our conversation, but I needed more time. *Maybe at dinner.*

"SIR, PERHAPS I can prove my claim to you." Lee gestured for me to continue. I had ID in my wallet, so I handed my driver's license to him.

"I see your likeness. It is different from the pictures we see in our newspapers, and your picture has color, matching your own. But there is nothing else here."

I looked at the license. He was right. No address, no date of birth. So I pulled other identification from my wallet—my Social Security card, credit cards, health insurance card, auto registration. None had dates, and dates could have verified what I'd told the general. Or convinced him I had invested mightily in a very peculiar joke. I was confused. My final thought, my final chance, was to reach into my pants pockets; I knew I had started the day with money in my pocket. I withdrew blank pieces of paper. Perplexed, I handed General Lee the items from my wallet. Lee looked them over, but didn't know what they were.

"These are things I have never seen, but they don't explain anything. What is an auto driver license?"

"General, I don't know how much time we have together, but if you can spare some, and if we could speak openly, my class may be able to convince you. I thought these items would help, but I was mistaken."

Lee said, "Like you, Mr. Russell, I have little time I can count on. You are aware there is a war going on?"

"Yes, General, but General Johnston will surrender to General Sherman on April 26, and in November of this year, your ship, the *Shenandoah* will offer the final surrender."

Lee again stared at me, his eyes wide, losing patience, more than skeptical. "That is preposterous. You are guessing, sir. No one can know for sure what is happening in the other theaters of this infernal conflict." Yet I sensed he was curious.

"I understand your skepticism, General, but perhaps there are other ways for me to prove it to you? May I bring my students back?" When Lee nodded yes, I waved the class back. When they were all gathered and quiet, I said, "Boys and girls, may I present to you, General Robert E. Lee, Commander of the Army of Northern Virginia of the Confederate States of America."

In spite of the shocked and doubtful looks on their faces, and the general's own uncertainty, Lee smiled and said gently, "It is a pleasure to meet y'all."

I explained that we had discussed my lack of money and the missing name or address on my identification. Dan Wilkinson raised his hand. "Mr. Russell, we have our textbooks." I took one and opened to a random page. Looking at the page upside down, Dan said, "Wow! The pages are blank." I asked the kids to see if they had anything written in any of their books. Reaching into her book bag, Carol Murray took out her laptop.

The general observed all the activity and spotting the computer, asked, "Young lady, what is that?"

"It's called a computer, General," I said as I followed his glance to Carol. "It is one of our primary means of communication. Turn it on, Carol." She did, and the battery was working. "Carol, see if you can find anything on the Civil War." She clicked on Know It All, her browser, but a message appeared, "No Connection." When I saw that, I told her, "Open a new word doc. Type something. Let's show the general something of how it works. Can you open pictures?"

Another girl, Pat Leslie, said, "Mr. Russell, I have my cell phone." I was oddly thankful she'd brought it with her.

"Pat, would you bring it here, please?" I looked at my watch, knowing that the period would be ending soon but not sure what would happen then.

Lee asked, "Mr. Russell, what is that on your arm?"

"We call it a wristwatch, General. It is a timepiece."

"May I look at it?" I slid the expandable band and handed it to Lee, who removed his own watch from his pocket to compare. I was grateful to have refused to buy a digital model. "How do you wind it?" asked Lee.

I wasn't sure how to answer. I said, "It's run by a battery, General."

"I am familiar with those. The battery was invented by Mr. Benjamin Franklin and then improved to create electric current. We have those batteries now, but I believe they only function in liquid and need a sizable container." Knowing he would be surprised again, I removed the battery, a thin metal disk, and placed it in his hand. "This is quite amazing. Do you have other uses for batteries?" he asked.

I took Pat's cell phone. "General, this device allows people to speak to each other. Over long distances."

"Ah, like a speaking trumpet. I can speak to those men across that field. Sometimes hearing is difficult if the wind is up, but if they are closer it is quite acceptable, even when there is wind."

"General, this device allows us to speak to someone in California, or Europe, or even farther distances, regardless of the weather. And we can hear their response."

"If that is true, could you show me?" Lee asked.

"I'm sorry, sir, but the transmitters we need haven't been created yet." I handed the phone back to Pat.

Lee asked, "And that operates with a battery?" Pat removed the battery and handed it to Lee. The general passed it from hand to hand, held it between his index finger and thumb. "As confounding as this is, clearly you do not live near here, and perhaps are not from this time." He lowered his eyebrows and sucked in his lips, at least that's what it looked like. He was thinking, I think. "Quite interesting, I must say."

"Mr. Russell," said Carol, "I have some pictures, and I've typed a note about what's happening here."

"Thanks, Carol. Would you show them to General Lee?"

Carol walked over and offered him the laptop, saying, "If you'd like to hold it, sir…" He sat on a tree stump, and she knelt next to him. She tapped keys to move through her photo album. Lee looked at the pictures and then at Carol. He asked her if he could try. "Sure, General. Go ahead." As though he were touching a baby, General Lee tapped the keys as he had seen her do. He smiled and looked at me. "Battery?" he asked.

"Battery."

His curiosity overcame his reticence. "Mr. Russell, sir, why don't you sit down. It seems we may have a reason to talk for a bit more."

"Thank you, General. Class, sit!" The class crowded in close to the tree stumps where their teacher and their surprised host were sitting and found spots on the ground. The trees around us were bent, as if they were listening to this most unlikely conversation.

"Yuck" came from Jason James as he placed his hand on the undergrowth. Everyone looked at him, and he held up his hand. General Lee told us that there had been fighting there early the day before and handed his handkerchief to Jason.

"No thanks, General," said Jason.

"Please," said the general. "Those were my boys. It's all right."

"Okay, thanks," said Jason, reluctantly taking it and wiping his hand. He handed it back, muddy and marked with dried blood. The general's eyes blinked, and he looked down briefly, sighing, as he placed the handkerchief in his coat pocket.

A hand went up. "General, did you know George Washington?" asked Lauren Clinton. For the first time, the general chuckled. "I am sorry, young lady, but General Washington died before I was born. Although our families have been close for generations."

I asked General Lee if he would permit a few questions. Lee said, "As long as you don't tell me more about the near future, I'll answer what I can. But first, would you tell me about driving? Why is it necessary to have a license to drive cattle where you come from?"

I thought a moment. "Briefly, General, a variety of powered vehicles were, I mean will be, built later in this century. You are familiar with the internal combustion engine?"

Lee nodded, "I have seen schematics but nothing in operation, other than trains."

"Well, sir, a product called gasoline, is, um, will be, refined, from oil. It is highly combustible, and we have used it for more than a century to power vehicles. Take your wagons, as an example, General. Imagine if they were motorized instead of being drawn by horses or oxen. They might go ten miles per hour instead of ten miles in a day, and they could carry heavier loads." A breeze blew through the clearing, spraying us with day-old rain.

While the class did its best to dry off, Lee continued my thoughts, "Our tactics would have changed, certainly." He stroked his beard as he listened.

"Now General, picture that same vehicle traveling the seventy-five miles from Richmond to Appomattox in an hour.

"You can do that?" asked Lee.

"And faster, General." Lee sat up straight, once again shaking his head, amazed. "We have vehicles that can go over 400 miles per hour. Not sustained speed, but that is the land-speed record. Of course, not on roads like those." I pointed to the rutted, muddy trails off to our left.

"Land-speed record? Can you go very fast on water also?" At this, the students and I grinned at each other.

"Tell him, Mr. R," said Clayton Waters.

I told the general about airplanes, the Wright Brothers, Lucky Lindy, planes used in warfare, and that in 1969, Neil Armstrong would be the first man to walk on the moon. Abruptly, Lee stood up. "Now, sir, you have exceeded your believability!"

"It's true, General," said Marty Rose, jumping up. "My dad's a pilot in the Air Force. I have a picture of him with a plane here." Marty handed the photo to Lee, who looked at the picture, back to Marty, again at the picture, and sat back down. *The picture was there, the computer had pictures, why were the pages blank, and my ID?*

Turning to me, the general asked, "Air Force?"

"General, there will be an entire branch of the military devoted to flying airplanes, which is what we call them. Our Navy has ships that are large enough for a plane to land on. Even though they are from my own time, I find that remarkable."

"Mr. Russell, I think that would be quite an understatement."

At that moment, a bell rang clearly. The sound was muffled, as if it were far off. I told the general that the chime signaled the end of the class.

The kids had started to get up. "Kids, stay here. General, I'm not sure what is about to happen, but if you are willing, I have another group heading in, and I think they would benefit from our conversation."

Lee waved to bring them in but asked, "Where are they coming from?" I pointed, went to the outlined opening and, without leaving the grass, held the door open. One by one, the next class came in and looked around. I told them to follow me. When we reached the clearing, I said, "All of you take a seat. General, this is my next class. Class, it is my honor to introduce General Robert E. Lee."

"Right," said Johnny Clayton. His deep voice resonated. Slim and muscular, Johnny can be imposing, especially on the football field.

Dan Wilkinson said, "It is, Johnny, so shut up." He's shy but gritty. Dan and Johnny are good friends.

"You shut up," Johnny shot back.

"That's enough. Sorry, General. They are likely as skeptical as you."

"I can understand," said Lee, nodding his head.

"Fourth-period students, General Lee and the third-period class have been discussing some of our inventions. We were about to ask the general some questions. Just so you know, today is April 10, 1865, and we are at Appomattox. Third period, I will give you all excuses for your other teachers." *I'll have to figure out what I'm going to tell them.*

I heard soft knocking in the background and looked up to see Ashley peering through the window of the outlined door. *He never knocks,* I thought. *I wonder what he sees.* I turned and said, "General, yesterday you met with General Grant and surrendered the Army of Northern Virginia." Lee scrutinized me. His expression registered his surprise at how much I seemed to know. He sighed and nodded yes. "Are you at all relieved the war is basically over?"

Lee marshaled his emotions and replied thoughtfully, "Mr. Russell, I am exceeding glad to end these hostilities. My boys fought well, but there have been fewer and fewer of us over these past years." He spoke with a soft accent, adding "and the Union seems to have endless amounts of men and armament, food and supplies. For the past week, my soldiers have been living on fried bread and toasted corn, if they can find it. In fact, right now, General Grant's men are provisioning all of my boys in the field." Lee pointed across the valley, which the fourth-period class only then noticed.

Jack Massa asked, "General, don't you know General Grant?"

"I have known him in many ways, young man. We have faced each other in the field for these past many months. I fought with him in Mexico, although we served in different units. We met briefly yesterday, and truth be told, I didn't have a clear memory of having seen him before. He spoke a bit about those times. But I was not there to reminisce. Frankly, when I arrived, I was unsure how I would be received. I was, after all, the losing general and would be viewed as a traitor by many."

"Were you? A traitor, I mean?" asked Sean Little.

"I was an officer in the United States Army until 1861 and was offered command of the Union army by Mr. Lincoln. But I am a Virginian, young man, and when the Virginia legislature voted to secede, I believed it my sad duty to follow my fellow Virginians into the Confederacy. Am I a traitor?" He watched a flock of birds leaving the treetops. "I suppose I am," he said, stroking his beard.

Bob Bee asked, "How do you feel now?"

"Now? I feel tired and dispirited. I have been away from home for a long time. It is my ardent hope that this war will truly end soon and that the Union will be re-established. I have heard that Mr. Lincoln has spoken of reconciliation. I will do all I can to help that happen."

"Excuse me, General, but didn't you own slaves?" asked Matt Christopher. Sorrow again visited Lee's face. He said, "It does return as always to our peculiar institution, doesn't it?" It seemed almost like he was talking to himself. "At one time, my family did own slaves. But I released them years ago, before this war."

"But I don't understand. That's what the war was all about," said Cheryl See. "If you didn't own slaves, why did you fight to hold on to slavery?"

Addressing Cheryl and then scanning the intent, upturned faces, Lee said, "This war was also about allowing people to live without the government in Washington giving orders to the states. Even Mr. Lincoln said if he could keep the Union together without freeing the slaves, he would do that."

"But General," said Eric Silver, "he freed the slaves."

"He did that, but only when this war has ended will we truly determine the outcome. I believe slavery to be wrong, but what will these people do if they don't have the homes and food they received before? Where will they go? We will see if Mr. Lincoln has done more good than harm."

"What will you do now, General?" asked David Jewels. David's freckles bounced on his cheeks, his messy, blond head keeping step with each word.

"I will return to my family and my home. But first I must return to Richmond to speak with President Davis about ending the hostilities and reuniting our country. He will not be happy. A number of my men have offered to continue the fight, a guerrilla war from the hills. I hope I have convinced them otherwise. I hope Mr. Lincoln will soon complete what we began yesterday."

"But Lincoln was assassinated," exclaimed Amanda Lesetto. The class grew silent. Lee's jaw dropped; a sharp breath joined a mournful stare at Amanda.

"Sorry General," I said. "Amanda, we were not going to mention the near future."

Lee asked, "Is this true?"

"General, do you really want to know?"

"Now that the subject has been opened, please."

With a chest-heaving sigh, I told him that in four days, President and Mrs. Lincoln would go to Ford's Theater in Washington to see "Our American Cousin" and that the president would be shot by an actor, John Wilkes Booth, who hated that Lincoln had defeated his beloved South and was even talking about allowing the former slaves to vote one day. I added that attempts by his fellow conspirators to kill Vice President Johnson, Secretary Seward, and Secretary Stanton would fail, but the president would die the next morning.

"Then we of the South cannot look forward to what I had hoped would be a congenial reconciliation of this nation. It is a sad day now for many reasons—for all of us." The general stood and looked toward the valley and away from us.

A new question came from Johnny Clayton. "General, what was the worst battle, do you think?"

With his thumb and forefinger, Lee stroked his mustache. Turning back to us, he said, "At Gettysburg, I think I made a mistake, and a costly one it was. Too many were lost there, on both sides. So many of my best commanders. If only General Stuart had been nearby, perhaps the outcome might have been different. We fought at Sharpsburg in Maryland; some call it Antietam for the creek that runs through the field. We fought at Fredericksburg. We fought in the Shenandoah. I think the hardest loss for me was at Chancellorsville, when General Thomas Jackson fell." He hung his head.

Eric Silver asked, "Do you mean Stonewall, sir?"

"Yes, his men called him that and named their brigade the *Stonewall*." He had looked up at Eric's question. "I felt as though I had lost my right arm when he died."

"General, what does the E stand for?" asked Pat. "You know, Robert E. Lee;" she emphasized the general's middle initial.

"Ah, yes," he said. "Well, the E stands for Edward. But why do you know my name that way? Of course, these days I'm known as General Lee," a playful twinkle in his eyes. "But most people I know have called me only Robert Lee."

"General, historians refer to you using your initial," I said. "It has a sort of melodic sound—Robert E. Lee."

Lee smiled. "You know, Mr. Russell, I, too, have worked with students. I held the post of superintendent of the Military Academy at West Point, which is also my alma mater, as you appear to know."

From the trees, a horse whinnied. Walking toward us was a horse, gray with a black mane and long black tail, and a soldier. "Old Traveller, my horse, is always ready to tell me when I need to pay attention to the needs of the moment," said the general.

The scene surprised and confused the approaching soldier. Walking up to Lee, he whispered, "General, I've been worried. You've been gone for two hours." He peered at us, curious.

Lee waved toward us. "I would like to introduce Colonel Walter Taylor, my adjutant and close confidant throughout these years of war. Colonel, this is Mr. Russell and his students from New Jersey. I will tell you about them later." Turning to the class again, he said, "Mr. Russell, young people, it seems my time with you is over. Our conversation has been very enlightening for me, I assure you."

"General Lee, it has been our pleasure and honor to have met you. Thank you for your time."

Various members of the classes offered thanks in a variety of ways. David Jewels said, "See ya, General."

The general cocked his head. "I wonder." At that, he and Colonel Taylor headed back into the woods, and we left the clearing, squishing toward the door. Suddenly, our shadows danced in the newly arrived sunlight.

The bell rang. I opened the door, and as I stepped through ahead of them, Dan Wilkinson, his textbook open, said, "Mr. R, take a look at this. The words are back."

Chapter Six

AS THE KIDS LEFT, Ashley scurried down the hallway and through the crowd of book bags. "Where have you been?" he asked.

Johnny Clayton overheard and answered for me. "Mr. Gilbert, you gotta go in there and see. It's really cool. We just met Robert E. Lee. Mr. R, how did you do that?" Ashley glanced at Johnny, bemused, and turned to me. So, I guessed, he hadn't seen much when he looked in.

"I looked for you after last period. Your room was empty."

"I saw you look in the window. Dinner will be the most interesting meal you'll have this week, I promise. I'll tell you later."

"Tell me what?"

"You're not going to believe this. I'm not sure I do."

"WHAT are you talking about?" He sounded exasperated. He didn't understand. I knew I didn't.

"Too much to tell. Later." Looking through the window, I said, "Room looks like it always does."

Ashley asked, "And you were expecting something different? What did Johnny mean about meeting Robert E. Lee?"

"Ash, I really don't know what happened, but, yeah, we met Robert E. Lee on the day after he surrendered. I'll tell you the whole story, but later. I have to get through the rest of the day first."

As Ash walked away, I twisted the doorknob, again feeling a tingle. I stepped through and saw a large building with a Ford sign across the top. Before I could see more, a club rushed my vision, collided with my cheek, and knocked me backwards. I hit the floor with a groan, and Ashley ran back to help me up. He stopped laughing when he saw blood dripping down my face.

"Are you okay? What happened?"

With students gathering around me, I said I didn't know. "I must have tripped and hit my face on something." Fran Lawrence handed me a tissue.

"You need to go to the nurse, Mr. R. You have a gash on your cheek. And it's starting to swell."

Ashley took over. "One of you, go to the cafeteria and get some ice in a cup. And ask for a dish towel, a clean one." He pulled my hand away. "Stay put, Fritz. Will someone go get Ms. Wharton? Tell her what happened."

I tried to stand but Ashley held me down. Now surrounded by my class and his, I told him to let me move to a wall, so I could sit up. All the while, I kept thinking about what I had so briefly seen.

The ice arrived first, followed shortly by Nurse Wharton and the principal. *Just what I need.*

"What happened, Mr. Russell? Are you okay? Why are all you students standing around? Get to your classes." I told him the students were mine and Ashley's and we had told them to stay. "Well then, that's okay I guess, but what happened?

When I told him I didn't know, he said I needed to be more careful. And then he said he hoped nothing was seriously wrong, because he didn't want to be filling out accident reports. We could all tell how irritated he was from his deep red cheeks.

The nurse pried the icepack from my hand and with a none-too-gentle prod said that I had a bruise and a small cut. Mr. McAllister said he was glad to hear it. She asked if I could stand. Ash and one of the boys pulled me up.

"Keep pressure on it and come to my office. I'll bandage it there."

George said he would cover for me. From the rear of my group, a couple of moans irritated George even more. "Everyone inside NOW," he said.

A bandage and a couple of ibuprofens later, I opened my door. George hustled past me without a word. The kids clapped softly as the door clicked shut. Marion Hickok asked if I was okay. I assured her that no permanent damage had been done, and the ice was helping.

Joe DiVincenzo said, "Hey, Mr. R. We heard you turned the class into a forest, and we're going to speak to Robert E. Lee."

"Joe, do you really believe that?" I glanced at my notes. "Okay, class, open your books to page 287. With the time we have left, we'll discuss the events that led to World War II."

Marion Hickok raised her hand. "Yes, Marion?"

"Mr. R, while we were waiting, Johnny Clayton said you told Robert E. Lee about computers and cars." I watched the class waiting, watching me.

"We have other things to discuss. I'll tell you about it sometime. Today we're going to talk about the Treaty of Versailles." Outside, a stormy sky still filled the windows, but it wasn't as cloudy as the looks on the kids' faces. Close by, there was a flash followed by a rumble.

Fran Lawrence asked, "Mr. Russell, is it true that if you count the seconds from a lightning flash until thunder that the number of seconds will tell you how far away the storm is?"

"No, Fran," I said. "It will depend on temperature and humidity. Sound travels about one mile every five seconds in normal conditions, but that doesn't account for altitude. Now, Can We Discuss the Versailles Treaty? Steve Christopher, will you read the main points of the treaty?"

As Steve read, I stood at the windows and watched the cars go by. The rain bounced on their windshields like popcorn. I wondered what had just occurred. *I'm not a spectator to history. I'm an eyewitness. Why didn't this class find the same scene? What's different? And where WAS I when I got hit?* When I turned back, I realized that the classroom was deafeningly quiet.

Marion Hickok raised her hand tentatively. "Mr. Russell, are you sure you're okay?"

"Yes, thank you, Marion, I'm fine. Let's see hands. How did the treaty prepare the groundwork for the future?" Hands went up. Tom Wyle didn't usually volunteer. "Yes, Tom?"

"By creating the League of Nations, it gave us an organization that was supposed to prevent future wars."

"How did that work out, Tom?"

"Not too well, Mr. R," said Tom, a little pink, and then asserted, "but it was a good idea."

"It was, and it is," I agreed. "What do we have today that does something similar?"

"The United Nations," said three or four out loud.

"Why didn't the League work?" Again, hands went up. New hands. *Bill Taggert? Wow, something's going on. But what?* "Yes, Bill?"

"First of all, the United States didn't join." His voice cracked, unaccustomed to participating. "And the treaty made Germany accept blame for the war and took away land from them. So the Germans weren't really very happy."

"Good, Bill." Kevin Maher's hand was up. *What's happening here today?* "Kevin."

"They made Germany pay repairments."

"Reparations," I corrected.

"Yeah, that's it," said Kevin.

"Keep going, Kevin"

"Well, the treaty tried to make all countries reduce their arms."

A voice from the back of the class called out, "And their legs." Steve Christopher. I shook my head as the class laughed.

"Steve, other than body parts, what did disarming mean?"

"Well, I think it made all countries make their armies smaller to prevent another war. And it made countries tell each other what they were doing."

"Seems like a good idea, doesn't it?" I asked. "Transparency of action, communication between countries, reduction in military strength. The treaty also had an agreement between members to protect each other from outside aggression, like NATO today. Can anyone see any weaknesses here?" I looked around the room. "Sam Olberman, what do you think?" Sam had been staring out the window.

Looking back at me, he seemed not to be paying attention. Or maybe he was deep in thought. I gave him the benefit of the doubt. "Um, well, it's like there's no way to make a country agree."

"All the signers agreed. Could they change their minds?"

Sam said, "I guess so."

"Can you think of a country that did?"

Sam glanced at the maps on the front wall. "Germany?"

"Good one, Sam. We'll get into that more in a couple of weeks. Can anyone think of another?"

Sarah Bright spoke up and said, "Japan."

"Good, Sarah," I said. "Can you tell us more?"

Sarah continued, "So Japan was one of our allies in World War I, and the treaty gave Japan all the islands in the Pacific that Germany owned. And the Japanese were totally our enemies in World War II."

"Terrific answer, Sarah." I said. She smiled, and I decided to fill in some details. "The Germans had colonized islands in the Pacific. Not all the islands, but they had not really developed them. The Japanese wanted to build an empire in China and in the western and southern Pacific and were already developing control in the entire region. After World War I, the government in Japan came under control of pro-military politicians and military officers. As the Japanese developed the area, they came in conflict with the U.S. and Britain by the early1930s. We'll get to that later also. Can anyone think of another factor which influenced the outcome of the treaty?" No hands went up. "What about economically?"

"The Roaring Twenties," said Eddie Bauer.

"What about them?"

"Well, things were good."

"Where were they good, Eddie?"

"Uh, everywhere?"

It was time to teach. "The war had been devastating to Europe. Millions of young men on both sides were killed or wounded. It ruined much of France and Belgium, where most of the war was fought. Germany was slammed by reparations and losing territory, including the Rhineland, where it mined most of its coal and got most of its timber. That's where industry was, too. Terrible inflation crippled the German economy. Before the war, Germany was the strongest economy in Europe." I walked back and forth in front of the class. "In the U.S., where normal life was not interrupted by the battles, the recession ended more quickly. Before the war, the United States had owed more money to foreigners than foreigners owed it. During the war, that switched, and it stayed that way until the 1980s." The bell rang ending the class.

"Aren't you going to tell us what happened last period?" asked Sam.

"Not today, Sam, maybe later." It was the end of fifth period.

Before they made it out the door, I said "We'll continue this on Monday." I heard the usual groans.

Ashley walked in. "You look like you have an addition built on your face. So what did happen?"

Bewildered, I shook my head and said, "At the house. I'll tell you what happened there. Not here."

"You know, the kids have one hell of a tale they're telling, and it seems that some of the teachers are getting filled in, too."

"I wish I could explain, but I can't."

Tom Jaffrey walked in. "That must have been a very interesting class, Fritz. Three of my fourth-period students didn't show up, and when I saw them in the hall, they said you would explain."

"I kept them through the fourth, Tom. Sorry. We had a project with a special guest." General Lee sitting on a tree stump flashed in my mind. "I thought it would be worth their time. I suppose you've heard the story already?"

Mr. Jaffrey said, "Uh huh. You're going to have to show a bunch of us how you did it, 'cause I haven't seen them this excited about, well, anything."

"Tom, when I have it all figured out, I'll have the office set up an in-service for the whole staff. Promise. But I'm still working out some details."

"Sounds good to me. Gotta run." I was glad he left.

Ashley listened, befuddled. "You actually set that up?"

"Nope. You'd have known. I just told him that so he wouldn't keep pushing—like present company. Look, Ash, before today is over, I'm going to need to explain this, whatever it was, to a bunch of teachers and to George. I don't really know what happened." I put the icepack on my cheek. "So expect a good dinner and a long chat. But right now, I have to call Linda and let her know you're coming and bringing wine." Ashley gave me a thumbs-up.

I had lunch monitor duty the first half of sixth period, keeping order in the freed chaos. Three different teachers asked what had happened to their fourth-period students. I refined the story for each of them. It was good practice for what I suspected was coming. *Funny,* I thought, *I never thought of myself as a born liar.*

But I'm getting pretty good at this. Knowing I had almost made it through the day, I flipped through my notes and then picked up the book on the right side of my desk. I thumbed to the pages I had paperclipped. A Ford sign. At the bottom of the picture, inside a circle, two feet protruded from a foggy rectangle. The caption read, "This photograph taken at River Rouge that day has never been explained. Whose feet were they? And what was the strange rectangle?" I examined the shoes and lifted my right foot. They were the same. I put the book in my briefcase. *Is this a coincidence? Or is that really me? If I were wearing running shoes instead of wingtips, I'd know. And the puzzle would be even bigger. What made me put on good shoes this morning?*

Just before the start of seventh period, I went out in the hall to wait for the next class. Seniors. Most of them were already there, talking among themselves, unusually clamor free.

Mike Malloy said, "Mr. Russell, is it true, what everybody's saying?"

"Not now, Mike." He touched his cheek as though I had slapped him. "Sorry Mike, I didn't mean for it to come out like that."

"It's okay, Mr. R," said Mike, his eyes on his shoes.

"Okay, everyone, go into the classroom." My fingers got another shock. It was like static, but different, longer lasting. The class filed through the door. And joined a mass of people. As I followed them in, bells were clanging, sirens blowing, and the crowd wailing and screaming. I looked at the surroundings, tallish buildings, shops, and then I looked at the class, all students' eyes on me.

"Mr. R, where are we?" asked Jen Bennett.

"I don't know." I turned from side to side, then behind me, to see if I recognized anything.

One of the men in the crowd, derbied, turned to see who was behind him. He muttered, "Washington Place." Then I squinted across the smoky street. A sign on the building read "Triangle

Waist Company" and below it, "Meyers, Cronin and Wallach". There was too much smoke and disbelief to see more. Coughing everywhere. Eyes watering.

"Oh my God," shouted Rose McGowan, pointing. "Look!" A woman jumped from a ninth-floor window, her dress trailing flames, like a rocket heading the wrong way. Others followed. We heard the screams as they grabbed the air to stop their falls, the crushing sounds as the bodies hit, thuds on the sidewalk. The crowd groaned and howled. Tears added to the moisture in the air. My students were crying, too.

"Where are the fire escapes?" Jen asked.

"That's what we all want to know," said a man with a thick mustache. "It's always the same. They lock the exits and the staircase doors in that place."

"Can't we do something?" yelled Jacob Steinberg. As we watched, firemen went in and out, heads hung, trying to be useful but failing. Their ladders were too short to reach the upper floors.

I looked at my watch: 4:58. I knew that couldn't be right but didn't have a moment to think about it. Police arrived in front of us, holding back the crowd. From the ninth floor, another fireman signaled that the fire was out. Across the street, bodies of the jumpers were lying in a chaotic jumble on the sidewalk, blood sneaking to the curb.

"Kids, let's go." Nudging people out of the way, we headed through the crowd toward a storefront door that stood out like the rectangle I had seen with General Lee, except it was outlined in fluorescent blue. I opened the door and shepherded the kids through. But instead of the classroom or the school hallway, the door led to the front of a large building, larger than a warehouse, and another crowd.

The street corner sign told us we were at 26th Street. The jostling crowd pushed us into the building, into what appeared to be a dock, but there were no ships. The only light emanated from the upper windows and widely scattered electric bulbs ten feet above us. Some people carried lanterns. Others had flashlights. Sobs of grief gushed from the crowd. Moving further, we saw open coffins, filled with bodies, some burned beyond recognition. Murmurs engulfed the class, and a yell came from up ahead, a man, his agony loud and painful, in foreign-accented English, "That's my little girl."

The pink sky and dark horizon told us evening had arrived. I looked at my watch again. Seven o'clock. Time must have shifted somehow when we came in here. That would explain how they had already set up a morgue. Or was it morning? I gathered the class as best I could and, shouting above the din, I told them, "Keep moving through. Get a partner and stick together. Make sure everyone is here." I moved them all ahead of me, trying to count them. "Go to the door. Let's get out of here." Exiting through the pandemonium, the class gathered outside. Nearby, newsboys shouted "Extra, extra. Read all about the fire at Triangle."

"Follow me," I said. We walked away from the crowd, led by a force I neither controlled nor understood. Finally, a door with a brightly lit outline. I twisted the handle. The hallway. "Everyone in here. NOW." I pushed the door shut. Hard. I opened it again, and there was our classroom, empty, normal. I hurried everyone in.

Jacob Steinberg, his voice trembling, asked, "What did you do, Mr. R?"

"It looks like we walked in on the Triangle Shirtwaist Company fire. We haven't studied that yet. Listen, you guys all have your last class in a few minutes. If you can, I want you to come back for a few minutes after eighth period. It's not detention. We need to talk about this." The class mumbled in agreement. Jen Bennett asked for a tissue. "But do us all a favor. Don't say anything to anyone yet, not even your friends. Until we talk." Short of breath myself, I saw on their faces that they had returned from a distant place. "I know it's going to be hard, but it's only one period. Then come right back here. All right?" I examined the stunned faces, some with tears remaining. "It's really important not to say anything. I need you to do this. Please." Reluctant okay's whispered from around the room. The bell rang. "I'll see you in forty-five minutes."

Chapter Seven

WHAT HAPPENED? How did it happen? Why? I sat at my desk, staring out the window. Talk about confused. *Lee was kind of fun, but not the Ford plant and the Battle of the Overpass. And the Triangle Fire was Horrific. What if something had happened to one of the kids? What if we couldn't get back? How did we get there?*

From the middle of my desk, under a handful of student papers, a labor history book beckoned. Blazing from the first marked section was "The Triangle Fire." I looked at the doorway and rubbed my chin. My right hand brushed my shirt pocket. An old reflex. *I could use a cigarette.* The classroom door jerked open. The next class began entering with none of the usual greetings; they stared instead. At me. Quieter than I'd ever seen this bunch. I ignored them.

Ashley poked his head in the door. "Are you okay, Fritz?"

"I forgot to call Linda." While Ashley looked on, I speed dialed home. As it rang, I said to Ashley, "Gonna be a great dinner." When Linda answered, I said, "Hi hon. I forgot to call earlier. I asked Ashley to come to dinner. OK? Good. I'll tell him." I stuck up a thumb and focused on my silent ninth graders. They inspected me, maybe for defects.

A hand went up. "Is it true, Mr. Russell?"

"Is what true?"

From the other side of the room, Jason Mayer said, "Come on, Mr. R. It's all over school that you changed the class into a forest."

He didn't know it, but Jason had just bailed me out. I leaned on the front edge of my desk. "Will one of you please show me the tree stumps? Obviously, I've also cut down all the trees." Reluctantly, the class laughed, albeit briefly.

"Okay class. Pick sides—Barney and Alan, you're the captains. I'm the pitcher." Baseball was a good way to take my mind off the trips to 1937 and 1911. They moved the desks. "OK, ready?"

First up was Tom O'Brien. "Single," he said.

"Who's the senior U.S. Senator from New Jersey?"

"Christie," said Tom, naming the governor instead.

"You're out." Tom frowned and went to the end of the line. "One out, next batter."

Mary Mitchell asked for a double. But she said please.

"Who is president of Russia?"

"Uh, Putin?"

"Go to second base. Next batter."

Jacob Krugman asked for a double. "What is the vernal equinox?" I asked.

"The what?"

"You heard me." I realized my tone was a bit sharp. "Sorry, Jacob."

With a puzzled look, Jacob ventured a guess, "Is that the equation for the Mars rocket fuel?"

"Swing and a miss, you're out." Groans came from his team and laughter came from the other. Barney Shera, the cleanup hitter, asked for a triple.

"What South American river has had an outbreak of man-eating fish?"

"The Amazon?"

"Well, it's a river, but you're out. Home team, batter up."

The new batter was Brandy Levine. She asked for a single, but then she said, "Mr. R, what's wrong. You're never like this. Are you okay?"

"I'm fine thanks, Brandy." She was right, and it wasn't them distracting me. "Who is president of England?"

Brandy, looking stumped, said, "Mr. Russell, there isn't a president in England; it's the Prime Minister in charge, isn't it?"

"Take first base, Brandy. You can hit a curve ball." She smiled and went to first.

Dennis Rogers, next up, asked for a single.

"Into what country did NATO just send troops?"

"Spain, no wait." Dennis reached out his hand, trying to retrieve his answer.

"You're out. Sorry."

Brandy then said, "Mr. R, can I steal a base?"

"What does NATO stand for?"

She thought for a moment, and said, "Truth, justice, and the American way!"

Everyone laughed, me included. "Caught stealing. Two outs." But the answer took the edge off.

Next up was Alan Goodman, who said "Home run, please, Mr. R."

"What ancient civilization miscalculated the end of the earth, which is now supposed to happen this year?"

"The Aztecs?"

"Nope. You're out. Nice try, Alan."

The game succeeded in distracting me—despite the ice melting down my face. "Class, those of you who got hits have no homework. Those of you who were out should write a paragraph about the question you missed for Monday." I smiled when they booed.

As the bell rang, I began to pack my briefcase. Ash squeezed past the exiting kids. "Want to get out quick?"

"Hang on a bit, can you, Ash. I have the seventh period coming back for a few minutes."

"Sure, I'll be in my room. Just come down."

The seniors began to shuffle in and sit down. No one was talking. I felt their eyes boring through me. Jennifer Bennett said, "Mr. Russell, seriously, what happened in our class?" She sounded ferocious. Heads bobbed.

I gave them two answers. First, a version of the truth. "You know we witnessed the Triangle Fire in New York City. The Triangle Fire was the deadliest industrial disaster in New York City history. In 1911, it was the second deadliest disaster of any kind in New York City, and it stayed that way until the World Trade Center was attacked in 2001. Doors to the stairwells and exits were locked, which was not uncommon at the time, supposedly to prevent stealing and unauthorized work breaks. Most of the victims were young immigrant women, mostly Jewish and Italian, mostly around your ages."

"As a result, new laws were enacted for fire safety, such as fireproofing, improved exits, and sprinkler systems. The fire was also the impetus for the growth of the International Ladies' Garment Workers' Union. The owners were prosecuted, but they were acquitted. Now, how we found ourselves there, I don't know. That's answer number 1." Answer number 2 was that I had a friend who invented a projection system that recreates events and that he had asked me to try it out in my class. I told them he worked in Hollywood.

Jennifer said, "Which is it, Mr. R?" She barked at me, ready to bite.

"Which do you think?" The students looked around at each other.

Larry Singer said, "How are we supposed to know?" His bark was lower pitched.

"What do you THINK?" I barked back.

Leigh Cohen, looking at the clock, said, "Well, none of us is hurt, and no one got lost. But it was pretty realistic, whatever it was."

Larry went on, "I don't think time travel is likely, so the Hollywood guy must be the answer."

"Thanks, guys; you're right. I want you all to think about what you saw, what you know, and what is most likely. I don't want to keep you any longer. I know you all have better things to do on a weekend. We'll talk more on Monday. You're dismissed. Have a nice weekend."

"Mr. R, some people had flashlights. That didn't seem real either," said Jacob.

"Jacob, dry cell batteries and the little bulbs were invented in the late 1890s, and the casing we're used to first appeared a few years later. Good observation."

Mike asked as his classmates rattled out, "Mr. Russell, what's a shirtwaist?"

"It's a kind of woman's blouse, Mike. Good question. Remind me to show you next week."

As the class emptied, Jen Bennett stopped and whispered, "Mr. Russell, I think we were actually there. I think you know how to time travel."

"You know, Jen," I whispered back, "it felt that way to me too. Pretty good system, huh?" I smiled at her, and she gave me a weak, unconvinced smile in return. "Have a nice weekend, Jennifer."

"You too, Mr. R."

Before I left, I put the books on my chair to take home and look through over the weekend. I walked to Ashley's open door. "Ash, I've got to go to the office for a second. I'll be right back."

"Okay. I'll be here."

I walked down the hall. I'd never really noticed how remarkably quiet it is after school, with only the occasional kid at a locker. *It's amazing how quickly this place empties on a Friday.*

George McAllister walked out of his office. His face was red. "Mr. Russell, may I have a word?"

"You haven't called me 'Mr. Russell' in five years. What is it, George?"

"It's come to my attention that there were some strange activities in your classroom today."

My arms were crossed, holding me back. I've known George for almost nine years. He can be irritating when he plays the boss. Outside, away from school influences or activities, George is a considerate, thoughtful guy, although not very exciting. He taught middle-school math before he became a principal. At school, well, that's another story. He once asked if I had any interest in being a principal. I was a little insulted since he also said he thought he'd gotten the job because his predecessor had been "innovative." George said that he was sure they liked him because he believed in following the rules. I told him I liked teaching but thanked him for thinking of me. "George, do you want to see for yourself? I promise there are no trees growing through the floor."

"Well I suppose I should check into it."

Reaching my classroom, I peered in the window. Everything seemed normal. But the buzz on my fingertips was there again as I opened the door. We walked through and into the White House Oval Office. The president was sitting at his desk, his rising eyebrows pulling his head up.

I knew right away we were in trouble, so I said quickly, "Mr. President, please, we're not a threat. When we stepped over the threshold, we thought we were going into my classroom. My name is Fritz Russell. I'm a high school teacher in Riverboro, New Jersey and somehow I have opened a time-travel portal. This is George McAllister, my principal. This is the fourth time today this has happened."

"Fourth time?" George sputtered. "You told me it was nonsense!"

"What did you expect me to say?" Another door swung open abruptly, and a secret service agent entered, drawing a pistol.

George started to object. I said, "Quiet, George. This is my fault, I think. Mr. President, if you'll give me a moment to explain, I think I'll be able to convince you that we're no threat to you."

The secret service agent said, "Sir, I think you should leave. I'll take care of this."

"Mr. President, we are not armed." I stared right at him. "I have ID, and I have a story to tell."

The president said, "Tom, check them for weapons."

George grumbled, and though Tom was a bit rough, I said, "George, we just walked in on the president of the United States. Stop complaining. This is the most interesting thing that's happened to you in the last ten years." The president chuckled.

It was hard not to look around. We were in the Oval Office. And it really is oval. I glanced at the portraits and the Resolute Desk, and looked over the president's shoulder at the gardens. I felt like twins, one who just walked in on the president and another who inhaled the history of the place.

The agent turned to the president and said that we had no weapons. "Tom," said the president, "check their identification and then put out an all-clear."

"Yes, sir." We handed him our drivers' licenses and told him our phone numbers.

The president stepped out from behind his desk, and said, "Won't you sit down?" as he motioned to a couch. He sat across from us. "You said you had a story. The fourth time today?"

I wanted to look around at the architecture, the paintings, the bookcase, but I met his stare.

"Mr. President, I can't explain this, but right now that door," pointing to where we came through, "is a passageway. What I'm about to tell you happened today, but I can't tell you how or why." When the president said that he was skeptical, George chimed in with "me, too."

"Yet here we are," I said, looking from one to the other. "And George can verify that we were just in New Jersey a couple of minutes ago." George shook his head in agreement. Then I recounted the events of the day, including my wound, watching the growing look of amazement on each man's face.

When finished, I said, "Mr. President, I apologize that we've taken up so much of your time. The only way to prove where we came from is to leave. If you're as curious as I am, maybe your secret service agent can take us to the door. Then we all can see what happens. We're clearly not a threat."

"Mr. Russell, that's not what concerns me. If somehow you've made an entry into the space-time continuum, then you've proven part of Einstein's theories, and I really need proof of your proof. Why Mr. Russell, you could be top secret!" the president said.

I felt my stomach tighten. Although spoken with a smile, our surprise appearance had to concern him. His secret service agents would be worried. I was. I suggested we try to return to the school so he could see for himself and have Tom check that it was a school. "You can stand by your door and watch. I think that as long as the door is open, we have a connection. And once the door closes on our side, everything will go back to normal."

"Tom, what about it?" asked the president.

"Mr. President, they don't seem dangerous. We've verified their personal information. We have locations. If this is real, we'll know in a second."

"You're game?" asked the president.

"Yes, sir."

"Okay, let's try. But first, Tom Andrews, meet Mr. Russell and George, uh, sorry, didn't get the name." George mumbled, "McAllister" and started to reach out his hand, but then thought better of it when Tom's hand moved to his waist.

We moved toward the door. I said, "I think I probably have to be the one who opens the door." Tom gestured for me to go first. Through the doorway, we saw a hallway, granite floor, light green tiling bordering lockers on the walls. "Wow," Tom said. Locking stares with him, I said, "You should be in my shoes."

Standing behind, the president, seeing the familiar view of a typical school, said, "Amazing. Tom, I want to take a look."

"Mr. President, I don't think that's a good idea. At least, let me go and check it out further." Tom walked down the hall, looked in classroom windows, and turned the corner.

I told the president I didn't think it was a good idea either, that I didn't know how to control it. "Mr. President, I don't know if I can get you back. I think I'm in enough trouble already."

Tom returned and told the president he had seen the trophy case with the name of the school on it. The president told him to call James. Tom pulled out a phone and spoke briefly. In less than five seconds, another agent ran in, with his hand on his pistol.

The president said, "It's cool, James, no gun," and held up his hand. James walked to the door, but his eyebrows rose when he saw the lockers. He kept his hand where it was and looked questioningly at the president. "I'll explain later." Looking to Tom, he got a nod telling him it was ok.

"This is what I want to do," said the president. "If closing the door breaks the link, we need to keep it open. Tom, you and I can go through, just to look, and James, you'll stay here at the door to keep it open."

"Mr. President, I really don't think the risk is worth it," I said. "I don't know what will happen."

"James, if I don't reappear in five," said the president, "call for the helicopter to head to Riverboro High School in New Jersey. Was it April tenth when you left?" I nodded. I also showed him my watch. "We're both on today's date and our watches show the same time, so we know we can get back. Also, James, if something happens, tell them I wanted a hotdog from Nathan's, the original in Brooklyn, so that's where we went."

James looked at Tom, who said, "It'll be fine, James. I'll be with them." James said, "Yes, sir."

The president said, "Mr. Russell, I've been taking risks since I took office. You must be aware of the constant shelling I've taken from Congress." He smiled. "Okay. Let's go. Oh, by the way, the fellow in the door is James Williams. We'll do the rest of the intros later."

The president stepped through into the hallway, George lagging behind. James stuck his head through just to see. "This is SO cool," said the president. Tom and James shared an anxious look of understanding. The president had taken a risk, and they needed to be alert. The president looked through the door into the Oval Office, whispering, "wow." He looked at George and me and said, "There are a number of considerations here. First, we need to document this. Does anyone have a phone?" Everyone did. "James, call Lily Evans and ask her to bring her camera." When Lily, the president's secretary, rushed into the office, she halted, her hand over her mouth. The president said, "Lily, I'll explain later. Please take pictures of us here and make sure you get the lockers. And we won't be mentioning this for tonight's news."

"No, sir," she answered. "No, sir," said Tom and James in unison.

"Lily, James, stay in the doorway. Tom, please take pictures of all of us from here."

I told the president that I'd like one, and after Tom took his, I photographed all five of my unlikely companions.

The president was thinking, an unfocused look on his face. That look makes Tom itchy, I later discovered. The president asked, "I'd like to walk around the school, if that's all right."

"Mr. President, to do that I think we have to shut the door and that will break the connection," I said. "I think right now we are still in your office, like we're in a tunnel. I don't think we should leave it open to anyone who wanders by, but I don't know if I can open it again."

"Hmmm. I'm in New Jersey now. Right?"

"Well, yeah, sort of. I guess so."

The president took out his phone, pushed a number. The phone rang on his desk. "So now we know that I can call home. Like E.T." He alone thought that was funny, but he shrugged off the lack of response. "Tom, the helicopter is on its way?" Tom nodded. "So, George, want to show me around?"

Tom begged him not to go further. "Mr. President, please sir, don't do this. Mr. Russell has said he can't be sure he can get you back."

"Tom, this could be more important than anything else I do in office. Tell you what. I want you and James to come with me. Lily, when the door shuts, I'm going to call you immediately."

He told her he wanted her to call him back to have a record of the outbound call. James stepped into the hallway, and the door clicked shut. Through the window, my classroom reappeared. The president motioned for Tom to open the door, and we went in.

"Interesting," said the president. "Looks like a classroom to me. Interesting color, Mr. Russell." George frowned. I had been asking him for years to have my room painted. The president and the agents scanned the room. Despite the strangeness, he was smiling at me. We had a connection.

"Mr. President, you need to make that call," said Tom.

As the president dialed, a face appeared at the door, clearly startled by what he was seeing. Both agents reached for their waists.

"Mr. President, that's Ashley Gilbert," I said. "He teaches here, his classroom is down the hall, and he's my ride home." I raised my hand to tell Ashley to wait and looked at the president, who nodded OK. I waved him in. Ashley walked in. He was followed by Sandy Horton, an English teacher with a quick brain and fast wit. They each took one step and stopped. Ashley gave me a quizzical look as he entered. The president walked toward them as Ash watched James and Tom.

"Come on in. Ash, Sandy. I'd like to introduce you to the president. These gentlemen are secret service agents. This is Tom Andrews. And this is James Williams." The president shook hands with the new arrivals. Ashley glanced at George and the agents and then turned to me.

"So it's true?" said Ash. In his left hand, he had a book, his finger as his bookmark. "Sandy and I were talking and heard noise in the hallway."

"I told you it was going to be an interesting dinner."

"What's the book?" asked the president. The question combined caution and curiosity.

"Just an old yearbook I found. I was showing it to Sandy."

"Can I see it?" the president asked.

Ashley opened the book and laid it on a desk. The president checked the pictures and laughed.

"That's a foul, for sure," he said. "Charging." The picture showed two young teachers playing basketball. "I play too, you know."

"What year was that, Ash?" I asked.

"2006, my first year. You've gotten better under my tutelage."

"Do you have portraits in here?" asked the president. Ashley turned to the English Department and his picture, then flipped to the History Department and mine. "I played in high school, you know."

"You were pretty good, they say," said Ash. The president smiled and looked at Sandy.

"I'm guessing you're not in here. Ms. Horton, is it?"

"I was in high school in 2006, Mr. President."

"This sure brings back some memories. Your book is in pretty good shape."

"I was digging through a closet last night. Didn't find what I was looking for, but I figured Fritz might like to see it, too. His is probably buried in his garage." I nodded. We have a lot of pictures in yearbooks, Ash and I. The chronicles of our careers. Ashley's annual poetry readings, the chess club he supervises, and my history baseball.

"I look a lot younger," said George.

"You were never young, George," Ashley said. "You were born a principal."

The president said, "We were about to tour your school." We suddenly heard "Hail to the Chief" coming from his phone. He looked at everyone and said, "Still don't know who did that. Yes, Lily, it's me." He asked her to stay by the phone and said he would call again in ten minutes. "If the world appears to be ending, please call me back." Then he looked back at us. "So let's go." All seven of us walked out of the classroom and turned into the heart of the school.

"You know," said Ashley, "according to all the laws of physics, including the theory of relativity, this is impossible."

I said, "I thought you teach English. When did physics become your thing?"

Twitching like he had bugs in his shirt, George said, "If you turn left here, we'll get to the gym. The core of the school was built by the WPA in 1936. We added wings, three of them, plus the cafeteria, the gym, and the auditorium in the 1950s and 60s, as Riverboro's population swelled from the baby boomers." George kept turning around while he lectured. "We keep the gym open after school for pickup basketball. One corner has mats and a couple of gymnastic pieces, and we use it in inclement weather for team practices, Mr. President. This is our cafeteria," gesturing to his left. George was nervous; his voice rose and fell, but there was pride in it.

George led us to the gym and held open the door. "Looks like a gym to me," the president said. Heads had turned as the door opened, and when the players began to look, the basketball game slowed and then stopped. A ripple of silence washed over the visitors. The president held out his hands, asking to be passed the ball.

Before there was time to react, he said, "Hold on a second." He slipped off his suit jacket and handed it to Tom. Turning back, he signaled for the ball. Jerry Warner passed it to him, and the president turned in one smooth motion and shot. A low arc and a barely audible swish. Jack Dylan retrieved the ball and threw it back to the president, who stepped to his left and shot again. The net barely moved. Ash whispered, "I can do that."

Clapping and a few whistles reverberated through the gym. When the students moved closer, the president said, "Sorry to interrupt. We're just looking around, guys."

Chris Brothers asked, "Could we get your autograph, Mr. President?" He held out the basketball and then glanced at George for an okay. George nodded. The president took his jacket back, pulled out his pen, and scrawled "To all the gym rats at Riverboro High." He scribbled his name and handed the ball back. As he was putting his jacket back on, a couple of students walked up, holding notebooks, with a "would you sign my book?" look on their faces.

He asked them their names and chatted with them. *Just like General Lee,* I thought. Other students had disappeared into locker rooms to find their own objects for autographs, and in a short time, a group of kids spread out in front of the president.

As he began to sign, I said, "Mr. President, you need to make a phone call." The president nodded.

"Hang on kids. Gotta make a call." It was answered instantaneously, and he said, "Everything is fine, Lily." Then he said, "Where is the helicopter? OK, see you soon."

Turning back to the kids, he asked, "Okay, who's next?"

While the president greeted and signed, Ashley whispered to me, "What's going on?"

I whispered back, "Dinner."

Although the line was still a dozen long, George said, "We really should move along, Mr. President." In contrast to the president's calm, George was fidgeting, shifting foot to foot, his hands going from pants to jacket pocket and back.

The president said, without stopping, "There are only a few more," and continued signing. He seemed less offended than I was that George would try to tell him what to do. He stopped for a moment to exercise his hand. When he had signed all the notebooks and other objects handed to him, including Jack Dylan's left sneaker, he said, "I've gotta go, guys. Nice to see you all."

"Thanks" and "thank yous" echoed as we walked out. Applause reached us from behind. He poked his head back in, smiled and waved, and let the door close with its usual clang.

George took the lead again, but the president hesitated and spoke to me. "I'd like to go back to the classroom." George skittered to a stop and turned around.

Backtracking, we returned to my classroom, stopping at the door. I said, "Keep your fingers crossed." Not knowing what would happen, I hoped for a shock, although I wasn't sure why. I grabbed the doorknob and pulled, knowing it would open to the Oval Office. From behind me came the sound of exhaled relief. I straddled the doorway, one foot in the corridor and the other in the Oval Office. Lily Evans stood by the president's desk. Many staff members filled the room.

The president stepped through and turned to us. "I don't think I'll be able to walk through this door again without being apprehensive."

George said, "Before you go, Mr. President, would you consider coming to our graduation? It's on June twenty-third, a Tuesday.

"Lily, please note my schedule to see if we can do graduation on June twenty-third," the president said. "George, we'll have to get back to you, but believe me, I'll try." He then turned to me. "Mr. Russell, I believe you and I will need to have another conversation soon. Thanks for a most interesting afternoon." When he shook hands with Ashley, I realized they were about the same height. So was Tom Andrews. His secret service agents shook our hands and headed through the door. The president ushered them in and, for a final handshake, took my hand in both of his and whispered, "I'll be in touch." He walked back into his office. I waved, stepped back into the hall, and let the door close.

* * *

AFTER THE INTRUDERS had departed, the president scrutinized the stunned crowd in his office. They were all waiting for an explanation, a story, something. He had no doubt that they all would have something to say to someone. "Everyone, this has become top secret as of right now. You are all sworn to secrecy. Who'd believe you anyway?" he shrugged and then smiled. He went from person to person asking for a verbal answer, not just a head nod. "We don't know what just happened and we'll investigate. What you just witnessed, whatever it is, however it happened, is important. But you will say nothing. Now, we all have other things to do. Before you leave, give your name to Mr. Clemmons," he said, referring to his chief of staff. "Back to work." As the room cleared and his chief of staff took names, the president wrote notes on a yellow legal pad, trying to recall the exact details of his visit to a high school in New Jersey through a door in his office. He was interrupted by a throat clearing.

"Mr. President, may I take a few minutes," asked his national security advisor. "We need to act now. This intrusion can't be ignored. I suggest using my ops squad tonight. If they can get here, they can get anywhere. Our security is in jeopardy."

"Mr. Koppler, I was just there. It's a high school. They're teachers. They're less dangerous than you are. We have a discovery that may lead us to a better world and a better understanding of the universe."

"Sir, I've seen a lot in my career, and nothing good ever comes when science runs amok. Better to end it now and not have consequences."

"Jim, before I consider that, I want to know more. I will handle this. If we really have a problem, you'll have plenty of opportunity to advise me."

"Mr. President, I've dealt with bad actors my entire working life. None of them appear to be what they really are. At least let me take them into custody for more questioning. I am responsible for the security of this country. You CAN'T let it be."

Gripping the edge of his desk, the president said, "You are not singlehandedly responsible for anything more than keeping your office analyzing the world. I CAN let it be. And so will you. If I need further assistance, and if you can provide it, I'll ask. Until then, leave them alone. Is my point taken?"

"It is, sir, but with deep misgivings. Your safety has just been jeopardized, and everyone has his price. That endangers the security of the United States."

"Jim, if you prove to be right, then I, not you, will be responsible. No one will blame you. But, I'll say it again. I will take care of this. Now if you'll excuse me, I have work to do."

The president stared at the door his visitors had come through and sighed. He finished his notes and asked Lily Evans to join him. He handed her the pad, told her he was safe, and that everything would be fine. He hoped he was right.

* * *

MUTED BUMP AND CLICK. I grabbed my jacket and briefcase. I needed to get away. But George started shouting immediately. I put my stuff down again.

"How could you not let me know that this was happening in one of my classrooms? Your students could have been in danger. The school could be sued."

Not hearing a word, I focused on what had happened. When George ran out of rant, I said, "George, if I had told you, what would you have done? Would you have believed me? Or had me arrested? Or called a shrink?"

"Well … well, I don't know, but," and he stopped. Ashley watched silently, glanced at Sandy, understood I wanted to escape. After I suggested that they sit down, George said, "Well, I really should report this."

"George, think about what you're saying. Please sit down. Now." Surprised at my tone, George sat. I moved the books from my chair back to my desk and sat. Ashley grabbed a chair three desks over and one row behind, out of George's sight. Sandy sat in front of me.

George said, "What did he say to you when he was leaving?"

"He said he'd see us at graduation." My cheeks, not liking the falsehoods, twinged.

"Did he really?" I heard the voice of a kid offered chocolate.

"He'll be here if he can." I told him to think how impressive he would be sitting on the stage with the president. I warned him that a secret service detail would be with him. I suggested George might plan a dinner. "George, imagine the pictures in the newspapers, the national TV coverage. You might even be on YouTube."

All in a dither, George said, "Fritz, you're right." I was 'Fritz' again. "I have a lot to do. Will you help me?"

"Of course. We'll all help. But don't start telling anyone yet." Ashley's smirk let me know he got it.

George turned to Ashley. "Sure, George, you can count on me."

"I think we need to go and think about what just happened. George, it's the weekend. Take a break, and as hard as it will be, I don't think you should tell Lois."

"She won't like that much," said George. George and Lois had been married for over thirty years, and she always knew when George had something on his mind.

Ashley stood, and the uncomfortable chair's scraping against the floor prompted George to stand. "This has been a very confusing afternoon," said George. "Do you really think he'll come?"

I said, "I think he feels a strange connection to us." I know I thought so. "I think he'll want to come."

Looking around as he left, he said, "Have a nice weekend."

"You too," we said.

As the door shut, Ashley started to ask, but I cut him off. "Let's get out of here." I grabbed my jacket and briefcase, made sure the books were there, took the keys out of the desk lock, and flipped off the light as we left. We hustled out and headed for Ashley's car, an almost new Mustang convertible. The top was up and puddled. Sandy was right behind.

"Sandy, Ash is coming for dinner, and we need to talk about this. Want to join us?"

"This is too weird, Fritz. Yeah, I'll go home and change and be right over. Do you want me to bring something?"

"Just yourself. I think we're set. You know where I live."

As Sandy got in her car, a girl's voice traveled across the lot. "Mr. Russell." Jennifer Bennett, carrying her book bag, was coming toward me. Her face was smudged.

"What's the matter, Jen?"

She related what had happened when school ended. She told me that a group of kids were talking about what had happened in class, and she said she thought it was real. They started making fun of her, calling her names, and she started to tear up again.

I suspected there might be more. I glanced at Ashley and asked her, "Are you waiting for your ride home?"

She said, "I live just a few blocks away. I walk."

"I'd offer you a ride, but you know, school insurance rules. How about I walk with you for a bit? Give Mr. Gilbert your book bag."

"That's okay, Mr. R. It's not far."

"It's not a problem, Jen."

We started walking past newly manicured carpets and the copycat garden colorings of the copycat castles where the weekend warriors would soon appear. Spring in the 'burbs.

"Jen, can you keep a secret?"

"Uh huh."

"Good. I'm going to tell you the answer to the question I asked the class after school." As we walked, I invented the story of my Hollywood friend—a spontaneous assortment of lies, fabrications, tall tales, and untruths with each step. I try never to lie to my students. It's hard to backtrack, and I've worked hard over the years to build trust with my kids. Each year, that relationship has improved. And I didn't like adding tarnish. "That's why everyone from third period on was talking about the weird stuff in our class. Your class had a different scene programmed. I didn't think he would pick such a disturbing event. I'll have to tell him he needs to do his own censoring. That was pretty X-rated to me. What do you think?"

She halted, absorbing, processing, disbelieving. After a second, frowning, she asked, "That wasn't real?" I shook my head no. "Mr. R, you should have warned us. That was very upsetting," almost scolding me. "All those dead bodies, people jumping out of the building. We could hear them hit the ground. And the smoke."

Ashley kept up with us, careful not to splash the puddles. He leaned toward the window, and I told him, "Jen's class witnessed the Triangle Fire." I hadn't had a chance to tell him.

"Jeez, you're kidding." We reached Jennifer's house, and I opened the car door. Ashley slid her book bag over. She hoisted it to her shoulder, questions growing like the spring flowers that were surrounding us, almost ready to burst, but said nothing.

I asked, "Got a piece of paper?" She took out a notebook. "Call me if you want to discuss this some more. But don't give my number out," I said lightly. I climbed into the car. "Have a nice weekend, Jen. Really."

As I started to close the door, she said, "Thanks, Mr. R."

"No problem. See you on Monday." Ashley stepped on the gas.

"Now will you tell me what the hell is going on?" I could only laugh. "What's so funny?"

"You can't imagine how glad I am to be able to talk sanely about this. Would you believe I don't have a clue what happened? The story about my Hollywood friend, pure BS."

"I know," said Ashley, "but how did you get to the White House?"

"I don't know. Look Ash, let's get to my house. I want Linda to hear this too. We need to figure this out."

* * *

Returning to his office, the national security adviser passed Tom Andrews headed for the president's office. "Mr. Andrews, a moment. You went with him. Where did you go?"

"A high school in New Jersey, sir. Riverboro. They are what they say, Mr. Koppler. Mr. Russell is a teacher, and the other guy is the principal."

"You might think so, but I'm not convinced. The president doesn't seem to realize how exposed he's left us all." Koppler eyed the agent. "Keep me informed." Tom Andrews sighed as Koppler walked away.

Chapter Eight

AS WE STRODE up the sidewalk under an arch of new leaves, the garden flowers greeted us. I hadn't really noticed when I'd left home that morning, but the tulips had joined my daffodils in a parade of bright colors. I had planted almost two hundred bulbs in the fall, and the flowers were now waving in red, yellow, white, and purple. There were some multi-colored ones, yellow and purple, and a few that looked like candy canes. Ash said, "When winter comes, can spring be far behind?" The flowers were a perfect foreground to my white house. I reached into my pocket for my keys, but a soft metallic ping on the walkway made me stop. My desk key. "I forgot to lock my desk."

"Anything worth stealing?"

"Probably, but only I would steal it."

I dropped the key back in my pocket as we climbed the steps. Linda was there, waiting.

"Hi, honey, I'm home," I said, smiling as I kissed her.

"Fritz, what happened to your face? What's going on? George McAllister has called twice in the last twenty minutes. He sounded upset."

"Lots to tell you. It's been a strange day. Garden looks great."

She looked from me to Ashley, who nodded in agreement. "Well?" she questioned.

"Hey, let me get my coat off, okay?" I pleaded.

"You're not wearing a coat!"

"I was speaking of my figurative coat." I hung the jacket in the hall closet. "Did George want me to call him?"

"No, he said he'll call back."

Ashley, sniffing, said, "Something smells tasty."

"Lasagna," she said, anticipating his next question.

"Oh, goody!" said Ashley. Linda's lasagna had won a cooking contest, and Ashley loves it. So do I.

"Linda, I have a lot to tell you, and Ash hasn't heard the whole story yet. Sandy Horton is coming, too. She was talking to Ash, so I invited her." Ashley and I sat at the kitchen table.

Linda frowned at me, her eyebrows lowered and her head cocked. She said, "You can tell it again when she gets here. What's happened? Want something to drink, Ash?"

"Diet soda."

"Like you need it," I said, as she opened the bottle. "Lin, when we settle down, I'll tell you the whole thing."

"Do you want a soda?" she asked me.

"No, thanks." I walked to the liquor cabinet and took out a bottle.

"Fritz, it's not even five o'clock."

"It's five o'clock somewhere. It'll take some the ache away." I removed my watch and changed the time. "See, five o'clock. At least in my little world." I poured and got a couple of ice cubes. "OK, let's talk."

"Sandy should be here any minute." Ashley said. With that, there was a knock.

"Sorry it took so long, Fritz." Sandy handed me a paper bag. "I bought wine for dinner. Hi, Linda. Hi, Ash."

After Sandy settled in, I started.

"At the start of third period, I opened the door to my room, and we walked into the woods. And met Robert E. Lee."

"Oh come on," Linda said, looking at Ash, who shrugged. "You walked through the door and into the woods?"

"Yeah, but I could still see a door outlined on the scenery. It was just there, a rectangular outline. The doorway has to be the entrance to a portal. Let me keep going." I related the conversation and the class questions and how the fourth-period class joined us. I told them everything I could recall. "When the period ended, we could hear the bell ring. The classroom door was always visible, right there in the forest. I don't know if that scene traveled to now or if we went back in time. I wonder if General Lee told anyone else."

"What happened next?" asked Linda.

"Well, after class ended, we walked back through the door and back into the hall. Ash, that's when I told you dinner would be interesting. Anyway, I walked back into my classroom, but it wasn't there. I had just enough time to see a group of men and a large Ford sign over a building that looked like a factory. Before I had time to react, I got hit in the face. I fell backwards into the hallway."

"You told me you tripped. And the cut was from hitting something."

"We were surrounded by kids, Ash." I brought my briefcase to the table, and took out the books. "After lunch, I spotted this book under some papers." I flipped to the marked page. "This picture was taken in 1937. The photographer said later that a man appeared and disappeared before he could take more pictures of him. Other onlookers described a similar sighting. Here. Read the caption." I took off a shoe and held it next to the book. "Look at these. I think that's me."

"Fritz, that's nuts," Linda said. "That picture is almost eighty years old. How could that be you today, when it's been in that book since it was published?"

"That's just one thing we need to talk about."

"And if that really happened, it's dangerous," she said. "Not something you should be fooling around with. Have you looked in a mirror?"

I told her I hadn't, but I wanted to finish the story. I'd gotten patched up, I said, and went back to class, and everything about the room was normal. "Ash, that's when you told me the kids were talking."

Ashley said, "And they were telling it pretty much like you just did. At least about meeting Lee. Other teachers know the story now too. You're gonna have some serious 'splaining' to do."

I knew he was right, but what could I say? I couldn't get my brain around what had happened. I told them that the only things I could do were guess or lie, and lying had filled my day. "If I told them what really happened..."

My phone rang. "It's George," I said, looking at the caller ID. "Hi, George. What's up?"

"Fritz, this is getting serious." His sentences came like rockets. "I've had calls from six teachers and some parents in the past half hour. I don't know what to tell them."

"What did you say, George?"

"I said I was aware of the situation, and that I would investigate further. Fritz, if they start calling the superintendent, this could get out of hand."

"Hmm. George, hold on a second," holding my phone against my shirt. I looked at Linda. She recognized the look and told me to invite them over. Come for dinner, I told him. That way Lois would know everything, and he could avoid calls.

"Good idea. Thanks. What time?"

"How about six?" Linda had raised six fingers.

"I'll bring some wine. See you then."

I turned off my phone. "They can leave messages. Now where was I?"

Looking at my watch, I said, "It's 5:15. Should we wait until George gets here? Do you want some help setting up, Lin?"

She said, "All I have to do is get out a couple more plates and glasses. Let's talk about what's important. I want to know now.

You can tell it again, but let's get the story so we can think about what to do before George and Lois arrive. Two heads are better than one," looking at Ashley, his chin in his hand, listening, "and in this case, four heads."

Ashley said, "Four heads. Sounds like a real monster." He made a face and took a long, noisy breath. The monster said, "Dinner smells really good, Lin."

"Monster is right," I said. "When seventh period started, I opened the door." I hesitated and looked at my hand. I told them what had happened, including my story about a friend in Hollywood. "Actually that was pretty good, given short notice, don't you think? I wish that were true."

Ashley took over. "That's when you came to my classroom and said you needed to go to the office."

Now impatient, Linda asked, "And?" Her arms crossed, she was waiting for the punch line.

"So I went to the office and George stopped me, you know how he is, 'we have a problem, what's going on? Blah, blah, blah.' I told him to think about what he had heard, did it make any sense? Then, and here's the mistake, or maybe it wasn't a mistake, I told him he could see for himself. We went to the classroom." I paused again and wiggled my fingers.

Linda asked, "What's wrong with your hand?"

"Nothing. But I got a shock, you know, static, and when I opened the door, we were somewhere else. That might be part of this." I looked at my hand again. "Anyway, George and I walked into the Oval Office, met the president, got checked out by a secret service agent, and I told the president and George what happened today. Then he came back through with me and George into the school. That's when Ash and Sandy turned up."

Ashley picked up the story. He said he and Sandy had been waiting for me in his classroom, and when they heard talking in the hallway, they went out and saw my door close. He looked in the window and felt like his eyes were popping from his head.

"Talk about weird. Lin, I was looking at the president. We went in, Fritz introduced us. All of us took a tour of the school. The president shot a couple of baskets in the gym and signed some autographs. Then we reconnected him to the White House."

My turn again. "When he went back and the door closed, the Oval Office disappeared. So here we are now, and I have no idea how any of this happened."

"Good. So now we have the outline, and all we need to do is figure out how to stop it from happening again." Linda answered. She left the kitchen, and checked the dining room. "We have a few minutes until George and Lois get here, so let's stop and set the table. We can think about this as we go."

"Dining room?" I asked Linda.

"Of course," she said as she opened the oven.

The dining room is the only formal room in the house. Linda's grandmother had wanted her to have the furniture. A mahogany table, oval with three leaves, and matching buffet, breakfront, and server. Hand carved legs and drawers. Antique knobs and handles. Leather-covered chairs with clawed feet and extra padding, which I really like. Twelve people can sit at the table and keep their elbows unscathed. I took out the special silverware and handed it to Ashley. Linda had taught him to set a table long after his mother had given up trying. Ashley and I had visited his parents in Connecticut once, before Linda and I got married. His mother kept referring to him as "the uncivilized one." He laughed, a sound that has become as familiar to me as the changing seasons.

I grabbed the crystal glasses and followed him to the table. Sandy helped Ash.

"Do you think that the static has anything to do with the lightning?" Ashley asked, now that he knew what had happened.

"No talking without me," Linda called from the kitchen. "No fair."

"Okay, hon." I knew that she wanted to know and, more important, that she could help put the pieces in place. She's got a great analytic mind.

The doorbell rang. George was there with Lois, who asked "So what trouble are you causing today?" She smiled. "C'mon in," I said, smiling back.

Linda and Ashley came to the door, Sandy right behind. When Lois saw Ashley, she said, "So both the troublemakers are at it, I see! Hello, Sandy, Linda."

"Nice to see you too, Lois," Ashley replied. Sandy waved.

Lois is in her late 50s. Some think her pushy. To those who don't know her, she is an obnoxious, abrasive annoyance attached to the school principal. But we know her well as a smart, reasonable, and reasoning woman whose opinion and insight would be valuable. She's also an awful tease. Although her husband often doesn't, she can be counted on to "get it". Now everyone had arrived. "Lovely flowers, Linda," Lois said, pointing to the vase of red tulips and yellow daffodils at the center of the table.

"Do you want something to drink?" I asked.

George said, "Oops, I left the wine in the car," and got up to retrieve it.

While he was out, Lois said, "George is upset. He's received about a dozen calls since he got home, and he won't tell me anything more than there was a problem at school, and he's handling it. And now here we are. So you two are up to something."

"Lois, when you leave tonight, you'll know everything." I said. "We haven't had time to consider this puzzle, and we need to solve it."

George returned with a merlot and a chardonnay, red and white, and put them on the table. Ashley reached for them. "May I take a look?" George handed him the bottles. "Nice. Have you had these before?"

"Yes. I think you'll enjoy them. Since I didn't ask what we were having, I brought both." Ashley liked wine; he had taken a wine tasting class and then gone to Europe a couple of summers ago on a tasting tour.

I said, "I think they'll be gone before too long."

Still in the dark about all this "mystery", as she called it, Lois was getting annoyed. "Yes, yes, we can drink all the wine later, but I want … to know … what's … going on!"

"Dinner's ready," said Linda. Lois's tight lips and finger tapping showed her increasing impatience. Ash followed Linda into the kitchen.

I said, "Lois, Linda is a great cook, and I want you to eat. I'll tell you all what happened, during dinner. Then we can discuss this. Okay?" I called to the kitchen and asked Linda to wait with my plate for now. "Ash, would you open the wine while I help serve."

"Stay there," Lois ordered and got up to help. The wine poured, plates delivered, and everyone waiting, I took a deep breath. The mixed aromas of garlic and meat sauce grabbed my nose and whispered to my stomach. I looked at everyone enviously, a variety of cheeses still percolating on their plates.

When Ashley sat down, I raised my glass in a toast, "to answers," and sipped. "Go ahead and eat," I said. "I'll talk." I retold the story of the day's events, adding some details, trying to picture the scenes as they occurred, looking for clues. The one person who had heard none of this before, Lois, listened intently and kept looking at George for corroboration, and he nodded yes when he could.

When I finished, Lois said, "Well, you boys have had a busy day, haven't you?"

"Lois," I asked, "if you had heard this without the whole story, would you have believed it?"

"I'm not sure I do now," she answered. "It's just so completely … unbelievable."

"You should be in my shoes. It was strange enough just to have it happen. But four times, with the kids involved, this isn't just strange, it's scary. And I have no idea what it's all about."

Ashley said, "What I said earlier. Do you think it had anything to do with the lightning?"

Puzzled, Lois asked, "Lightning?"

"You know Fritz was hit by lightning a couple of weeks ago." Talking and eating paused. "And we had lightning and thunder all day long today. Fritz felt static each time he opened the door to an adventure."

Lois said, "George, now I understand why you're upset, and why all those calls came in." George nodded.

The story told, I sighed and leaned back into the padding, took a sip of wine, and said, "I wonder why we went where we did? Or did they come here? Or did we meet in some middle?"

It was quiet again. With her voice soft but convinced, Lois said, "Just looking at you all, I don't think you're kidding." She examined me, then Ash. "We DO have a problem and not just about time travel. The students will tell everyone, and we have to deal with the parents, the administration. I think we might hear from the newspapers at some point, probably soon." George and I looked at her and then at each other. "And clearly, your little trip to the past did some damage. You're going to have a sizeable black eye."

"I hadn't thought about that," I said. "And the newspapers could be a problem."

Linda said, "And don't forget the White House."

"We're not going to get away with the Hollywood friend story, either," Ashley said.

Running my hand through my hair, I said, "Then we need to do two things. First, we need a plausible story for everyone outside the government. Second, I've got to figure out how this portal thing works, fast, so I can keep it from happening. I don't want the kids to go through anything like the Triangle

Fire again." Everyone was eating again. "Talking to Robert E. Lee was pretty cool though."

Lois injected, "But what if you'd met him at Gettysburg instead? That wouldn't have been so 'cool'"

"No, you're right Lois. Sorry." But I wasn't really sorry. *It was fascinating. But why Appomattox and not Gettysburg?*

Lois said, "George, you haven't said anything. What do you think?"

Chapter Nine

GEORGE'S ANSWER never emerged. The doorbell rang, but we weren't expecting anyone. I looked at Linda, who shrugged. Standing on the step, hands behind his back, James Williams waited. He told me the president was in the Suburban at the curb. Tom had come too, and the First Lady was with them. I held the door open in a gesture of invitation. On the front steps, an imitation of composure, I shook hands with the president, the agents, and the First Lady. When Linda saw the procession, she said, "Oh, my God."

"Mr. President, this is my wife, Linda, and George's wife, Lois. You've met the rest of us." The president handed a shopping bag to Tom, introduced the First Lady, and shook hands. "I don't believe this," Lois said.

"Sorry to barge in like this. We tried to call a number of times, but you seem to have turned off your phones." The half-eaten dinner plates surprised the president. "Oh, we're interrupting your dinner. I'm so sorry."

"We were just discussing today's events," I said, taking their coats. "Ash, grab some chairs, will you?" As everyone returned to the dining room, Linda asked, "Can I get you some lasagna? There's plenty." No one said no.

The president took the package from Tom, handed it to Linda, and smiled. "Some wine. From the White House collection."

"Thank you, Mr. President. Please everyone, sit. I'll bring the lasagna. Fritz, get the glasses and silver."

Lois and Ash helped Linda carry plates to the table. "This smells delicious," said the president.

"It tastes even better, Mr. President," said Sandy.

"I'm actually glad you're here," I said. "We've been talking about how to present this thing. George was getting calls from teachers and parents, and Linda just said the White House would be concerned."

Twisting his fork in his fingers, the president said, "She's right. When we got back, a little stunned I can tell you, we started to talk about what security issues this poses. You saw the crowd in my office, and I'm worried someone might leak it. I hope what happened is so weird that no one would really believe it anyway. My national security advisor is especially troubled." He frowned. "When I told the First Lady what happened, she was skeptical, but with so many people having seen it, she pointed out that we all need to use the same plausible story. Mr. Russell, would you go over it again, all four occurrences?"

"Of course, Mr. President. Ash, pour the wine please. I'll tell you the entire story while you eat." So, I described the day one more time. Tom recorded everything.

As I spoke, I surveyed the table. George, to my right, was eating, but he watched me, flounder-like. The president, next to George, leaned toward me, taking forkfuls when I paused. Ashley watched the newcomers. The agents sat across from each other, watching every move. Both seemed to have natural radar leading the food to their mouths. Linda bit her lip. Before I began, I retrieved the book about the United Auto Workers.

"Mr. President, I didn't find this until after you left the school." I opened to the picture. "When I stepped into my room, I saw what's in this picture. The Ford sign, the group of men. I didn't have time to recognize who they were or where I was."

"It's a famous shot. That's Walter Reuther and other organizers for the auto workers before he became head of the UAW and later the CIO. No one could ever explain the feet or the rectangle."

"I think that's me."

"Why?" asked the secret service agent.

I took off my shoe, and passed him the book. "It's hard to tell in a black and white picture, but you had that same rectangle. What happened when we left the Oval Office?"

"It vanished. Instantly."

I completed the rest of my story, the rest of the day. When I finished, the president turned to the First Lady and said, "I told you. This is amazing."

"When you arrived we were talking about the story we'll need and how to prevent whatever happened from happening again. I'm guessing that's why you're here. You obviously weren't home very long."

The president contemplated his answer. "When we returned, you saw that my office was full. We can't make up a story like your Hollywood one. But the truth is worse. If the news gets out, you could become a target. Anyone who wants to commit a crime, from bank robbery to assassination, might want to use you. It's not just my security."

"I hadn't even thought of that, Mr. President. We haven't had a chance to think this whole thing through yet. I don't know how or why it happened, but there has to be a reason the portal opens when it does. And the places we went to, all four, are about as random as they could be, except that they did fit my curricula and interests."

Ashley mentioned the lightning again. "Oh yeah. Ashley and I were playing basketball a couple of weeks ago, and I was struck by lightning. I was holding open a metal door when the school was hit."

Tom said, "You were lucky."

"True, but is this time-travel business related? Or just a co-incidence?"

George finally ended his non-participation. Looking slowly around the table, he said, "I think we need to find an explanation for the school first. There are too many people—students, staff, parents—who are going to hear versions of what happened. We can't swear them to secrecy. We really need to clamp down by Monday, or who knows how widespread this story will be." Everyone listened. "Fritz, your Hollywood fiction was enough to hold the fort for an afternoon, but it won't hold up if the story gets out. Everyone in Hollywood will want to know who your friend is."

Quiet thought followed a buzz of agreement. I watched the president scratch gently behind his left ear.

Linda asked, "Mr. President, the government does all sorts of secret stuff. Has there been some kind of study of time travel? At the Defense Department or the CIA, something like that. You know, like Area 51?"

That brought his attention back to the table. He said that one of the first questions he had asked when he was elected was if there was really an Area 51. "I was told there wasn't. Then, a few years ago, the information on Area 51was declassified. No aliens."

Lois said, "Yeah, plausible deniability!" The president threw her a big smile.

Ash said, "I saw that movie."

"To the best of my knowledge, we don't have any work on any of this, but," he hesitated, scratching again, "maybe there should be." He went from scratching his ear to rubbing his chin. He glanced at me.

"Mr. President, excuse me for chiming in, but even if there isn't," said Tom, wiping his mouth, "maybe that's the cover story." Tom said he had been listening to stories for almost twenty years as a secret service agent. "Try this. Mr. Russell agreed to cooperate in our study. Someone would have to come up with a reason why he was chosen. Or maybe the reason could be unstated. He couldn't tell anyone the truth, so he invented the Hollywood connection. No one but us knows about his trip to the Oval Office."

"And everyone at the White House," said Lois.

The president turned to Lois, frowning. "The folks at the White House have been told that this is a matter of national security. They all know what that means—no talking to anyone. Or I'll disappear them." Shocked looks and sharp breaths surrounded him. "I'm just kidding, sorry." The stunned silence was broken by the nervous clank of forks on plates and an audible rumble from my stomach.

"Excuse me. I forgot. I haven't eaten yet."

"I'll get you a plate," said Linda, rising from the table. "I'll help," said the First Lady.

"Could I have some more?" asked the president. "This is really good."

Linda smiled. "Sure."

"I'd love to get your recipe," the First Lady said. "One of these days I'm going to have to cook again."

I touched my shirt pocket and said, "You know, I quit smoking six years ago, but I sure could use a cigarette right now."

The president said, "You should be in my shoes."

"You know, you're easy to convince this is real, Mr. President. We barged in on you," I said. "But for anyone else, no simple explanation will work."

"And looking at your face, we can be assured that whatever happens on the other side can be brought back to the present. That's worrisome."

Linda returned from the kitchen with two plates of lasagna. "Anyone else? There's plenty."

Looking around the table, waiting, Ashley finally said, "You know me, I'd love some. I'll get it, though."

Linda turned to Tom and James, "Gentlemen?"

"Yes please, ma'am," said Tom.

"Me too, ma'am" said James. "This is delicious."

"Thank you." She scanned the table. "George?"

"Why not," he said.

Linda called to the kitchen, where water was running and dishes were clanking. "Four more plates, Ash and Lois." More clatter in the kitchen was followed by the scraping of a spatula, and the First Lady and Ashley returned with the lasagna, the First Lady sporting an apron, and Ash with a dish towel draped over his shoulder. Linda said, "Ash, wine." It wasn't a suggestion.

I passed my glass to Ashley while I thought about my options. The secret service agents declined. Wine splashed in the rest of our glasses.

"Do you guys want some soda or water?" asked Linda.

"Yes please, ma'am," said James.

"Which? We have Diet Coke."

"That would be fine, ma'am," said James. "Yes, please," said Tom.

"James, you need to stop calling me ma'am. My name is Linda."

James said, "Yes ma'am. Sorry, ma'am." Grins surfaced around the table. "Sorry, uh, Linda, it's a habit. Part of training."

We were getting closer, but the story needed editing. Linda said, "I think that George is right. The truth needs to be bundled and wrapped up so tightly that it's fully believable if it does get out. We need a story by Monday, and George, you will probably need to talk to the teachers first thing and have some kind of meeting with the students and probably the parents, too."

George swallowed, and with another forkful in his hand, said, "I'm afraid if we publicize it, the story will grow even bigger. Maybe we should only talk with Fritz's classes. Maybe, Mr. President, we should get someone to come from Washington?"

"If we do that, then we have the White House connection and the government involved," Sandy said. Sandy had been almost invisible. "Don't we want to avoid that? It seems to me we can't use Hollywood and shouldn't use the White House. I think we need something in between."

The First Lady said, "I think Sandy is right. We're talking about new technology. Why not invent an inventor?"

The president put down his fork and looked at his watch. 7:45. "How about I call the Secretary of Energy and get her here. She may have a thought on how to create an inventor."

The First Lady asked, "Does she need to know?"

Wiping his mouth, the president said, "You're right about that, but it would add someone who has dealt with this stuff, inventors, ideas, pretty often."

"You could brief her tomorrow rather than getting her here now," said the First Lady.

Plate scraping slowed, and forks were lowered. Mouths wiped with napkins signaled surrender from the meal. Our guests leaned forward, ready for the next course of conversation.

Lois asked, "Fritz, the kids all love you; do you think an inventor would be enough for them? George, you could have a meeting with the teachers on Monday and tell them the same thing. Some parents are still going to be upset, but you can tell them that Fritz didn't know which of his lessons the guy would pick. Or when. And you can say that Fritz has called him and told him off for surprising the teacher and traumatizing a high school class."

The First Lady agreed. "I think that will work. The story is limited and the outcome is controlled."

Linda said, "I think it would be helpful to have someone check out the room, but I think any mention of the government could expand this out of control. I think the Hollywood guy works. You know they are working on hologames now, and there was a holodeck on *Star Trek*, so it's not new."

"But maybe better?" I questioned. "New technology. Next generation."

"I agree with Linda and Fritz," said Lois. "If we're dealing with a fantasy, we should keep it in that realm."

Linda added, "Fritz, if you apologize to the teachers for the disturbance, they should leave it at that. Ash, Sandy?"

Ashley looked at Sandy, a little longer than I would have expected. "If you don't give them too much to think about…" He turned his focus back to Sandy.

With Monday resolved, we still had a problem. I didn't know how the portal opened or if it would happen again. I said I was trying to grasp that time travel was real. And I was simultaneously figuring out how to prevent what had happened and wanting to visit the past again.

"Mr. Russell, your first concern has to be the security of the country," said Tom Andrews.

"Hold on a second, Tom. He's a history teacher." The president told me he could appreciate my dilemma. That this discovery could be dangerous had already been shown. But there could also be benefits. "I'll have to think about that," he said, rubbing behind his left ear.

"Well, I could suspend you until you figure it out," suggested George.

Lois said, "Honestly, George! Don't be silly! If the classroom is the portal entrance, someone else might stumble through it and not handle it as well as Fritz has. And he needs to be there to figure it out. If he just disappears, the story will look suspicious."

"Good point, Lois," said Linda. "If that happens, people are going to come to me to find out what happened to Fritz. I can see a trail of news cameras on the sidewalk. That doesn't keep things quiet."

"So what do we do?" asked George.

Ashley, who had been unusually close-mouthed, almost distracted, said, "I hate to keep harping on it, but we have two electrical events that I think are connected. Lightning and static on the doorknob. Today's weather was thunder and lightning. I think that's what we need to explore. Maybe the Energy Secretary would have some helpful suggestions."

"But not tonight!' said Lois.

With that, the conversation lulled.

Ashley said, "Wine, anyone?" He held a bottle in each hand. I handed him my glass, but the others merely shook their heads no.

The president looked around. "We still have to have scientists investigate the portal. There are serious security issues."

James said, "Mr. President, couldn't we send some people to check out the classroom for out-of-the-ordinary power surges or something like that? We could do it over the weekend."

Tom added, "The Energy Secretary might have someone who could shed some light and come here. Or maybe the science advisor?"

"Those are good ideas. I just think I should call her now."

From the kitchen came a loud, "I think you should wait." It was Lois. She then came back in carrying four plates of cannoli. Sandy brought the rest of the plates on a tray.

"Coffee, anyone?" Linda asked.

As she looked around, James said, "Ma'am, I mean, Linda. Please." Nods all around.

I got up, held up my hand to stop the president, who had also started to get up. "I'll get them."

Linda and I went back to the kitchen. We didn't speak, but her wrinkled forehead said she was anxious. I brought out sugar, sweetener, and a pitcher of milk. No one spoke; everyone was considering what had been said so far. The president broke the quiet. "These are great," pointing at his plate with his fork.

"Thanks, I made them myself," said Ashley.

"No he did not," said Linda. "I bought them this afternoon. If anyone wants another, there are three left."

George said, "I'll have another if it's okay." Lois glared at him.

"I can cut them in half if you all want more."

"No, thanks," said the president. "Gotta watch what I eat, you know."

"Anyone?" said Linda, looking at Ashley, who nodded yes. "Fritz?"

"Maybe later, if there are any left. George, can we get into the building over the weekend?"

"Of course. If you let me know when, I'll meet you there."

George and I looked at the president.

He said, "I'll call the secretary on our way back to Washington. I'll have her meet me in the morning. I'm sure she'll find someone and, knowing her, she'll want to come up herself. Early afternoon is probably the soonest we can get all the pieces in place."

"Can we get in in the morning, George?" I looked at Ashley, who mouthed "sure."

The president said, "I would appreciate if you waited. I'd like to get some guidance first, especially since you don't know what will happen."

"Sure, Mr. President."

"Oh, and be sure you have your phones on."

With dinner done and a plan in place, the president's visit was over. He said, "I think it's time to go." He rose, placing his hand on my shoulder. He said he appreciated our cooperation and thanked Linda for dinner.

The First Lady said, "I think we ought to help clean up first. We were uninvited guests, you know."

"Actually, you were invited," I said. "You know those raffles to have dinner with you at the White House? Well, I responded to one and invited you to come to my house instead. Never heard back though. I was thinking about a barbecue, but this was nice too."

In the hallway to bid our guests goodbye, George said, "You won't forget about graduation, will you, Mr. President?"

Lois said, "George, what are you talking about?"

"I forgot to tell you. I asked the president if he could come to our graduation ceremonies."

The president frowned. "We forgot about the gym. We signed autographs and spoke to the kids. The inventor story won't work for that."

George said, "You could say you stopped to use the bathroom and then toured the school."

"That would work. Tom, when we get back, we're going to have to change the appointment book. Would you call Lily Evans and ask her if she would mind coming back to the office in about two hours?"

"Yes, sir."

We waved as they drove away.

Chapter Ten

"I'LL HELP YOU clean up, Linda," Lois said and began collecting the empty glasses. Sandy already had a handful of plates, and Ash was rinsing and loading the dishwasher when we came in with the last plates and glasses. I asked if there was any lasagna left.

"Nope. Sorry, Fritz. No leftovers. But anyone want more coffee?"

"That's just more dishes for you," said Lois. "George, I think we should leave these three NICE people, and Ashley, to have a little quiet."

I disagreed. "I think another cup of coffee is a good idea, Lois. We still have a few things to discuss, just us." We all sat at the kitchen table. I said, "Is anyone else not sure of what just happened?" They all looked unsure. "Look, we haven't had time to think about what went on, and the government is already involved. DISAPPEAR. Now there's a word. Doesn't make ME comfortable."

"I think he was kidding, Fritz," said George, fidgeting.

"Was he?" I asked, glancing at Lois. "We have some pretty smart people right here at this table. Something in the classroom opened the portal. I think Ash is right that lightning, or electricity was somehow involved. I got shocks when I touched the doorknob. I'm trying to remember what I was doing or thinking that might explain the locations we went to. You all know I'm interested in the Civil War, always have been. And I teach the course on workers in America. So there's a relationship, but why travel to those specific sites. And how did the Oval Office open up?"

Lois said, "Fritz, at least for the moment, we have a plan to give us time to figure it out."

But Linda picked up my thread. "I'm not sure how much time we really have, Lois. They must be rattled. It only took three hours from the time Fritz left school until the president showed up."

"Less actually," I muttered. "Lois, we have a story for school, and we have a guaranteed visit tomorrow. Unless there's a simple answer and they find it, we have a problem."

"What worries me," said Ashley, "is that whole business about national security. I really think the president thought your visit and his were cool. 'Amazing', he said. But I watched him the whole time. He was listening, but he was staring like he was seeing what you were saying. He seems really shaken about your just walking into his office." He sipped his coffee. "Look, so far as we all know, time travel and teleportation are impossible. But Fritz, you did it and then took him along with you. They aren't going to let this go." Ashley looked at himself in the back of his spoon. "Did you pick up on changing the president's calendar for today?" he continued.

"They really do need to explain his being here," said Lois.

"And I think they're afraid we may say something they can't explain away or cover up. We need to get on top of this, or we're all in trouble, maybe everyone in this town is at risk."

George said, "Don't you think you're exaggerating, Ashley?"

"Not if he believes what he said about security, you know, bank robbers and terrorists. I mean, Fritz is number one, but we're all involved."

I wasn't that anxious, but I was glad that Ashley understood. George on the other hand had, well, the train had left the station while he decided which car to get on. I worried about the kids. We'd been lucky today. "We've got to figure this out fast."

Lois said, "It's starting to get late. Linda, let me help clean up. You TWO," she glowered at Ashley, "need some time to talk, I'm sure."

Linda said, "Lois, really, I'm fine." Lois got up anyway and headed for the sink. Sandy was stuck in the corner. George, shaking his head, said, "I've been very careful for years about when to tell her no. Mostly, she just does it anyway." Lois scowled.

We talked about the teachers' meeting on Monday, and after about ten minutes, Lois said, "George, let's go. You'll see these two delinquents tomorrow." To me she said, "Someday, maybe, I'll live to see you two act your ages, not like your ninth graders."

"Well, let's see. Hmm. Sorry, Lois. Don't think that will happen. Possibly for me. Definitely not for him." I pointed my thumb at Ashley.

Lois frowned, and then we all laughed. Except George, whose face reflected his trying to figure out what I meant. We laughed harder. George got up, followed by Ashley and me, and all three of us followed Lois and Linda to the door. Sandy worked her way out of the corner and caught up.

"Linda, thank you so much for a lovely dinner," said Lois. "I was certainly skeptical about this story, but I'm not now. George and I will work on the teachers' meeting, and he'll get back to you by Sunday night. If either of us has a thought or question, we should call each other. Okay?"

Linda said, "I think that's a good idea. We have your number, don't we, Fritz?"

"Yup," I said.

"Then we're off," said Lois. She looked at me, shaking her head as she stepped toward the door. "Time travel. What next?"

George shook my hand, kissed Linda's cheek, and said, "You're a good cook. Thanks. Good night, Ashley, Sandy. See you tomorrow." He followed his wife out the door. We stood on the porch and watched them drive away.

* * *

"DID YOUR RECORDER get all that, Tom?" asked the president.

"Yes, sir."

"Well, they certainly get it, don't they?" said the First Lady. "They're nice people, caught up in something no one understands. I don't think they're a threat to anyone."

"Not intentionally, anyway," said the president. "Where did you put the device, Tom?"

"In the table leg where the screw hole is. Someone would have to look very closely to find it. Unless you know what it is, it looks like a button, so even if it's found, it'll get thrown away. If they do move it, we'll know."

"Let's go home," said the president. They boarded the jet and headed for Andrews Air Force Base.

"Tom, did you reach Lily Evans?" asked the president.

"Yes, sir. She'll be waiting. Frankly, I don't think she had left yet."

He told the First Lady he wanted to call the Energy Secretary. She said, "It's not even late. Call her."

"Yes, Mr. President, good evening," she said.

"Hi Brenda, sorry to bother you, but I need to speak with you in person tomorrow at 8 a.m."

"Certainly, Mr. President."

"Before the meeting, I want you to consider this. I need a person who is an expert in electricity, electromagnetic fields, recording electrical events, things like that. Power surges. That kind of thing. I'll fill in the details tomorrow."

"Mr. President, as you know, I worked with those kinds of topics before you appointed me. Besides myself, there are two young people on staff who fit your description. Would you like me to get in touch with them?"

"Can they be at the White House tomorrow morning?"

"I don't know either of their schedules, but I'll call. If they're in Washington, they'll be there."

"Thanks. See you all in the morning. Oh, and you may need to spend the night in New Jersey."

"Yes sir. Good night, Mr. President."

The president returned to the seat beside his wife and said, "She's got a couple of tech jocks who'll be there in the morning."

* * *

"I FEEL like I've been awake for two days."

"We'll go," said Ashley. Sandy pushed her chair back and started to get up.

"That's not what I meant. I can't wait to look around. What I didn't say was that I had planned to talk about the end of the Civil War. And I was considering the different labor tragedies of the early 1900s, including Triangle. I still don't know what happened, but I can't imagine that it was brain waves that got us there."

"Well, in your case, brain waves don't explain it," Ashley grinned. "Linda, can I have that last cannoli and another coffee?"

"No way," I said. "That cannoli is mine. And you can get your own coffee."

"I wasn't asking her to get it, only if I could have it. I'll split the cannoli with you."

"No. It's mine."

"Split it with him, Fritz. I'll get more tomorrow while you're at the school."

"Good," said Ashley, going to the refrigerator. "Anyone want coffee?"

"Sure," I said.

"Get it yourself," said Ashley.

"No wonder Lois keeps calling you two delinquents," Linda said, handing me the cannoli and a knife. "When you've finished eating, drinking, cleaning up, and fooling around, it's time for you to go home, Ash." I cut the cannoli in half and took the bigger piece. Ashley pouted.

"Okay," he said. "Throwing me out into the cold dark night. I get it."

Linda said, "Good. It's about time you got something."

Ashley and Sandy left about a half hour later. When she was leaving, Sandy whispered to me that she'd love to meet William Shakespeare.

"Quiet at last," I sighed. I pushed my cup away.

"Fritz, I don't know if I should be scared or not, it's so unreal." said Linda, sitting down again.

"You don't know? I met Robert E. Lee, who died in 1870. What I did today is in a picture from a Detroit newspaper from 1937. My class witnessed the Triangle Fire in 1911. The President of the United States just had dinner with us. Any one of those would be reason to be scared. And not knowing why or how it happened, or what might make it happen again, that's not my typical day. Lin, we need to figure this out."

Linda's feelings are right more often than not, and I've learned to pay attention. Most of the time she understands pretty much everything before me. As an editor, she sees plots unfold. But we weren't dealing with fiction. She said, "I don't think we have to be afraid yet. Think about all the things they have to deal with every day. You have to be a special kind of crazy to want to be president. Fritz, what scares me the most is despite all the things he has to deal with, he took the time to come here. And brought his wife."

"I think they had three reasons. First, to check if we were regular people; second, to get away from Washington; and third, for a home cooked meal." She still frowned. "Seriously, I think he trusts the First Lady more than his closest appointed advisors.

My guess is she came to size us up for him and help him analyze the whole thing. She's smart, and she's a well-trained thinker. But, I'll bet they can't get lasagna this good even at the White House."

"Be serious."

"I am. Think about it. When you're the president, you've got to deal with every backstabber in the world. No wonder presidents go gray so fast. Congress, taxes, wars, special interests, the media. Did I mention Congress? I teach this stuff and it makes me crazy. I can't guess what it's like to be on 24/7."

"You never told me what Lee was like," she said. Her eyes shone with the same intelligent curiosity I had discovered early in our time in New York. I grew up across the Hudson and had visited the city a lot. It was a playground. But with Linda, New York became a classroom. We did the Bronx Zoo and Yankee Stadium; we visited the Cloisters and Battery Park. We went to lectures at Columbia and N.Y.U, visited the Brooklyn and Bronx Botanical Gardens, and got seats for the U.S. Open tennis tournament for a day.

We went to a Michelangelo exhibit at The Metropolitan Museum of Art, "Don Giovanni" at the Metropolitan Opera and, well, New York Mets games. We skated at Rockefeller Center, laughed at the comedy clubs, drank at McSorley's Old Ale House and, of course, saw a few Broadway shows. We even took the Staten Island ferry just to go for a ride. And we went out into the harbor to visit the Ellis Island Museum.

We watched the Thanksgiving parade before I took her to my parent's house for dinner. At Christmas, we shopped and window shopped. And of course we went to the UN and the Empire State Building. I came to appreciate that "the Bronx is up and the Battery's down." I'd lived nearby my whole life and had never seen New York like I did that year.

In answer to her question about Lee, I said, "We didn't have any time to discuss that. I haven't even had a chance to tell Ash.

Anyway, we interrupted Lee's first chance to get away from the chaos. Lin, the gunpowder smell hung in the air like a thick curtain. One of the kids got blood on his hand." I paused, visualizing Lee sitting on a stump with a laptop. "I was surprised at how receptive he was, though, once we got him curious."

"After what he'd been through the last four years, I think he enjoyed the distraction and the kids. He's slim for an older man, but he probably hasn't eaten a regular meal in years. I think he was fascinated that so much would change in the future. We showed him a computer and cell phone, and he was captivated by the idea of cars. He's a pretty smart guy, you know. He was up at the top of his class at West Point."

"You're talking about him in the present tense, like he was alive."

"Well, today, at least, he was. But I forgot to mention that when we first met him, Dan Wilkinson started to show Lee his textbook, but it didn't have any words. The words came back as we were leaving. It's like history caught up." I winced when I started to lean my cheek on my hand.

"What happened when you got hit?"

"I opened my door and looked to my left. The big Ford sign was clear, but the presence of other men was more a feeling than my actually seeing them. I got blindsided. I think I surprised the guy who hit me, and my face got in the way as he raised his club. I don't know for sure, but I think he pushed me and I fell backwards."

"But the picture? How is that possible?"

"From everything we know, it's not. I can't prove those are my feet, but the setting, the rectangly thing, and the Ford sign sure match. I wish I'd had even a couple of seconds more to look around. Lin, if this is real, why me?"

"Right now, I don't know. What about Triangle?"

My mind jumped. I could still the smell charred wood and burning cloth. "It was awful. We got there toward the end. Some people were escaping from the roof, but we watched as women jumped from the top floors. Some were on fire. They were like a meteor shower. All I wanted to do was get the kids out of there, so I was completely surprised when we entered the morgue, not only because it was so gruesome, but because it meant we also went to still another time that day, much later than the fire. I think it was that night. You know what was weird though? Even though it was the end of March, we didn't need jackets. I'll have to look up the weather that day. The kids were really upset."

Linda said calmly, "You got them back unharmed. That's the most important thing."

"Thank God. So how was YOUR day?

Chapter Eleven

SATURDAY MORNING brought jacket weather. We sat with our first cups. The spring leaves were rattling when brakes on the driveway made me snap to. "Now what?" I said. When I got to the back door, there stood Ashley, his arms around a full paper bag.

"I brought breakfast," he said, peeling off his scarf and rubbing his hands against red cheeks. His early morning arrivals had been a part of our weekends for years, and were usually accompanied by a story.

"You're up early. Couldn't sleep?"

"Nope. I kept going over the classroom layout in my head. The bookcases are steel, you know. And that ugly green rag you call a rug. Always charges me up for a static shock when I touch metal. I think we really need to get in there and look around."

"Is Sandy coming?" asked Linda.

"She said she'll meet us at school. I need to call her."

"I'm not going anywhere until we find out what the president's doing," I said. "But I'm glad you're here. We're going to need to help George with the story, I'm sure. Grab a cup of coffee. It's hot, and it tastes as good as it smells."

"I brought bagels, the deli's lumpy cream cheese, and coffee cake. What do you want?"

With bagels in the toaster, and Ashley finally sitting down with his mug, I said, "We can explain away the time-travel trips, but the kids in the gym saw the president, so we're tied in to his explanation of that." Ashley had already managed to get crumbs on the table and was picking some off his sweater, one at a time, and putting them in a neat pile on the corner of his plate.

"Maybe you can explain away time travel. I can't. You say you met a man who's been dead for a hundred-and-fifty years. You took a class to an event in 1911. You can explain it away. Explain it to me first."

I told him I couldn't, but both had happened. And we had to find out why and how before the government took steps to erase any evidence. Including me.

Linda pointed out that the president was changing his schedule book to say he'd stopped as he was driving by. "But there were no cars," she added. "I wonder if the school's security cameras were on when they didn't arrive."

"Wow, I forgot about the cameras," I said. "We need to let him know."

* * *

THE PRESIDENT, joined by the Secretary of Energy and the two analysts, was also having coffee. Served from silver and holding china cups by an original Remington cast of *The Bronco Buster*, they discussed the troubling science of Fritz's travels. "That's some story, Mr. President. I share your concern, especially since it violates everything we know about physics," said Secretary Stevens.

"Well, not everything, Madam Secretary," said Kim Bishell, a tall woman with a serious face and red glasses. "Mr. President, we have been studying time as a tangible substance, as more than a concept alone. We have used every energy-detecting device we have, and although we haven't actually produced a picture yet, we have found that at low frequencies, we are able to discern what seems to be time's residual particulate matter. It's really early, but it's interesting."

The president asked, "Do you think you could find anything in that classroom?"

"Don't know, sir, but we can give it a shot," Tony Almeida responded. "But first, Mr. President, we can check your door before we go to the school. I have one of the wave counters in my lab. It's about the size of a pack of cigarettes, and we can collect data on a laptop. I'll go get it, if you want."

The secretary took charge. "Tony, go get it quickly. We can start here, if that's okay, Mr. President."

"That's why we're here." He called the secret service agents into the room. "James, give him a ride so he can get back through the gates quickly."

"Yes, sir."

The president continued, "I'm going to ask the three of you to go to New Jersey today and check out the school. We'll arrange for you to meet Mr. Russell while you're there. Does that data collector have any use on people?"

Kim replied, "We've never tried it, sir. It would be interesting to see." Tony and James left the Oval Office.

Pondering the doorway of elegant white panels, the secretary asked that no one use it until it was scanned. "If there is something there, we don't want to add additional energy patterns."

"Being able to trace someone through time, extraordinary," the president mused. "A time imprint, like a fingerprint. This is exciting, even for me as a non-scientist. But as a lawyer and a citizen, I worry about the privacy implications. It raises as many issues as it might solve. I have a call I need to make. Would you mind waiting in the outer office? Tom, show them where and get them some coffee."

"Thank you, Mr. President," said the secretary, as she and Kim followed Tom out the door.

Tom returned immediately. "Mr. President, we've continued to monitor Mr. Russell's conversations. I think you should hear this."

As he listened, the president's legal pad was filling up. Tom clicked off the recorder. "Two things hit me, Tom. First, the cameras. We need them to 'malfunction'. Ask George if they have cameras and then let him show you the system. The second thing is what Mr. Russell said about his brain causing his travel. I'll have to think about that. Tom, sorry to lay this all on you this way. We've seen a lot together, haven't we?"

"We have, Mr. President. It's been an honor to work with you."

Within minutes, Tom's beeper notified him that James was back. "Bring them all in. And Tom, we're also going to need listening devices at Gilbert's and McAllister's, and Horton's, just in case. I think redundancy is appropriate."

"I was thinking the same thing, sir. I'll take care of it. If they do find one or two, they may be less cooperative, but they're not likely to look for additional ones. I was thinking of putting one in the kitchen also."

The president frowned. "I think you should avoid the kitchen, Tom. The First Lady was in there and we weren't, so they would suspect her immediately. I would rather keep her out of this. I don't think she would approve."

"I'll take care of it, sir." Tom left through one of the other three doors in the Oval Office. The president turned in his chair and gazed out at the spring morning in the Rose Garden. The first roses were blossoming.

"Interesting," he said.

When the group returned to the room, the president spun his chair around. Tony removed the wave counter from his briefcase. Before Kim's laptop was connected, the president asked, "Can I see that thing?"

"Sure, Mr. President. I designed it myself," said Tony.

The scanning lasted only a couple of minutes. When Tony finished, Kim said, "I think we have some activity, but I can't tell if it's from normal traffic or something else. It's all recorded. We need to boost the transmission and check the various frequencies."

"Good. Are you all ready to go to see the school?" Tony tapped his knapsack. The president told them they would leave from Andrews with Tom and James. "The classroom is the focus, but I want you to go to the gym, too. We'll need to buy time for some other things, so I want you to check the rest of the school." He sat down at his desk again, leaning on his fists. "None of this is to be discussed, even when they ask—and they will. Mr. Russell is anxious to examine his classroom. Get this done as quickly and quietly as possible but keep scanning after you've finished if James hasn't let you know it's ok to go."

"Yes, sir."

Final instructions given, the president asked if arrangements had been made at the other end. Informed that everything was set, he told them that Mr. Russell would meet them at 1:30. "OK, get going and let me know when you're on the way back."

* * *

THE PHONE STARTLED me. I spilled some coffee down my chin. "Good morning, Mr. President," I said, wiping my face. "We've been waiting for your call." The president filled me in on the schedule. He asked if that would work for us. "1:30. No problem, sir." I glanced at Ash and Linda. "I'll call George and let him know. Uh, before you go, Mr. President, were you able to fix your calendar?" Ash dropped his bagel, scattering the onion chips. "That's good. Goodbye, sir."

"I wonder what they think they'll find," Linda said. "Ash, call Sandy."

AT 1:10, WE HEADED OUT. Linda had decided she wanted a first-hand view. George and Lois were already waiting in the parking lot when we arrived ten minutes later. Sandy pulled in right behind us. Slapping feet drew our attention to the volleying on the tennis courts across the lot.

Precisely at 1:30, a black Suburban turned into the curved driveway and unloaded James and three strangers. One face was familiar from the news. James introduced Secretary of Energy Brenda Stevens, Kim, and Tony. All business, they were all in suits.

James said, "Thank you for a delicious meal last night. When I told my wife how good it was, she asked if I could get the recipe."

Linda said, "Gladly, James." Linda shared the recipe regularly. "Give me your email or street address."

"Thank you, ma'am." Linda scowled at him. "Sorry. Linda." We headed right for my classroom. There was no static when I touched the doorknob.

The secretary explained that Kim and Tony would test for electrical fields to see if there was an anomaly. As we watched Tony begin scanning, Ashley asked, "What is that thing?"

"A scanner. It detects electromagnetic charges that we wouldn't expect to be there," said the secretary.

Linda asked, "What happens after you collect the data?"

"We'll return to the lab and analyze it."

Linda asked, "Do you expect to find anything? Do you have a hypothesis?"

"We're working at very low frequencies, which we think would be the energy range for your husband's contact with the time portal." Tony scanned the door first from inside the classroom and then from the hallway, up and down the entire surface.

AS TONY WORKED, Tom was walking up to the Russell's front door. He covered his shoes with booties and picked the lock. He first checked the original bug and then placed two more. It took less than two minutes. When he opened the front door, he heard snipping and noticed a neighbor trimming his shrubbery, Tom said, "Thanks, I'll be in touch." The neighbor paid no attention, and he drove away.

His next stop was the McAllisters, about ten minutes away. Then he went to Ashley's house, a comfortable Cape Cod with uncut grass outside and unwashed dishes, undusted everything, scattered newspapers and magazines, and stacks of books everywhere. He left through the back door, repeating "I'll be in touch," although Ashley's car was gone. If anyone were watching, they would have known he was an intruder. He walked quickly to the Suburban and headed back to the airport.

AFTER TONY HAD FINISHED the door, he swept the entire classroom. He ran the sensor along each row, checked every desk and chair and then, holding his arm up, scanned nothing but air. Ashley asked him if he could pick up the baseball game. Finally he scoured my desk, the sides, crawled underneath, and finally scanned the desktop. After he covered the classroom, he scanned George, Ashley, Sandy, and me.

Tony turned to the secretary, "I've got it all here, ma'am. We should follow the route through the school." George led the way.

As we entered the gym, Tony asked, "Where was the president in here?"

I tried to duplicate the president's steps and showed where he'd stood signing autographs. Tony scanned the floor, walked to the basket, held the scanner up to trace the arc of the basketball behind my hand as I demonstrated. Then he examined the gym door again. "Done here, Madam Secretary."

"Mr. McAllister, we'd like to check other parts of the school, just to be thorough," she said.

George finally chimed in, "Well, I don't get it, but I guess you know what you're looking for." That statement was so typically George. He is a smart man, but he assumes people in authority know more than he does. He reacts to what affects him, the school, and then everything else. Sometimes he seems like he's somewhere else, even when he's talking directly to someone.

Nobody answered him, but we all left the gym after Tony said, "Madam Secretary, I'd like to go check the classroom once more, alone with Mr. Russell."

"Go ahead."

When we got there, he had me open the door and scanned the doorknob as I pulled. Then he scanned me as we walked through the doorway and the door as it clicked shut.

"Okay, I'm done," said Tony, opening the door to the others.

"Find anything, do you think?" I asked.

"Don't know yet," said Tony, returning his scanner to his briefcase.

"Thank you all for your trouble today," said the secretary, as the staffers packed up. "We'll let the president know our results."

Lois, who had been quiet the entire time, asked "What about us? Aren't you going to let us know if you find anything?"

"The president will be in touch, ma'am" said James. "He instructed me to let you know he is grateful for your cooperation, and he will be sure to follow up with you when the data has been reviewed. There is one other thing, though. I noticed security cameras running both inside and out. Are they on today?"

George said, "They're on during the school day and are motion activated when the school is closed."

James asked, "How are the shots stored?"

"Well, we keep tapes for two weeks and then they're downloaded to a data storage company. I've been principal for eighteen years, and we've only looked at old pictures once."

"Can I look at yesterday afternoon's recording?" It didn't sound like a request.

"Well, I guess so, sure. They're in the office."

In a closet where three monitors showed split screen images, George explained that there were three cameras that would have picked up the president. He logged in and entered the security codes. The grainy black and white pictures lit up the screen.

James asked to see the shots of the street and parking lot. He told George that he was making it appear that the camera had failed while the president was at the school since they hadn't come by car. George thought a moment and nodded. When the shots of the president were finished showing, George said, "That's all we have."

James said, "Thank you, Mr. McAllister. That should take care of everything. We'll let you get on with your weekends."

When we rejoined the others, I asked, "Did you drive from Washington?"

James said, "No, we flew."

I assumed he meant into Philly or Newark, but Ashley said "Really! There's no airport around here, at least none that I know of."

James looked at him. "You wouldn't."

I looked at Ashley and then at Linda. I said nothing, but Lois said, "So a top-secret government airport? Fascinating."

James said, "Not top secret, just convenient."

The car door clanged shut. "Well that was pretty boring," said Ashley, hands in his pockets. Ash talks with his hands, so that seemed strange to me.

"George, are you set for Monday? Do you need any help?" Sandy asked.

"Thanks Sandy. I don't know what we'll need yet, but I'll let you know."

Lois took over. She said George would call a mandatory meeting of all staff after school on Monday and so after-school activities would have to be cancelled. George glowered at her. "That's what we thought would disrupt the day the least. What about you, Fritz? What are you going to tell the kids?"

I glanced at the tennis matches while we crossed to our cars. "Like we discussed last night, Lois, I'll go with the story of a friend, the Hollywood version, who developed a new, advanced imaging system. I think they'll believe it."

"You'll have to talk at the meeting too," said George.

"By then we'll have the whole story, George. Don't worry. I'll work on it today, and I'll call you and let you know by tomorrow night. Okay?"

"That's good," said Lois, waiting to climb in. "Let's go home, George."

* * *

THE PRESIDENT FILLED Koppler in about the day's activities in New Jersey. The national security adviser was a Washington fixture, highly regarded in the intelligence community, and well connected. He had risen through Treasury investigating questionable foreign funds, done well on Wall Street, and returned to Washington as an intelligence consultant. Wealthy and well groomed, he had an imposing personality.

Although the president had appointed Koppler because of his experience in the politics of intelligence, he hesitated to speak his mind about the portal. His advisor wasn't his friend. He wasn't even in the same party. They talked about imminent danger and the ability of the teachers to maintain secrecy. The national security advisor suggested putting bugs in their homes, and he said again he thought the president should consider ending the threat.

"Jim, I want to see where this leads. It's important. If there's reason to be concerned, I'll let you know."

Chapter Twelve

ONCE WE GOT HOME, Linda broke the silence of the drive. "I think we have more than a problem. Look at what happened. They sent the Secretary of Energy to investigate. They have a device that they think might detect the portal." She stopped short, I could tell she was thinking, and then asked, "You don't think they bugged us last night, do you?" she asked.

* * *

THE SUBURBAN ROLLED through the parking lot and stopped at the baby jet waiting at the edge of the runway. The open field surrounding the landing strip was protected north and south by woods that blocked the view from the road. Piles of brick and lumber sat by two small trailers. Tom took out his phone. "Mr. President, we're done here. We'll be back in about an hour." A group of robins landed on the grass next to the tarmac. "Yes, sir. I took care of everything. We were lucky. Ms. Russell and Ms. McAllister came to the school, so I got all three houses. I didn't do Ms. Horton's place, though. Too much traffic. She lives in an apartment complex. Yes. Madam Secretary," he held the phone out. "The president wants to speak to you."

"Hello, Mr. President." In response to his question, she said, "Tony recorded everything, sir. Kim left the computer in the car. They were interested, wanted to know how things worked.

We'll look at the data on the plane, and we'll show you whatever we have when we get back. Yes, sir. We'll see you then."

* * *

"I HOPE they haven't been that stupid. We're not a threat to the president or national security." Looking at Ashley, I said, "Well you and I aren't, Lin. Can't be sure about Ash."

"I can't believe you said that," Ashley sputtered. "Say stuff like that and if they do have a bug, the president is going to have me disappeared."

I shouted, "I was just kidding, Mr. President."

Although she knew Ash and I were engaged in harmless banter, Linda sensed that there was a serious if not sinister possibility which neither Ash nor I was seeing. No longer willing to listen, Linda said, "Honestly! You two are nuts! What if they HAVE bugged us? What are we supposed to do?"

"Nothing different," I said. "We haven't done anything wrong. We're dealing with something that no one understands. They can't seriously think we're dangerous."

"But Fritz," said Linda, "they ARE obviously worried. They came here last night. And came back today. There's nothing usual about any of this." I heard the intensity as her sentences sped up.

"Lin, all that may be true, but I'm not going to get paranoid about it. I'm still wondering what the trigger is for opening the portal. I'll leave the paranoia to Ash."

* * *

"DO YOU THINK you got anything, Tony?" Kim asked from across the aisle.

"We'll know in a minute." He sat back and found himself sucked into the soft seat.

The plane reached cruising altitude, bright sun shining through the right side windows. "We don't have much time now.

We'll be home in a few minutes. This plane really moves," said Tony. He took out the scanner, connected it to the laptop, and downloaded the images. They both watched. Kim turned in her seat, and told Secretary Stevens they had found something.

Without getting up, the secretary said, "We'll look at it together when we land. We're going back to the White House, and we can show the president. But I want to see what you have first."

* * *

ASHLEY SAID, "I don't know about you, but I'm hungry. Got anything to eat?"

"You brought a dozen bagels," I said, pointing to the crumpled brown bag on the counter.

"Yeah, so I had that for breakfast."

I said, "If you keep eating our food, we'll go broke." As I spoke, I wrote on a piece of scrap paper, "Let's go out for lunch." Linda and Ashley nodded. Then I said, just in case, "Nah, expense be damned. Let's go out. I have a craving for a pastrami sandwich."

* * *

IN ANOTHER BLACK Suburban parked beside the plane, the secretary looked at Kim's computer. She said, "Kim, can you slow down the images?" She did. "Good! Now you know why I hired you guys. James, we need to go to the lab. Tony has to pick up some equipment."

Tom took his phone from his pocket. "We're on the ground, Mr. President. We're stopping by the lab, and we'll be there in about an hour." James started the car. "Yes, sir. We'll see you then." He disconnected. "James, we need to stop in Foggy Bottom on the way. POTUS wants a pastrami sandwich."

* * *

"I WONDER IF they found anything," I said. "They ought to be back by now." I took a bite out of a heaping pastrami on rye. "This is so good," I said with my mouth full.

Ashley took a bite of his and said, "It's not polite to talk with your mouth full." Linda raised her eyebrows and shook her head. Over the years, her head shaking had been a regular part of our relationship.

"Okay, Ash, assume you're right that electricity is the key. They were looking for electrical images. So where would electrical charges come from?" I asked.

Ashley was chewing, but Linda said, "The electricity comes from you. The static on the doorknob opens the portal or signals that it's open. What else would conduct electricity?" She has a way of directing a conversation by asking the right question.

"Water, metal," said Ash, thinking of options. "There's no water in the classroom. So what about metal? What's metal in the class?"

"Besides your robotic self?" I said.

"Very funny," said Ash. "Besides, I'm not metal. I'm a new age polymer."

"You must be because no one could eat like you and never gain a pound."

Ash winked. "It's my workout routine."

"Okay, okay," said Linda. "Metal in the classroom. Desks, window latches, the door hardware, the cabinets, bookcases. What else?"

We stopped talking, thinking while eating.

"I want a pickle," said Ashley.

"Fritz, metal probably has something to do with opening the portal," Linda said. "But that still doesn't explain where you went. The charge may get you through, but why Appomattox, New York? Why the Oval Office?"

I put down my sandwich. "At first, I thought it had to do with the date. But that doesn't work. Triangle was in March and the

Ford thing was in May. But like I said before, I was reading about the Triangle Fire in a book, and I was..." Suspended between words, I visualized the book.

"What?"

"You know how I use paperclips as bookmarks."

"Metal. Again."

"I've got to get back into my classroom."

Ashley asked why.

Linda said, "He uses paperclips to mark pages."

"Metal!" said Ash. "And?"

"Okay, picklehead, if it's metal that opens the portal, and I use paperclips to mark books, then maybe that's how I got to Appomattox and Triangle." I pondered for a moment. "But I don't have any books about the Oval Office or the White House."

"What about the president?" Linda asked. "Do you have any books about him—or the one he wrote?"

"We need to get back in the classroom," said Ashley, about to bite a pickle.

* * *

THE SECRETARY, her staffers, and the two agents entered the Oval Office. The president, gesturing that they should all sit, walked to one of the tan couches. "So?" he asked.

Tony and Kim set up the booster and the computer on the coffee table in front of the president and then sat on the floor, ready to start. James and Tom stood behind them. The office door opened again. Jim Koppler. "Sorry to interrupt, Mr. President. I heard the secretary was back. May I watch?"

"Grab a seat." Though he couldn't say anything, the president wasn't happy. Talk about uninvited guests, he thought.

The secretary said, "Mr. President, we haven't seen this with the booster yet, but there are images or at least some electrical impulses detected. Tony built an image booster, and Kim set the computer to let us change speeds on the images."

"Great. So let's see it."

Tony switched on the booster, and the screen came alive. The president watched the scanner image pass over the classroom door. "Stop it there," said the president at the same spot where Tony had first reacted. "What's this?" he said.

"I'm scanning the door from the inside, sir. Kim, can you back up the image a few clicks?" A twinkle glimmered, and she stopped the image. Multiple human forms appeared in the doorway, none of them discernible. A vague image of two feet pointing skyward. Attached to legs that stopped at the knees. The president made a note on a new sheet, and flipped back to the prior page.

"Can you focus on any of these?" asked the president.

"I'll try sir, but we haven't done this before." She hit a number of keys and the images grew larger but were still not identifiable.

"Keep going," said the president. The screen showed Russell's desk, and once again, there was a flash of light. Kim reversed the recording and tapped it forward until the light flashed.

"The scanner was on the middle drawer?" asked the president. "Can you go frame by frame?"

Kim moved the recording, one frame at a time, until the flash disappeared.

"There's nothing here, Mr. President." She tapped another key, and the recording resumed its normal speed. When the light occurred, Kim stopped the computer and reversed the pictures.

"Can you make it clearer?" asked the president.

She did. "What is that?" the president asked.

"It looks like kids sitting at desks, Mr. President, but there's a background image I can't make out," said Tony. Kim tried to enhance the picture still more, but the background didn't come into focus.

"Well, you got something, but who knows what it is. It doesn't seem to show anything that would help," said the president.

The secretary said, "Mr. President, I think we'll need to massage this in the lab. And we do have some positives, particularly Mr. Russell's desk. Let's get another look at it." The president studied Secretary Stevens, considering that option, while the others watched him.

Jim Koppler said, "Sir, we could switch the desk and bring it here. I'm certain we could do it without Mr. Russell's realizing it. We could do it at night."

"I don't know. If the desk is tied to the portal, wouldn't taking it disrupt the connection?"

"Why do we even care, Mr. President?" said Koppler. "If we get rid of the desk, we solve the problem." The president held up his hand to stop him.

Tony responded, "I could go in at night and take more readings, Mr. President, Madam Secretary."

"We only have until Monday before they get back in there," said the national security advisor.

The secretary said, "How about this? Let us look at the data more carefully over at the lab. We can go back tomorrow night if we need to."

* * *

"I WONDER IF the president will call us if they find anything," said Linda.

"If they find something, he may call, but I doubt it. I need to get back in. I want to look at the books, see what I marked. I want to know how that portal works."

Ashley interrupted. "It sounds like you want to go through the portal again on your own terms." He picked up another pickle.

"Ashley, the only way to prevent another classroom episode is to know what causes it. If I can figure it out, then I can stop it."

Linda, knowing that Ash was right, said, "Fritz, you can keep the kids out, but you want to go through again. Don't deny it.

I know you too well. We both do. Promise me you won't go through if you find out how. What if you can't get back?"

"I promise," I said, a knee-jerk answer. I'm sure Linda and Ashley knew I was lying. I slid off the vinyl seat and said, "Let's go home."

Linda drove and I sat in the back seat, listening. Ashley suggested calling George to open up again. "I think he's intimidated. His sense of order is disrupted."

Linda said, "Ash, he's concerned about the kids."

"Lois is concerned about the kids. George is concerned about how this makes him look," he said as Linda turned into the driveway.

Getting out of the car, I said, "George wants this to end." I glanced at the lawn, adding cutting the grass to my to-do list. "I'll tell him I may have a solution. He'll open up. My problem is I don't want him there. I'll call him and tell him I'll pick up the key. I really just want to look at the books and any other metal objects in there."

"What if he wants to come?" asked Linda. "Because I'm coming too."

"Me too," said Ash.

"Then I guess it doesn't matter if he comes." I was outvoted. I knew Linda wouldn't give in. I dialed, and Lois picked up. "Hi, Lois. It's Fritz Russell. Is George there?"

She said, "I was wondering how long it would be before you called. You want to go back into the room, don't you?"

"Lois, you always amaze me."

"We'll be at the school in fifteen minutes," and she hung up.

I just stared at my phone. "Fifteen minutes," I said. "But they'll be there"

"That was easy," said Ashley.

Chapter Thirteen

AT THE ENERGY DEPARTMENT laboratory, the secretary and her assistants viewed the recording. It was grainy and staticky. "Like a 1950s TV show," Tony commented. Secretary Stevens thought an antenna might clear up the pictures and asked how else they might try to enhance the recording. Tony said, "We're definitely going to need to get back in. I think Kim and I can put together a low frequency antenna, but we need new data. We can't do it with what we have."

At the White House, Tom told the president that Fritz and the others were going back into the school.

"I'm not surprised," said the First Lady.

"Me neither," said the president. A yellow pad sat on the coffee table in front of him.

Tom continued, "They are looking at metal objects and books. Oh, and they suspect we've bugged them."

"You didn't bug them all, did you?" asked the First Lady.

The president nodded yes, not looking at her.

"Why? They're not trying to hurt anyone."

"I don't want to hurt them, but I don't want uninvited visitors again, either. We're trying to contain this."

She shook her head. "That's just a bad idea. If they find the bugs, they'll never trust us."

Tom said, "They're also concerned about your 'disappearing' comment, sir."

"Yeah, that was dumb. But I'm the good guy."

"They might not think so," said the First Lady.

* * *

WHEN WE REACHED my classroom, I hesitated. There was no shock. George asked what I had found. Without answering, I went to the bookcase and started pulling out books and stacking them on the window sill. I told him I wasn't concerned about the portal but with how we ended up where we went. I began opening whatever had paperclips.

George said, "You NEED to be concerned about the portal, Fritz. I can't risk the school getting mixed up in this." I didn't say anything, but my back and neck muscles yelled at him.

Crossing to the stack of books, Lois asked, "What are you looking for?"

"Paperclips." She picked up a book.

"What do paperclips have to do with this?"

"I'm trying to see if I marked the pages for Appomattox and the fire. I know I did in the Auto Workers book. Electricity is involved somehow, and metal conducts electricity. If I marked the locations with paperclips, it could have had something to do with it."

"Here's one," said Ashley. He flipped open to the page. "It's Fort Sumter."

Linda, thumbing through another Civil War book said, "I have one here at … OH," she exclaimed. "Andersonville." Lois looked like she'd never heard of it.

"Andersonville was the Georgia prison camp for Union soldiers," I explained. "Over 12,000 died in brutal conditions. Good we didn't go there." She gave me her I-told-you-so stare.

"Here it is, Fritz," said Linda, holding up another open book. "Appomattox. Lee surrenders."

I took the book. A paperclip marked four pages about Grant meeting Lee. I flipped to the last page connected by the paperclip and read about the aftermath of the surrender, including Union soldiers providing food to Lee's men. I checked the title, then looked at the bookcase. "Lin, where was this book?"

"Right here, bottom of the pile," she said, pointing to the corner of my desk.

I looked at another book from the desk. *Triangle: The Fire that Changed America.* Another paperclip. I turned to those pages. "I clipped these because Frances Perkins, FDR's Labor secretary, the first woman in the cabinet, was an eyewitness." I wanted to discuss the impact of the fire on public policy and the law with the kids. "Did you know that she was the force behind the creation of Social Security?"

Lois said, "Always teaching!" She smiled at me, and I appreciated her comment, especially in front of George. I smiled back.

"Well what have we accomplished?" said George.

"Nothing yet," I said. I examined everything on the desk, one piece at a time, until I reached the bottom of the pile. "Here it is."

"What?" Linda asked.

I held out a travel brochure for the White House tour. A photo of the Oval Office had a paperclip on it. "So it really does look like my paperclips have something to do with it." I went to the stack of books on the windowsill. "None of these," I said. I looked at the desk again. It wasn't messy, but books and papers covered the perimeter. "I need to take all the paperclips off everything on the desk." I took out my desk key to unlock the desk, but it was already open. I had forgotten to lock it again when we were there earlier.

"Do you want us to help?" asked Ash.

"Yes. And stick in scraps of paper as placeholders." My tone of voice registered. I was barking like George. Looking at them, I said, "Sorry. Thanks." They took books and papers, and the paperclips piled up. I opened the drawers and looked for more clipped items, but there were none. "Interesting," I said.

"What is?" asked George.

"I'm not sure, George, but it seems that the only paperclips are ON the desk."

"There are paperclips in books on the shelf, Fritz," said Linda.

I glanced at the bookcase. "But not involving places we went. I think that means the connection includes the desktop somehow." I tapped it a couple of times.

"But there are at least fifty clips in the stuff on the desk," said Ash.

"It doesn't seem random," said Linda.

"Maybe, maybe not." Linda told me my forehead looked like a ploughed field. I stared at the top of the desk, wondering how the connections were made. I walked to the door and then looked from the door to the desk.

"What are you looking at?" said George.

"I'm not sure, George. Just looking."

"Do you think the desk has something to do with the door?" asked Lois.

"You're ahead of me again, Lois. Yes, but I don't know what or how." I continued looking back and forth. Then I said, "Lin, where exactly was that Civil War book?"

"Right here," she replied, pointing to the left side of my desk.

"And the Triangle book was in the middle, I'd just looked at it before class. The brochure was in a pile near the book with Lee's surrender. The UAW book was under the homework papers on the right. Left, right, center."

"So?" said George.

"So?" I said. "Sew buttons." My arms folded, I looked from the desk to the door and back, like a slow motion tennis volley.

"Buttons? What buttons?" George asked, sounding confused.

"I don't know, George. Maybe there is a pattern. There's no electrical connection between the door and the desk. I just don't know." I looked at the floor. "George, do you know if there is wiring under the floor?"

"I don't think so. This wing was built on a slab; there's no basement here. I think the wiring's all above ground. I've never seen them, but I'm sure the administration must have the original plans somewhere."

"If there's no basement, there are no wires from the door to the desk that we won't see. Just a thought."

"Do you want me to check about the plans?"

"No. No reason to. Thanks anyway, George. It must be something else."

"Let's get some coffee," said Ashley, watching me grind my teeth.

"Good idea," said Linda.

Lois told George that it was time to go. They still had work to finish for the meeting. George wasn't paying attention. When we started to leave, he just followed. At our cars, I told George that everything would work out and not to worry. "I have some things to think about. But I think I have a way to avoid getting the kids involved again. Thanks for coming, and thanks for coming, too, Lois." She waved.

* * *

WHILE HE WAS CONCENTRATING on Tom's report, the president's phone rang. He flinched and refocused. Secretary Stevens told him they had a solution but needed new data.

"Good. Can you go back tonight? Our friends went back to the school this afternoon, looking for clues."

"Mr. President, we're good."

"Good luck, and I'll speak with you tomorrow." The president hung up. "You'll get everything arranged, Tom?"

"Yes sir. I'll take care of it."

* * *

STRAIGHT HOME, no stop for coffee. "Fritz, what were you looking at?" asked Linda.

"There has to be a connection between opening the portal and the desk. After I saw the books on the desk, I just knew."

"Knew what?" asked Ash.

"I think there's a two-way connection between the door," I pointed with my left hand, "and the desk," I pointed with my right. "Something about the desk is causing the portal to open. Then, when the connection is made, the door connects back to something on the desk, like the paperclips. Or maybe vice versa. But what? Why?"

"You said, 'left, right, center' " said Linda.

"The order of events. The books were on the left, then the right, and then the center. The brochure was on the left again. The order of the trips."

"Then you don't think it was random."

"It could be random, Lin, or maybe there is an order. I don't know. Not enough information."

"Stop right now," Linda was edgy "You are not, I repeat, not, going to test this theory, if it's even a theory. I know you too well. Forget it." She turned to Ashley. "And don't you go helping him."

"Lin, the only way to find out, to be sure it's not random, is to be deliberate." I was trying to sound reasonable and calm, in spite of my anticipation. And her discomfort. "But if my guess is right, I still need the static from the doorknob to open the portal. Now I'm sure that happened each time. But does it depend on the weather?"

"You promised me," she said. She walked out of the kitchen.

I called her, but the stairs squeaked from climbing footsteps. I said, "You know, Ash, if we hadn't gone to the White House, this would just be a field trip. A weird one, but that's all. What bothers me is not having the time to figure out what happened. The White House has so many resources to use against us. I don't think they're bad guys. Hell, I voted for him twice. But I think they're trying to find the portal."

"That makes sense."

"Nothing makes sense, but I could be in trouble with them." I realized I was chewing my bottom lip. The events of the past day ran through my head again, and I recounted them to Ashley.

"Are you getting paranoid?" asked Ashley

"Remember, even paranoids have enemies. Maybe I'm making too much of this, but I'd like to be sure. I can trust the president will act on this. He's more important than me."

"Not to me," Linda said from the doorway.

* * *

TOM WAS WAITING near the gate, his jacket zipped half way to conceal the bulge, when James arrived at Andrews. The guard raised the gate, no questions asked, and Tom followed them in. At the guard booth, he rolled down his window and said that they would be returning around 4:30. "We'll park by the plane. If there are any problems, call the agent on duty at the White House."

"Yes, sir," said the guard. When they boarded, the secretary asked the scientists if everything was ready.

"Yes. Actually, we have a couple of options," said Tony, now wearing jeans and a leather jacket. The secretary smiled at that answer. Tony pushed the seat cushion. "Nice ride."

As the plane rose, the Energy Secretary said, "So. Tell me."

Kim looked over her glasses. "Madam Secretary, we worked on this until about an hour ago. We needed to find something to maximize conductivity as well as being sure we could adjust the computer image to highest resolution." Stevens listened, thinking she had the best geeks in Washington.

Tony swiveled side to side. "I wish I had one of these at home." Secretary Stevens tapped the seat arm, waiting. "Sorry. So TV antennas are made of aluminum and pick up high frequency transmissions. I tried one to see if they could handle the lower frequencies we're using. Nope." He shook his head. "To pick up lower frequencies, I made a ferrite wand. One of copper wire, too. I needed to make them pretty long. I also made one using sand in a glass cylinder. Silica. And one from peroxide, a little more unstable than water. Just guessing."

"Good thought," said the secretary. "So you're going to run through the sequence a couple of times?"

"At least four times, maybe more," Kim said. "Using different combinations."

The short flight ended quickly. They stowed the equipment and climbed into the Suburban they had left there. No one seemed to be around. "We're a little early," said Tom. "Let's go anyway and see. James, you're going to have to drive around. Madam Secretary, you'll stay with James. We can't park at the school. Someone might notice. See if you can find a quiet spot and park nearby."

"Got it," said James. They reached the school in about fifteen minutes. James drove around back, invisible to the street. The team took their tools and went to the side door. As they approached, a small light turned on. Tom made a mental note to visit the office. He picked the lock, and they were in. Ample light from the street allowed Tony and Kim to set up easily.

"Kim, hold the antennas," said Tony, breaking the silence. "We'll just do what we did this afternoon," and he started at the door. After the first pass, less than ten minutes, Kim picked up the second wand and Tony repeated the scan. They did a third pass and then another, using two wands.

"One more and we'll be done."

"That's fine, Tony," said Kim. "Let's finish and get out of here."

Tom said, "When you're packed up, go outside, away from the cameras, and head back to the car. Tell James to leave the parking lot and turn right, go about 100 yards, and I'll catch up with you." He went to the office, looking for the closest exit as he walked. Job completed, he checked for cars and pedestrians and then slipped into the cool, starry night. When he reached the Suburban, he climbed in and said, "Let's go home."

Kim said, "Madam Secretary, I think we may have a better picture than the earlier ones, but of what, I don't know."

"We'll need the computer at the lab," said Tony. "We had flashes and sparkles, so I'm optimistic."

"The president will want to know as soon as possible, so can you two keep going?"

Kim looked at Tony, who shrugged and said, "Sure, but I could use a bite to eat. We haven't been near food since yesterday's dinner."

James said, "We can hit the Airlift when we get home."

"Not there," said Tom. "A place closer to the District. Too many eyes and ears. Especially at this time of day."

They settled back for the rest of the short trip. Tony had a little time to sink into the cushions.

* * *

WHILE THE RUSSELLS and Ashley were spending a tense Saturday night and the Energy Department people were repeating their trip to New Jersey, the president and First Lady attended an official function at the Kennedy Center. Part politics, part social responsibility, he ate the chicken, cold and overcooked, shook hands, and made small talk. During a short break, he leaned over to his wife and said, "I really appreciated that lasagna."

She looked at him and frowned. "Remember, you may be the good guy, but so are they," she said.

He was in his office by 7:30 Sunday morning, with a pitcher of coffee, his first cup half gone. His gray jacket was folded over the arm of a chair, no tie. He was scanning the *Washington Post* Sports section, when the phone rang. "Good morning, Brenda. How was the trip?"

"Good morning, Mr. President. It went well." said the secretary. "The kids have been working all night to capture the images. They loaded the different scans on a CD, and we're ready to show them to you, if you'd like. But they're not dressed, sir."

"Me neither. Come on over." He told the agent outside his office that Secretary Stevens was on her way with two assistants and asked him to show them right in.

"Yes, sir. I'll let them know at the door."

The president was facing the Rose Garden, tulips and daffodils now in full bloom. His feet were on the window sill, his folded *Post* now open to the business news when the First Lady walked in. "Did you eat?" she asked. His chair creaked as he spun to answer.

"Not yet," pointing to his coffee cup. He told her Secretary Stevens was on the way, complete with the new scans. "I bet they haven't eaten either." He picked up his phone, pushed a button and said, "Good morning. Would you arrange to bring a couple of pitchers of coffee and maybe some coffee cake or Danish for seven people to my office. In about 15 minutes," he said. "Thank you." He turned back to the First Lady. "They got back about 4:30 with the new scans. Want to see them?"

"Absolutely. And if there's anything there, I think you should tell the Russells. He's clearly the catalyst. Let him help decide the best way to stop it." A knock on the door, and the national security advisor entered.

"Good morning. May I come in?"

"Sure. We were just talking about the Russells. Secretary Stevens is on the way. They just got back from rescanning the school."

"Mr. President, I think you should keep all new information away from the teachers. Any assistance we give them can backfire on you. That information could be sold, used against you."

The president saw the instant ripple on his wife's jaw but said, "From what we saw, I think he'll try to use the portal again, to figure out how it works. That worries me. He could be a target if the wrong people find out."

"So could you, Mr. President," said Koppler. "He's a teacher. How responsible can you expect him to be with this? He won't understand the implications."

"He won't be irresponsible. Especially because he is a teacher. Nor is he stupid," said the First Lady.

Koppler looked at her, but said, "Mr. President, I have a meeting now, but I'll be here most of the day. If you'll excuse me."

The president nodded, and when the door shut, he started to speak. A knock on the door interrupted him. Tom came in with the secretary, Tony, and Kim, a breakfast cart from the kitchen, and then James. Kim and Tony set up a portable screen, the computer and a projector.

"Go ahead," said the president.

"We took five readings, Mr. President," Kim said, now wearing khaki slacks. "We used different types of antennas in case one worked better. What you'll see is the same scenes, using the different antennas." Tony, still in his tee shirt, started the DVD.

"Will this continue on its own?" asked the president.

"Yes, sir," said Kim.

"Then get yourselves some coffee and something to eat. I'll guess you guys are hungry."

As the images played, Tony narrated the scenes, the same they had seen on the first try, again with split screen images. "Stop there!"

Kim halted the images and backed up, frame by frame. "Is that me? There." The president rose from his seat and walked to the screen. In the hazy background, there were images.

"We think so, Mr. President," said the secretary.

"This looks like when they first came through into my office." The recording started again. As new images appeared, the president asked, "Is that ... Robert E. Lee?" pointing to the left side of the screen, "and is that a building on fire?"

"Mr. President, we think we have the images, but we didn't want to say anything and possibly affect your perception," Stevens answered. "One has us baffled. Here, Mr. President." She pointed to the feet extending through the door way. "It looks too antiseptic to be an amputation or an accident. We have no idea what it could be."

"Nothing like this has ever been done before, has it?" asked the First Lady.

"There's never been an event like this before, ever," said Secretary Stevens.

"It's almost like ghost hunting," said Tony, his eye on the platter of pastries.

"Is there more?" asked the president.

"We picked up these images only once, Mr. President, and there were other spikes in the recordings, registering energy levels out of the ordinary," said the secretary. "But no other images. Kim, keep running the program. We'll show you, sir." There were various bright lights on each scan from different places in the classroom, and each scan showed a brief energy spike around the desk.

The president said, "The desk. I wonder if it controls the portal."

"Mr. President, as sensitive as this instrument is, there could be some kind of power source inside the desk," said Secretary Stevens. "We tested the scanner on things like batteries, cell phones, laptops, and they all emitted similar patterns. It's not clear that the desk has any involvement."

"You could ask him what's in the desk," the First Lady said, offhandedly.

"I'm not sure I want him to know what we've found. At least not yet. I need to think about this for a bit. Thank you all for your efforts. Would you all mind waiting outside?" Tony took a raspberry Danish as they left.

The room cleared, except for the First Lady and Tom, who shut the door. "Mr. President, I haven't checked the recording yet today. I'll do that now and let you know if anything's on it."

The president nodded as Tom left the Oval Office. "Tom, ask Mr. Koppler to come back, please."

Chapter Fourteen

LINDA AND I were talking in the kitchen, drinking coffee. I chomped on one of the bagels and cream cheese that Ashley had brought. We were trying to avoid more discussion of the events of the past two days, but it wasn't possible. Linda hoped the president would call.

"I was thinking of going to the driving range. No storm clouds today." We glanced out the window. Birds chattering, wispy clouds, and an azure sky, it was a beautiful morning, a good day to hit a bucket or two.

"You're not leaving me here to answer when he calls."

"If he calls, he'll call my cell. Have you seen it?"

"Your phone?"

"Yeah. I don't know what I did with it. I checked my pants and my jacket. I looked in the car earlier. Nowhere." I sipped my coffee.

"You didn't leave it at school, did you?"

"If I did, I put it inside my desk. If he calls, he'll think I turned it off." I scratched behind my left ear. "But he won't call."

"Why do you say that?" She set her cup down.

"Because if they didn't find anything, there's no reason to call, and if they did, the president's probably trying to figure out how to use me." I recognized my discomfort; it was the same feeling I had the first time I met Linda's father.

"That's ridiculous, Fritz."

"DISAPPEAR," I reminded her as I got up. "You want more coffee?"

"No," she said. "When they look at all that's happened, Fritz, they have to know you're not a threat."

I told her they weren't afraid of me. They were afraid I might do something or go somewhere I shouldn't. Or that someone would find out and use me. My coffee poured, sitting back down, I said, "They always think worst case. This is an important scientific discovery. More so if we learn to harness it or even stop it. I'd like to look some more. But I don't want to call George. Besides, I still need to get prepped for tomorrow. That's why I want to hit some golf balls." The doorbell rang.

"Ashley, I'll bet," said Linda. "But why the front door?"

"Sorry to barge in," said Lois, alone. "I told George I was going shopping." Ashley was just pulling up to the curb.

"There's hot coffee in the kitchen. Go ahead. I'll wait for him."

Ashley sauntered to the door. "Hi, another party?"

"Now that you're here."

We walked into the kitchen as Lois was sitting down. "I'm concerned that George is misreading all this. He's so worried about the kids telling people, and he doesn't know what to say. I really am sorry to bother you; I know you're trying to figure this out too. But he can make it so much worse if he says the wrong things. And he's scared the president will do something awful." Lois said it all in a single breath.

I agreed but said the story was plausible and that George only needed to introduce me. "I'll take care of the rest. If I can convince the teachers, George doesn't have to worry. And I think I know how to avoid another trip."

"How?"

"A different classroom. Since my door opens the portal, a different room should keep it from happening again. I'll talk to George about that later."

Lois sighed, "Well, he'll be glad about that."

"Lois, tell George that the president's a good guy and he doesn't want to make more out of this than we do," said Linda.

Lois replied, "I hope you're right."

"So do we," said Linda, looking at me. Again, I silently agreed.

* * *

TOM KNOCKED AND WALKED into the Oval Office. Koppler had returned, and the First Lady was still there. She had been telling the president that the most important thing was to let Mr. Russell know what had happened, disagreeing with the national security advisor. "He's smart, and he'll try to figure it out. He wants to keep his students safe. He wants them to learn history, not witness it."

Waiting for a lull, Tom finally said, "We've got some conversation, Mr. President."

"Let's hear it."

The four of them listened as the Russells and Gilbert discussed the desk, paperclips, and the pile of books.

"They think it's the desk, too," said the president.

"And they're not sure you're the good guy," said the First Lady. "Call him. He needs to know he can trust you. If you need to do some tests on him, maybe you can invite them here, for dinner or something."

"I AM the good guy," said the president. "I want this over with, ASAP."

"Mr. President," said Mr. Koppler, "I can work with Tom and make sure it is." The president ignored him.

Tom said, "Sir, at the end of the recording, it seems that Mr. Russell has misplaced his phone. Possibly in the desk."

"Where the energy surges were, so maybe the desk has nothing to do with this," said the president, completing Tom's thought.

"I'm going back upstairs," said the First Lady. "Call him," she admonished as she left.

"I don't think the guy is dangerous, at least not on purpose." His comment was aimed at his national security advisor. "Ask Secretary Stevens to come in, will you?"

When she entered, the president asked her to think about what might trigger the portal. He added that they should think about how to short circuit Mr. Russell. "Now go home and get some sleep. Tom, you and James should get some shut-eye too." He went to his desk and picked up the phone, then put it down. He didn't want to talk to the desk in New Jersey. He walked a couple of laps around his office and then went to the door. "Lily, would you get Mr. Russell's phone number for me please?" He turned to Koppler.

"Jim, I know what you're thinking."

"Mr. President, I want to bring him here, question him, maybe keep him out of play for a while. That will give me a chance to do in-depth checking on all of them."

"Jim, it's a small-town school. I don't want to raise suspicion."

"We might find other connections, Mr. President. He could be a plant, an agent. He could be a spy. Another country could have found this portal and be employing it against us."

The president stopped him. "I need to think about what the implications are. Jim, he's been teaching there for ten years. I saw his picture in the year book. You can't seriously think they had a special book made on the off-chance we might check for it. I think you may be short-changing Mr. Russell. If anything, we may need to protect him. So sit tight. And really, Jim, if another country were controlling this, they wouldn't have walked into this room." The national security advisor knew he had been dismissed.

The president returned to watching the White House grounds. He wondered what he would say. Lily Evans entered and said, "Mr. President, they don't have a home phone. But I have both Russells' cell phone numbers."

"Thanks, Lily."

* * *

Koppler had his cell to his ear as he shut his office door. "Riverboro High School in New Jersey. Fritz Russell, a history teacher. You know what to do." And then, "I don't care. Just do it."

* * *

LINDA'S RINGTONE SANG, and we all looked up. She grabbed her purse from the counter behind her and looked at the caller ID. "The White House," she said. "Hello? Yes hello, Mr. President." She listened, a frown reappearing. "He can't find it. He's right here, hold on."

"Yes, Mr. President, good morning. No bother."

The president told me that there were images, but they were still analyzing them. "Mr. Russell, we don't think you're a threat, but in the wrong hands, you might stumble on something that could be a problem. That's about as candid as I can be. For me, not knowing means that I have to be concerned." I told him we had been talking, too, and thought we might have figured out the connection.

"The desk?" the president asked.

"Yes, sir. We can't prove it yet, but I think that we have a strategy to keep it quiet."

"Good. Can you tell me?"

"I can control the students, I think. Only three classes witnessed the portal firsthand. I'm pretty sure they'll believe me. As we discussed Friday night, I'll tell them about my friend, the special effects guy in California. I was thinking he could be from the team that worked on *Star Trek* special effects. That guy Tony who was here yesterday could be the guy, for instance.

He seemed to know about this stuff. That way, no one else gets roped in."

"Great idea. I can let him know. He's got clearance, and he's smart. Of course, if you don't need to use a name, so much the better."

"All I remember is 'Tony', sir. I also think I can avoid the kids being involved again. The static from the doorknob activates the opening, I think. Or maybe it's a sign that the portal is open. If I feel the static and don't open the door, I can take my class to another room. George will agree to that. But beyond the doorknob, of course, we still haven't figured out how the portal is directing me to wherever."

"Mr. Russell, that's why we're concerned. If your travel isn't random…" The president stopped mid-sentence, but his message was clear. He continued, "I don't know what use it would be, but I'd like my medical people to do some tests to see if they can find any unusual emissions, radiation, surges, you know."

"That sounds pretty menacing, Mr. President."

"Not at all, just tests. In fact, why don't you and Ms. Russell come down here? We'll do the tests, and you can join us here for dinner. We'll be even in the hospitality department."

"When?" I asked. The call was making me uneasy and suspicious.

The president paused, and I heard pages turning. "Well, we don't want to be too obvious. How about next weekend? In fact, why don't you bring Mr. Gilbert, Ms. Horton, and the McAllisters? Maybe we can solve this finally."

"I'll ask, Mr. President. Can I get back to you?"

"Sure. Call this number. Enjoy your bagels."

He waited while I grabbed a pen and piece of paper. "Thank you, Mr. President. I'll call back later, if that's okay."

"That'll be fine. Have a nice day."

"Yeah. You too." *You have to be kidding.*

I said, "He wants to do tests on me. They think I might have some anomaly that controls the portal's opening."

"At the White House?" asked Ashley.

"He didn't say." I gave him a knowing look. Linda looked astonished.

Breaking the silence, Lois said, "Well, that won't make George feel better. He'll be beside himself. I'd better go." She put on a light coat and picked up her matching green handbag.

"Don't tell him yet, Lois." I cautioned. "I'll call later. That way he won't know you were here."

"Right," she said, as we walked to the door. "Bye, everyone."

Returning to the kitchen, I motioned Linda and Ashley to come out the back door. After telling them the president had mentioned bagels, I asked, "Are you thinking what I'm thinking?"

"A bug?" asked Linda. "Fritz, they're smart people, and they're thinking about this just like we are. I hope it's coincidental."

Ashley asked, "So? What should we do?"

"Look for it. We know we have to be careful even if we don't find it," I said. "I guess we shouldn't be surprised. But we've already told him everything we know."

Linda asked, "Have we said anything that they would worry about?"

"If the president knows about the desk, he probably knows about the paperclips too."

"But even if he knows, did we say anything that would worry him?" Linda repeated.

"Only that we weren't sure we could trust him," I said. "Could be we were right!"

"Actually," said Ash, "I'm kind of sorry to hear that." Ash looked up at the birds perched on the wires overhead. They watched us, too.

"They could be anywhere," I said. "But I want to know if that's what we're dealing with."

"They were only in the dining room," said Linda.

"The First Lady was in the kitchen," I reminded her. "It would be clever, someone we wouldn't suspect."

"You don't think?"

"Why not?" said Ashley. "If they did bug us, she could have been the one, as easily as anyone."

"Okay." She sighed. "Let's check the dining room first," said Linda.

* * *

THE PRESIDENT LOOKED UP. "I thought you were going home, Tom. You really should. Do I need to order you?"

"Sorry to interrupt, sir, but the Russells suspect bugs. I stopped to check before I left. They started talking about it yesterday."

"How could they have guessed?"

"You said bagels. I think they're being cautious, but if they find a device, we could have some trouble with them. And Mr. President," Tom hesitated, "Mr. Koppler asked me to keep him informed of what Mr. Russell is doing. Thought you should know."

"Thanks, Tom. Right now, don't tell him anything important."

When the president returned to the residence, he told the First Lady that he had called. He had told Mr. Russell about the images and that he wanted to have some tests performed and invited all of them to come for dinner the next Saturday.

"All in one conversation. A lot for Mr. Russell to take in," said the First Lady. "And he said?"

"He didn't seem to like it much, the test part, and said he would call later. He wanted to tell the others, I'm sure. But he was pretty forthcoming about what they did and talked about. He also thinks the desk is part of this."

"I told you he was a good guy. He's into something big, doesn't know how to fix it yet, and he's afraid of the president of the United States. Sounds very normal to me. It's a good thing he doesn't know how involved the NSA has become. And now he has to look forward to not just his meeting tomorrow, but tests, whatever that means. I think I might be a little worried, wouldn't you?"

"At least if they're all here, maybe we can discuss this openly and reduce their suspicion."

The First Lady merely raised her eyebrows. Tom knocked. When he came in, he was crinkling his forehead.

"Mr. President, they're looking for the bugs. They think there's only one, but they're looking at everything."

"How can you tell, Tom?' asked the First Lady.

"They're not talking, they have a baseball game on very loud, and I can hear drawers opening and other non-normal sounds." He frowned and finished his thought, "Like crawling under the table."

"Oh boy," the president sighed. "I really hope they don't find them. I thought I had the trust issue under control. Thanks, Tom. Please go home, at least for a while. Your shift must be long over."

Tom said, "I'm fine, sir. I'll keep you informed."

When Tom left, the First Lady frowned at her husband, shook her head, and returned to her reading.

* * *

"HERE'S SOMETHING," said Linda, pointing to a drawer in the china cabinet. "How could this have gotten here?" Stuck on the rear of a drawer was a button-like object.

"I found something," said Ashley from under the dining room table. He had a flashlight and said, "What does yours look like?"

"A button."

"Can I have a knife or screwdriver, Fritz?" asked Ashley. "Lin, I'm glad you got the carpet. I'll be sore after this but not nearly as much as I would've been on hardwood."

I went to the kitchen, returned with a steak knife, and handed it to Ashley.

"Hey Fritz, I'm looking at a button, not a cow."

"Sorry."

"I can't believe this," said Linda. "What do they think we are? A foreign country? This is really annoying."

I returned with a small screwdriver. "What's annoying?"

"That they would bug us," said Linda, her complexion changing from pink to red. It reminded me of the last time she stayed at the beach too long. Ashley fished the button from the screw hole under the table and got up. Showing us the button, Linda said, "Same thing." Handing both to me, I rubbed one between my fingers.

"Well, they know we've found them. So, I guess it's time for a phone call," I said. I felt my stomach clench, and my fists did, too.

"I'll bet it was Tom who planted them. That's the spot where he was sitting," said Ashley.

"You're probably right," I said. "Well, that takes care of going to Washington." Then speaking to the buttons, "You really let me down, Mr. President. As much as I would have liked to visit the White House and cooperate, no way that happens now. You tell him that, secret service."

* * *

TOM WAS BACK at the residence shortly after he heard this. "Mr. President, they found two of the bugs."

"Two?" questioned the First Lady.

"Tom placed them yesterday when they were at the school. I've got to call him and explain."

"Sir, Mr. Russell said he's not coming to Washington and won't cooperate further."

"Thanks, Tom. This can't get worse tonight, so I am ordering you to go home."

"Yes, sir."

The president looked at his wife, "Now what?" he said.

She told him he needed to think very carefully what he was going to say and that he needed to apologize. "This changes the whole situation for them, and now he's angry, at you. Like I said, you're gonna have to make nice."

"I will," said the president, picking up the phone.

* * *

"I DON'T KNOW how mad to be," I said. Two squirrels ran across the back lawn. "Who knows? Next it'll be the IRS."

Just then, Linda's phone, sitting in front of us, rang. She looked at the screen and handed it to me.

I answered.

"Mr. Russell, this is the president. I know you found the bugs, and I want to apologize to you. We didn't know what we were dealing with. I hope you'll understand the security importance. I really am sorry. Just to show you I'm on the level, I checked with the security team. There's a third one, under the chair Tom sat on."

"A third one?" I asked, looking at the others. "Under Tom's chair? Mr. President, aside from being disappointed, I'm pissed! I did everything you asked, I was open about what we found, and you're treating me like a criminal. This all happened TO me. I've figured out as much as I can in two days, without the full power and resources of the federal government." I realized I was yelling and being more than a little disingenuous. We'd never told him about the paper clips. "At the moment, Mr. President, I don't feel much like talking to you." I hung up.

"You just hung up on the president," said Ashley. "Pretty cool."

"Shut up, Ashley," snapped Linda. "You need to call him back, Fritz, and apologize."

Embarrassed by her scolding, I said, "Well, he deserved it. Let's get the other bug out first. I guess they'll want them back."

"You're not serious," said Ashley. "Give them back?"

"Ash, they probably cost the taxpayers a bundle."

We went to the dining room. I turned over the chair, but I couldn't see the button. Linda spotted it tucked into a groove where the leg joined the seat. "He hid that one well," she said.

* * *

"WELL, WHAT DID you expect?" said the First Lady. "He may be afraid of you, but he's not scared of you. Give him a few minutes to cool off and call him back."

The president grimaced. "I just stepped hard on the toes of a smart guy, a nice guy. Sometimes being president means you have to say you're sorry. What a mess," he sighed. The phone rang, and the switchboard operator told him who was calling. "It's him." He told the operator to put the call through.

"Mr. President, I'm calling to apologize. I lost my temper. I assume you want your bugs back."

"Hold on to them for me, please, Mr. Russell," said the president. He paused. "We'll disconnect them, I promise."

"I'll keep them safe—for the taxpayers."

"Then we'll see you on Saturday?" asked the president.

"Mr. President, I haven't spoken to the others yet, but frankly, at this point, I'm not ready to make that trip. Not even if you lived next door," I said sharply.

"Then Mr. Russell, will you let me know how your meeting went?"

"I'll give it some thought," and with that, I hung up.

SUNDAY CREPT TOWARD NIGHT, and I sat at the kitchen table, thinking, doing a quiet burn. I had been there most of the day. Linda studied for a while and straightened the family room. Ashley watched TV and helped her when she asked. I was in my own world, reviewing everything that had happened since the previous Friday. It had been a long couple of days.

"I need to write down what I'm going to say tomorrow and call George."

"Eat first, play later," said Ashley, drawing a scowl from me. Linda brought the salad and a loaf of Italian bread, already sliced, to the table.

"Ash, get the butter and dressings for me, please," she said. She sat down across from me, resting her arms on the table. She said that she and Ash had been thinking about our situation. "Try to put yourself in the president's position. He has to be concerned about the country. He's as concerned for himself and his family as you are for us and your students. He doesn't know you. You like how he has handled his job. He's a lot like you, and you know it. You even say the same things. And you hung up on him, twice." As I usually do, I listened to her carefully. Linda cuts to the chase.

"I'll bet that doesn't happen to him often," said Ash.

Ignoring Ashley, I asked Linda, "Do you think I should call him again? I really want to get past tomorrow and see what the fallout is."

"Then call him tomorrow. And apologize again."

"Do we get to go to the White House?" Ash smirked.

I scowled. "Look, they want to do experiments on me, like I'm an alien. Before I let them do that, I want a lot more info. If they BS me, I'll know. I know too much about politics to be baffled by it. I'll call tomorrow. Let's eat."

Knowing that the government would back up my story to the teachers, I laid out a plan. I would tell them how I had met a guy who worked in special effects, how he'd asked me to test the projections in an independent setting. I'd tell them I was upset about how it had turned out and its impact on my students. Linda and Ashley helped polish the plan. I told them I thought this was how politicians must write speeches. Linda said they had speechwriters. I stood in front of them and rehearsed the entire speech.

Ash said, "Not bad. And no teleprompters."

Then I called George, told him what I planned to say, and suggested some opening remarks for him to make. I wished him good luck and good night. "Thank Lois for me, will you? For her help."

"Sure," said George. "See you tomorrow."

"OK," I said to Linda and Ashley. "Now the kids. We have to explain Appomattox, the fire, and the president at the gym." Lying was the only practical option, but it didn't make me happy. Unless the topic came up, I decided I wouldn't talk about the president. Only a few students actually saw him, so I could say he had just stopped by to visit and we were at the office when he came in.

"That ought to work fine," said Ashley. "After all, it was Friday afternoon, and the school was pretty empty."

"I think we're set. Thanks for all your help, Ash," I said. "Now go home!"

Ash wiped away nonexistent tears. "I know when I'm not wanted."

"No you don't."

Linda and I walked him to the front door. "Thanks for the bagels."

"See you in the morning. Want a ride?"

"No thanks. I'm going to want to bolt when the meeting ends," I said.

* * *

THE WHITE HOUSE was not quiet. Late Sunday, after Fritz had hung up on him, the president was informed that Eledoria had bombed Jerusalem, supposedly in response to Israeli agents attempting to kill their ruler. Israel denied the accusation and sent planes over the Eledorian capital, Sooksamad, where they faced antiaircraft missiles and jet fire. The president had spoken to both leaders, as well as a number of others in the region.

He had also spoken to the Russian president and the Chinese ambassador, trying to prevent the conflict from escalating. He spoke to the Secretary of Defense and then to the Secretary of the Treasury about probable fallout in the markets, which were already volatile. After dinner with his family, he returned to his office for a meeting with the Secretary of Homeland Security. They discussed possible domestic terrorist activity as well as concern about severe storms expected in several parts of the country. He asked Sam Clemmons to arrange a cabinet meeting for 7:30 a.m. to get caught up on the evening's events. Finally, at about 11:30, Tom came to the Oval Office as the president was preparing to leave.

"Nice quiet weekend, Tom," said the president.

Tom grimaced in reply. "Mr. President, I know the thing with the Russells didn't go too well. And I haven't had a chance to fill you in, sir." Tom reported on his tasks in New Jersey. He told the president he had erased the tapes and left a bug in the classroom to monitor Russell directly. "Mr. Koppler knows about the bugs at the houses. I didn't tell him everything."

"I'm not sure I'm happy about his knowing, but it's too late to do anything about it now. It might actually calm him down a little. Keep me advised."

"Yes sir. Good night," said Tom.

The First Lady was reading in the sitting room next to the Lincoln Bedroom when he walked in and leaned over to kiss her.

"What a day," he said. "You know, with all this chaos, we haven't talked about the Russell thing. I think he has a lot of guts. He hung up on the president of the United States, twice."

She chuckled. "Hon, he hung up on you because you forgot he was on your team, and he got mad. I think I've seen you get mad like that before. It'll pass. I told you, he's a good guy, just like you."

* * *

VOTED "MOST LIKELY to Play for the Boston Celtics" by his class-mates ... sweet thought ... hadn't even liked basketball that much ... more focused on summer than graduation ... not much time before Kathy left for Stanford ... wished he could go that far ... money always got in the way but odd jobs, cutting grass ... maybe enough saved to visit a couple of times ... how different that year's prom was ... how much they'd taught each other that year.

Startled by night noises, Ashley left his reverie. "Damn, not again," he said to himself. He placed the book gently on his cluttered coffee table and went to bed.

Chapter Fifteen

THE MORNING BROUGHT clouds, humidity, wind, and predictions of thunderstorms. I had never before had an emotional relationship with the weather report. I switched channels. The TV news reported from Jerusalem, with evening videos and a live daylight feed. Linda said that the damage was horrible. A search and rescue operation was proceeding, the reporter said.

Since I didn't have a homeroom class, I still had a few minutes to consider what the day might be like. And what the president had done. Outside, the maples tossed their offspring, twirling into the air. When I was a kid, we attached the split seed pods with their sap to our noses. The daily announcements yanked me back inside. George listed the mandatory staff meeting first and then said, "Mr. Russell will discuss his adventures of last week."

Well, that guarantees a terrible day. Why did he add that? The kids all know the stories by now, and their principal just put the fat in the fire. "Time to change gears," I said aloud, as the bell rang ending homeroom. Within moments, the first period class began to arrive. My tenth graders are generally the noisiest of the day, especially on Mondays, but the quiet was otherworldly. Janet Abbott raised her hand. Normally, she smiled; not today. Her demeanor was a combination of curious and worried.

"Good morning, Janet."

"Hi, Mr. Russell. Mr. Russell, what are you going to tell the teachers?"

What I said now would set the stage for the rest of the day. "OK, let me ask you all a question. Raise your hand if you have heard any stories about Friday's classes." Every single eye was on me, and every hand went up. *No surprise there.* I said, "OK, tell me what you heard."

The class began to buzz. "One at a time, raise your hands."

Bill Carlson was first. "A lot of different stuff, Mr. R."

"Yeah," said Dylan Lake, no hand raised, not his usual style. "I heard you saw Robert E. Lee and a fire and lots of dead people."

"And the classroom was a forest," added Dana Goldsense. The buzz started again.

"Chill guys," I said, and to my surprise, they settled down right away. "Well it seems you've heard a lot. So now let me tell you how it happened." I knew I was going to have to repeat this story for each of my classes, so I needed to get it right. "Last summer, while we were at Cape Cod, we met..."

"Where's that, Mr. R?" said Bill.

"Someone tell him, please."

Johnny Autumn said, "It's that claw thing that sticks out of Massachusetts. Right, Mr. R?"

"That works," I said. "As I was saying, we met a guy who works for a special effects company in California and his team was developing a projection system that could create holographs able to fill entire rooms with different scenery. They had worked on movies and TV design for stuff like *Star Trek* and *Thor.* He asked if I would allow him to use my classroom to beta test their system as it was being developed. I told him it sounded interesting, but I would need to know more before I agreed.

"We stayed in contact, and last fall he called and asked if I could give him some idea of what we might be studying this month. Without being specific, I told him I was teaching about the Civil War, the period between the two world wars, and early twentieth-century labor history. He told me that they were technically ready to go, but he wanted specific subjects to develop for the classroom. We discussed how the system worked, as much as he could tell me." Hands went up.

"Let me finish." *Like Chris Matthews*, I thought. The hands went down. "Last week, he called again and said they had finished programming and needed to place the projection equipment in the room." *I'll need to tell George about this part.* "Anyway, they came in after school and installed the projectors around the room. I was surprised at how small they were." Heads turned, searching for something out of place. "They're gone now. They took everything out over the weekend."

Louise Butler asked, "Why didn't our class have it?" Her question reflected the genuine disappointment on the faces around her.

"I told my friend to pick the material he felt would work best. I didn't tell him what to use."

"So none of it was real?" asked Vicki Ann Brothers.

"All right, now," I said. "You're all old enough to know that what you heard happened is at best implausible, unlikely. If it really happened, where are the trees? Where are the charred dead bodies?"

"Gross" and "eew" rang out from different parts of the room.

"I agree. Time travel has been a source of lots of fictional adventures and lots of movies. Have any of you seen *The Time Machine* or *Bill and Ted's Excellent Adventure*?" A few hands went up, and blank stares appeared in heads nodding no. One hand remained raised.

"Yes, Janet."

"Mr. Russell, if holograms aren't real, then how come everything was solid. Why didn't everyone just fall through the dirt? Or the street?"

"Good question, Janet. I don't know how they did that, and I didn't think of it myself." She smiled at having come up with something her teacher hadn't. I thought, *I love her. Always thinking. These kids can help fill in the mystery and make my explanation better.* "I spoke to my friend on Saturday and told him he picked some pretty awful stuff, but I also told him it was incredibly realistic. Obviously, he was happy we were impressed."

"Mr. Russell, what was Robert E. Lee like?" asked Harry James.

"That's a really good question, Harry. General Lee was a little taller than me. He had a well-trimmed white beard." *Be careful,* I thought. "We met him the day after he surrendered to General Grant. He seemed a little depressed." That answer satisfied Harry, but other hands went up.

"I guess we aren't going to have that quiz today," I said. Cheers and clapping erupted briefly.

"Yes, Bill"

"Mr. R, you talked to Robert E. Lee. How do you know that what he said made sense?"

"Well, Bill, it made sense to me, and I've been studying General Lee and the Civil War for a long time."

Janet said, "But didn't you tell him about the world today?"

"Yes. We showed him cell phones and computers. He was fascinated. We talked about cars and planes, too."

Janet followed up. "Well, if you were really there, wouldn't that have changed the way the world is? I think it wasn't real."

"Another good point, Janet. Class? If it really happened, if it wasn't just a projection, wouldn't the world be different now?"

"How do we know it isn't?" said Sherry Steinberg. "Maybe all the changes took place before today."

"Still a bit skeptical are you, Sherry?"

"Not really. But if it was real, wouldn't all the changes have happened already?"

"I'd agree, Sherry, but nothing seems different to me today. Does it to you?"

Jumping in, Steven Chew said, "What if the changes haven't caught up yet? What if it's like a wave and has to get to the shore and that takes time?"

"If that's true, Steven, then we might see something happen down the road, if it were real. But that's a good point." *But maybe he's hit on something,* I thought. *Could that explain why my ID was blank but we could access computer pictures? Why I had no money? And the words reappearing in Dan's book. Did time catch up?*

Another smiling student. I think that if you want kids to learn to think, you have to compliment them when they do. Steven wasn't done. "Or what if the changes happened, but to us they're just normal. Because, like, we were born into them."

"I'm really proud of you all. Do you realize how quiet you've been and how much serious thought and analysis you've just completed? Well done! For homework..." They stopped being quiet. "Quiet down. For homework, write a minimum of two pages on whether you think what you've heard about was real or if the hologram is what happened. Write this down." I waited until the shuffling and scuffling for pens and notebooks had stopped. "I want you to discuss both options and why you reach the conclusion you do. Class is almost over. Does anyone else have a question?"

Bill once again raised his hand. "I don't have a question, but that whole thing must have been awesome. I wish I'd been there." A murmur of agreement went through the class.

"Maybe next time."

"You're gonna do it again?" asked Dylan Lake, who almost never said anything.

"We'll see, Dylan."

The bell ending the first period sounded. I thought, "*One down.*"

The next class began to come in, but something was different about them. They were too quiet. I prepared to tell the story again, but before I did, I asked, "What's up guys?"

Melissa Nicholas said, "Mr. Russell, we get our letters this week, and some people have already gotten some."

They were all seniors, and the letters were, of course, from colleges they hadn't heard from yet. "So, how's it going so far?" I asked, knowing I had a reprieve for a moment.

"Not so good for me so far," replied Melissa. "But I've still got three more to hear from."

I looked around as the kids looked at each other.

"I've heard from my safe school, Mr. R. Didn't get in," Josh Martin said. "It's been a terrible weekend at home, I can tell you."

"I know it's none of my business. If anyone wants to talk about your decisions, I would be happy to help if I can. Even if you just have questions."

Susan Adams said, "I got in early decision, Mr. R, but this is really hard for all of us."

"Mr. R, I got an athletic scholarship to a school in Kansas," said James Junior. "But my parents aren't sure they want me to go so far. I've still got a couple of schools in the east, but no scholarship, so I don't know yet."

A palpable fear of failure permeated the class. "Listen, guys," I said, "I know you're worried. You've done all this work, all these years, and now it's out of your hands. But trust me, the world isn't ending. Your futures are just beginning, so be optimistic. The worst that can happen is you don't end up where you want to go. When you get all your letters, then you can make decisions. If any of you want to talk when you're deciding, come and see me. If you want." A hand went up.

Josh asked, "Mr. R, did you like college?"

I hesitated, knowing it was a serious question. "Do you want a short, glib answer? Or do you really want to know what I think?"

"What you really think," answered Marjorie Cousins.

"Okay. When I reached this week in high school, I had all my letters but one. It took five days after I was supposed to hear when it finally arrived. I walked home at lunch each day to check the mail because no one was home for me to call. So I know how anxious it can make you, the waiting. I got into my first choice school."

"Where did you go, Mr. R?" asked Walt Bridges.

That's the first time since I started teaching that a student has asked. Maybe things are changing. "Cornell," I said. "Work's gonna change, guys. You'll have lots more time outside of class, but you'll have tons more reading and writing, and you'll have to study subjects you haven't seen before. They don't care how much work you have from other classes. So you'll need to plan your time. And you'll meet people from all sorts of backgrounds with stories of their own." A quick image of my dorm hallway flashed. "My only advice is to try new things."

"What was it like for you, Mr. R?" asked Terry Francis.

"Well, just to keep this short. The roommate I had my freshman year was also my roommate for our junior and senior years. We still keep in touch. I took classes in subjects I wasn't remotely interested in, but I also took a lot of history classes. In my last year, I was a manager of the hockey team. That was fun."

"You played hockey?" asked Josh, surprised.

"Nope. I love hockey, though. I kept statistics and picked up jock straps." The class snickered. "Anyway, there are four years of stories to collect for yourselves. And I have mine, but I am not going to tell you now," I said. A few ran through my head, and I grinned.

Walt raised his hand again. "Mr. R, will you tell us what happened on Friday?"

Finally. "We don't have much time left, so briefly..." I told the class what I had told the first period class. As the bell was about to end the class, Kimberly Goldstein said, "So everything we heard about the forest and Robert E. Lee and all, all that was fake?"

"Not fake. It was a projection of an event. It seemed real when we were part of it."

Kim said, "So it wasn't real. It was fake." The class laughed.

"I think you win the semantics battle, Kim. OK guys. Homework." Over the complaining, I said, "I want you to write a two-page analysis of the difference between fake and fiction, using Friday's events as you heard them to illustrate your arguments. Due tomorrow."

"But, Mr. R, there's so much to do already," said Susan.

I smiled. "Welcome to college." The bell rang.

As the second period class exited, Ashley walked in. "How's it going," he asked.

"Not bad so far, but the kids are much smarter about this stuff than I thought. The first- period bunch had some tough questions, but I think they believe my story."

"I hope so, 'cause George really put you on the spot."

"That's your fault. You provoked him."

"Me?" said Ashley. "He'd be provoked if I said 'hello' to him today. He really seems to be nervous."

"He'll be fine when the meeting is over."

"Gotta run. See you later," said Ashley, as the bell starting third period rang.

* * *

"WRITE THIS DOWN," said the voice. " 'On Friday, the president made a surprise stop at Riverboro High School in New Jersey.' Make up some kind of story around it. Got it? Good. Get it in the local paper up there." The man returned to the report he was writing.

Chapter Sixteen

MY NEXT CLASS SAT WAITING, each kid leaning forward, fuses lit. I asked if they'd had a good weekend. Then it started. Raising both hands to hold off the onslaught, I felt like a rookie goalie at hockey practice. "OK, OK, settle down. My first two classes heard my story, but they weren't there. You were. So let's go over what happened." For the third time, I told the same story. The class listened, ready to pounce when I finished. I took as much time as I could to run down the classroom clock.

Jason raised his hand. "Mr. Russell, if that's all true, how do you explain the blood I put my hand in? It was wet and kind of red, and it came off on the handkerchief."

"You know, I thought about that myself, Jason. I haven't spoken to my friend about that yet. That's a really good question. Tell you what. I'll be speaking to him again this week. I'll ask how he did that and let you know."

Carol said, "Mr. R, if it wasn't real, how did General Lee hold my computer on his lap? He seemed pretty solid to me."

"And the tree stumps and the ground seemed real to me," said Anthony.

"So you think it was real?"

"Well, I don't know Mr. R, but it sure seemed real. But that means we all time traveled, doesn't it?" replied Anthony.

"Does it?"

"Of course," said Dan Wilkinson.

"What if, let's say it was real," I said, "what if General Lee came to 2015, rather than our having gone back to 1865?" I was thinking aloud. I got up and walked to the front of my desk. "What if we opened an entrance for him? What if General Lee time traveled? When the bell rang, we just walked into the hallway, and the classroom was like it always is." *Like a scale coming to balance,* I thought. *Could time work the same way?*

The class settled into quiet thought.

"Are you saying that it was real, Mr. Russell?" asked Carol.

"No, but I want you to look at all the possibilities, especially if you're not convinced I'm telling you the truth.

"But what about the books having no writing and the dates on your license and all?" said Marty Rose.

"It was part of the projection, I think, Marty. Remember guys, this is all new stuff, and it's pretty advanced technology. I certainly don't understand it all. But like I said, I'll be asking questions this week. I'll let you know how they did it. That's if they'll tell me."

"Mr. R?" asked Pat Leslie. "This is all pretty weird. Why did you choose our class? And fourth period?"

"Pat, I didn't choose the class or the material. I was pretty surprised too. I did know that something was going happen at some point, but not when. I just gave them a list of dates that were out, because there was something scheduled. Let me ask you all, did you find the visit with the general interesting?"

The class was brought up short by the change of subject. Clayton Waters raised his hand.

"Yes, Clayt?"

"Mr. Russell, I don't know if it was real or not, but meeting Robert E. Lee was spectacular. I really liked it when we told him about cars and planes. And did you see his face when he heard about the moon landing? I think he was as surprised about being with us as we were with him. It might not have been real, but it sure felt like it."

"And his horse was there too," said Jason.

"Amazing as it was, I want to apologize to you all because I should have prepared you for something strange. I'm sorry," I said, "I really am."

"Mr. R, can we do it again?" said Dan Wilkinson.

I love how my students react to new ideas, even strange ones. If I could teach them anything, it would be to examine and analyze things before making judgments. Nothing makes me happier when they do. "Probably not, Dan. Mr. McAllister isn't very happy with me right now. Anyway. Homework." They grumbled, which didn't surprise me. I told them I wanted them to write a well-reasoned discussion of the visit to the past and to explain why they thought it was real or not. "Due on Wednesday." The bell rang, and the class began to pack up. I walked into the hall thinking, *this is getting harder as I go.*

Ashley left his classroom and walked toward me. His disheveled hair looked like it hadn't seen a comb in weeks, and his long shirt sleeves were rolled up, baring an ugly six-inch scar. Some of the kids knew the story. He had tried to break up a knife fight at the beach the summer before he started at Riverboro, earned twenty-six stitches, and carried a fierce credibility with the students. When I first asked him about it, he just said, "You should have seen the other guy."

Linda has a scar, too, from having pulled a bike messenger away from the taxi that had hit him in Manhattan. The broken spokes had torn into her leg. She and Ash still argue about who took the greater risk, who did the greater good, and who has the better cicatrix, as he insists on labeling his. In our short moment in the hall, he told me that his last class was a discussion of time travel. He assigned an essay for homework describing where they would go if they could, and why. He planned to give the same assignment to the rest of his classes and let them work on it in class. "I wonder if other classes are going crazy."

I wasn't really paying attention. I was thinking about the questions the kids had asked. *A wave?* "Ash, we need to talk." Before I could tell him, the bell rang.

I waited at the front of my desk, leaned back, and braced myself.

"Hands down." They were ready, but I knew I had to be cautious. "I want to tell you about Friday. You may have heard something already, but you were there, so we'll go over what really happened." I repeated the story, more smoothly now after three rehearsals. I was astounded that they let me finish. But as soon as I stopped, hands flew up.

"Mr. R?" Johnny Clayton, not waiting to be recognized, jumped right in. "I didn't see anything that looked like projections. I've seen holograms before, and those things had substance. It wasn't just a light, and you could smell gunpowder."

"And Jason put his hand in blood, and the ground was wet," added Cheryl See. They were off and running.

Amanda said, "Carol had the laptop on the general's lap."

Bob followed. "There was a horse and another soldier, walking in the woods."

David Jewels came with, "I could see other men in the valley moving around."

"General Lee was looking at pictures, he saw your license, Dan told me, and he talked about cars and the moon. Why would they have programmed him to talk about those random things?" asked Matt. One after the other, this skeptical class pummeled me with what they considered proof. But of what?

I let them go on for a few minutes. "So you all think we time traveled? Is that what you REALLY think?"

Eric Silver, probably the smartest student in the class, said, "I don't." Immediate silence. All heads turned to him. He said, "First, if Einstein is correct, time travels in only one direction, forward. Second, I've been reading about experiments the government is doing on image projection for defense purposes. They are trying to synthesize matter using local resources from where they're projecting. You said your friend makes advanced special effects. I wonder if the government and the special effects community are working together. I'll bet that's what he does. Third, nothing real could have been so cool. So I think that you're telling us exactly what happened."

Nothing I might have said could have been that convincing to the class. "Thank you, Eric. I'd like to read the materials you've been looking at." I could feel my anxiety ease, as if my toes were a drain spout.

"Sure, Mr. R. I'll give you the websites."

"Me, too" came from Johnny, Cheryl, Amanda, Jack and David, together.

"And you should look up interactive holography, too," added Eric.

"So, all you skeptics," I asked, pacing the front of the room, "what do you think now?" The class got quiet again.

Amanda said, "Time travel is a myth, I guess. No one has ever done it. No offense, Mr. R, but if scientists can't do it, why would you be able to?"

"Why, indeed," I said. "No offense taken. OK, for homework, due Wednesday." I had to raise my voice over the complaining. "For homework, describe what you would do if you could time travel. Minimum two pages. Tell me why and what you would do while you were there."

"Mr. R?" asked David. "If Eric is right, does that mean we can only travel to the future? Does that mean General Lee traveled to the present?"

"Good question. Think about what Eric said and part of the essay should be a discussion of whether you think Eric is right." Class ended. *Saved by the bell.*

As the class departed, I sat and stared at my now-clear desktop. Fifth period was going to be easier. The kids didn't realize it, but they had discussed some of the questions I still needed to answer. While I stared from the door to the desk, hoping for a clue, a voice said, "Mr. Russell? Your face looks awful. Are you all right?"

Returning to the present, I said, "Yes, I'm fine. Thanks for asking." But I still wasn't completely paying attention. I pictured my feet in the portal and the rest of me in the hallway.

Same voice, "Are you sure?"

This time I looked at Marion and said, "Just thinking."

"About Friday?" asked Sarah Bright.

I nodded yes. "Raise your hands if you've heard about what happened on Friday." All hands went up. "Tell me what you heard." Immediate cacophony. "Whoa. One at a time. Yes, Fran."

"I heard that third and fourth period went into a forest and met Robert E. Lee."

"And seventh period, you went to a fire," said Steve Christopher, Matt's younger brother.

"The fire was the Triangle Fire in New York," said Tom Wyle. His voice reflected his shyness. "But that was in 1911. I looked it up. How did you do it, Mr. R?"

"I told you on Friday I'd tell you when it was the right time. I've spoken to Mr. McAllister, and we think you should get the real story. So here goes." By now, I was able to deliver a detailed and more polished version of both visits to the past, better than I had yet. I dragged it out almost to the end of the period.

When I stopped, Sam asked, "What are you going to tell the other teachers, Mr. Russell?"

"The same thing that I just told you guys, Sam. Mr. Gilbert told me earlier that his classes have all been talking about it, so I'm probably going to apologize to the faculty for the disruption."

Bill said, "I wouldn't apologize. This is the most interesting thing I've ever heard, even if it isn't real. I'd like to have a class like that. Can you get one for us, Mr. R?"

Shouts of agreement bounced through the classroom. "That would be so cool, Mr. R," said Kevin Maher. "I'd like to go to…" I stopped him.

"Thanks, Kevin. I stopped you because that will be your homework for tomorrow. Everyone, minimum of two pages—where you would go and why if you could time travel? OK, pack up" as the bell rang. It hit me then that I would have a lot of essays to read.

"Lunch," I said to myself as Ash stuck his head around the corner.

"Still holding up?" he asked.

"So far, so good. But this has been a real effort. The kids are accepting the explanation, but I think some are unconvinced. Two classes want their own trips. And I don't know how to stop that."

He put his hand on my shoulder. "We'll figure it out."

* * *

THE DOOR TO THE OVAL OFFICE opened. "Mr. President, I think you should hear this," Tom said. The president stopped work on his speech. Tom reported that he had listened to five classes so far and picked the important parts. The president made notes.

When the recording ended, he grinned at Tom and said, "Well one thing is certain. He knows his students. I'm surprised he's not a lawyer or a politician. He avoids the truth as smoothly as the best of them on the Hill. Thanks, Tom. If anything else happens, let me know."

"Mr. President, Mr. Koppler listened too. I couldn't stop him. I think he's got a hookup to listen on his own."

"Thanks, Tom. On the way out, would you please ask Lily to come in?"

Ms. Evans had been on the president's staff before he was elected. She entered the Oval Office in a bright yellow blouse. "Yes, sir?"

"You are definitely brighter than it is outside," said the president. "Looks nice. Lily, would you see if you can find Jim Koppler and tell him I want to talk to him, as soon as possible.

"Right away, Mr. President." She didn't like Mr. Koppler.

* * *

AFTER CAFETERIA DUTY, I grabbed an oatmeal cookie and a bottle of apple juice and returned to my classroom. I tapped the doorknob. Nothing happened. Alone for the first time since the mysterious happenings on Friday, I unlocked my desk, and took out a pad and pencil. *What is it that I know?* I wondered and began to make notes. *Door knob, paperclips, stuff on the desk, maybe in a particular order. Friday was stormy. Are the kids more attentive?* I removed the books and the White House pamphlet from the desk drawer, put them where they were on Friday, and looked for the places that I had marked. *Maybe I should change the markers.* Although I didn't notice, I was being watched through the window in the door. Then the door swung open abruptly.

"ARE YOU NUTS?" I jumped. Ash glared at me.

"Maybe." I shrugged, not interested in a lecture at the moment. "I'm trying to see what the connections are. If I can find a safe way to do it again, then I'll know how to stop it." I took three paperclips from my middle drawer. "Ash, I'm the catalyst. You can't do it. No one else can. So I'm the only one who can stop it. If I can do it again, I will. It just doesn't seem to be random."

The next class began to enter. "See you at the meeting," said Ashley. I waved and cleared my desk, putting everything in the lower drawer. These kids concerned me most. They had witnessed the most upsetting event and might be less inclined to accept easy answers. Not telling them the truth would be the hardest because to make matters trickier, they were both older and a very bright group.

"So how was your weekend?" I said, trying to start on a light note. But the bombardment started immediately.

"Mr. R, you know how it was. You could have told us the truth on Friday," said Joe Norell.

"Yeah, we've heard from the other classes, a new special effects technology, interactive holograms?" added Larry.

"What I heard earlier doesn't answer a lot of questions for me, Mr. R. I could smell smoke. I heard those girls hit the ground. That was no light show," said Bill Robinson.

I'd expected this. "Do all of you think you time traveled? Raise your hands if you do."

The first hand up was Jennifer's. Then other hands went up, one at a time. I said, "Okay, but our having gone into the past is both improbable and scientifically unlikely." I felt more comfortable on my feet and stood in front of the blackboard. "Now let me tell you, as technically as I can, that we witnessed a new technology designed by people who have lots of experience with movies and TV. They have written algorithms to imitate sensory reactions—sight, sound, smell, et cetera. The group working on this is devising the technology for a series of movies." Taking a sip of my juice, I looked at my students to see if they were buying it. "So, still think you time traveled?"

One lone voice said softly, "Yes."

"Jen, I think you and I will have to agree to disagree."

"Mr. Russell," said Jennifer, "I know it sounds dumb, but I've thought about this all weekend. I searched the web for information on the Triangle Fire and time travel and energy transformation. And I looked at technical movie-making websites. There was nothing that would support my feelings. I went to the government, looking for technical info from the Energy Department, Department of Defense, the CIA (that was a waste), Homeland Security. There was nothing about any new findings either. So all I'm left with is that it seemed too real to be made up." She stopped.

"So everything you researched says what happened couldn't have, but you believe it anyway?"

"Yes." The class chuckled.

Mike said, "Jen, I tried to find stuff too. But when I read about time travel, and there's really a lot there, I just couldn't accept that it was real. It was a little scary, but I don't think it could have been real."

"Really, you guys, you need to get a life," said Bill Robinson.

I stepped in to keep from losing the class. "If you've done the research and found nothing, there is only one other possibility. It may be that scientists have not yet found a way to enter the space-time continuum. That might happen in the future. But, Jen, it hasn't happened yet." The class collectively exhaled, relieved, almost happy that what they had experienced had happened in history but that they hadn't been there. I could feel the tension in my shoulders release.

Leaning against my desk, I said, "Guys, I have a meeting with the teachers after school. I need to explain what's caused the chaos in every class so far today. Mr. Gilbert told me earlier that all his students wanted to talk about something none of them had seen. You did. I'll be talking to my friend this week to tell him how things went. Does anyone have a suggestion for me to pass along?"

"I have one," said Wendy Baer. "Don't do it in schools again." There were laughs, but there was also agreement.

"I'll tell him. But, Wendy, I've had three classes who said they wanted one of their own."

"That's because they weren't there," Wendy said. "They might think it was cool, but it wasn't. It was scary. I don't think I'll ever forget it."

"I know, Wendy, and I'm sorry. It's ironic, because I always want to make history come alive for you, but this may have been too much. But think what it was like for the people who were involved." The victims of the fire were, I pointed out, young women about their age with fire at their backs, some already on fire, no escape. Holding hands as they jumped, knowing they would probably die. "That's really scary. I believe we study history so we don't repeat our mistakes from the past."

"Doesn't work too well, does it?" Tim Andrews asked.

"Unfortunately, Tim, not always. But if you think about it, I bet you can find hundreds of things that do. As a teacher, I can only hope that a few students will understand and go on to make this world better for everyone." The class got quiet for the first time. "I think I have made my point today. Thanks, class. You may have just made my year."

A few smiles appeared around the class. As the period drew to an end, I said, "Tomorrow we will get back to normal. Be ready to talk about *The Jungle*, which you should have read for Friday's class. We'll talk about the point Sinclair tried to make and what occurred as a result." As the class shuffled out, Jennifer stopped.

"Mr. Russell, I got accepted by Cornell." Her radiant smile reminded me how much my kids had to look forward to.

"That's great, Jen. Congratulations. It's a fine school."

"Thanks, see ya," but I knew she had more she wanted to say.

* * *

MORE THAN A HALF HOUR had passed. The president was already annoyed when his national security advisor entered the Oval Office. Mr. Koppler appeared irritated to have been summoned. Keeping the president waiting had never worried him. The president knew his advisor had been the source of numerous leaks, but since no damage had been done, the president had kept him on, more to keep him close than because he valued his ideas. He'd get ahold of leakable info even out of office.

"Have a seat, Jim."

Koppler sat, yet to offer a greeting. He waited.

"I want to talk to you about Mr. Russell and the portal. I've had a couple of days to think about it, and I want to limit who finds out about it to those who know now. When I said on Friday everyone would remain silent, I meant it."

"Mr. President, are you suggesting that I have been talking?" said Koppler, ever arrogant and, this time, aggressive as well.

"I wasn't. Have you been?"

"I believe I am responsible for monitoring the security status of this country as well as the president's safety, sir. It's a big, dangerous world. I have people whom I trust to see that you get the best intelligence."

"So then you have spoken to people who didn't know?"

"No one without clearance."

"I thought I made myself clear." He appraised the man in front of him. Well dressed, scowling face, crossed arms. "Perhaps not. So I will now." His soft voice, barely above a whisper, was sharp and pointed. "First, no one else is to be included. Second, I want you to give Tom Andrews a list of the people you've told. Save him some time and include their home addresses and all phone numbers. Third, as of right now, all, I repeat, all analysis, discussion, reporting begins with me. And will be approved by me. Jim, this is not a typical national security issue. And I don't want it treated in the usual fashion. If you have ideas about how you might help me with this, by all means, let me know. Otherwise, let it be." The president glared. "Do we understand each other?"

"If I may speak openly, Mr. President…" He waited for the president's go-ahead. "This is potentially a weapon that can be used against this country. If it should fall into the wrong hands, we could have a perpetual crisis to deal with. I don't trust them. These teachers are shrimp in a shark's world. What do we know about them, really? How do we know we can count on them when the chips are down? Are you willing to place yourself or the country in jeopardy because they seem harmless? Mr. President, you may not like the way I do things, but I'm cautious, and I've been doing this for a long time."

The president was listening and gritting his teeth. Before answering, he made a note on a legal pad. "Jim, if I didn't respect your ability or your caution, we wouldn't be having this conversation. But I'll handle Mr. Russell and the others. I don't want to hurt them, or scare them so they won't cooperate. Until I can see all my options, I want them left alone and safe. I'll ask you again. Do we understand each other?"

"Yes, sir. Very clearly."

Chapter Seventeen

LAST PERIOD. Finally. I thought about the teachers' meeting. *They may be easier to convince than the kids, and they'll want to get out as fast as possible.* The bell rang. As they had been all day, this group, too, was uncommonly quiet, anticipating a discussion of Friday.

"You've all had a full day to hear tales of mystery and wonder. Anyone want to tell us the best version you've heard?" No hands went up. "Well, that's a first. As noisy as you usually are, no one has anything to say?" Mary Anne, whose sister was in the third-period class, raised her hand. "That's more like it. Yes, Mary Anne?"

"Mr. Russell, on Friday you said my sister was messing with me. But when we talked at lunch, she said your friend has a new invention that can make people see things that aren't really there. How will we ever know if what we see is real or not? We might not even be here now."

"Wow, Mary Anne, I hadn't thought of that," I said in earnest. "That's a completely new perspective." The class was still quiet. I surveyed all the young faces, which normally included mouths moving at full speed, now watching me with unusual focus. Once more, I told the story.

When I finished, Dennis Rogers' hand went up. "Mr. R, does that all mean that, well, that you didn't time travel? That all the stories aren't real?"

I knew that the tale had been defused. "Dennis, time travel might be a great fictional topic. But, so far at least, it hasn't happened." Then for the first time that day, I got blindsided.

Alan asked, "Was the president really here, Mr. R? I heard that he went in the gym and played basketball for a while. Then he signed autographs. Was he really here?" They all seemed to be holding their breath.

"He came just after school ended. He said he was driving by, saw a school, and wanted to stop and say hi. But the first thing he asked was to use the bathroom." The class laughed. "What's so funny? Don't you think the president goes to the bathroom?" This time the class wasn't sure whether to laugh or not. "But he really was here. Now for homework, I want an essay on what you would do if you could time travel, two-page minimum, for tomorrow."

Jacob asked, "If we could time travel, Mr. R, could we change history?"

"Jacob, you might want to include that as part of your discussion." The bell rang. "Class dismissed." I thought that was a good question, maybe the best one of the day. I thought again of the River Rouge photo. I'd gone back in time only this past Friday. The picture had remained a mystery for seventy-eight years. But my face hurt in the present. I knew then that I needed some lessons in the theories of time travel.

Before the class had emptied, book bags and knapsacks bumping from their shoulders, Ashley was there. "So. Now the teachers. Are you ready?" His sleeves were now inside the camel blazer that he's worn for as long as I've known him.

"Yup," I said.

"Yup? That's all?"

"Yup. Let's go."

We turned for the auditorium. Tom Jaffrey caught up at the cafeteria. "Fritz, this better be good. It's been a buzz all day. You're the teacher of the year to the kids."

"Should I say thanks, Tom? Or I'm sorry? I know you had your heart set on being teacher of the year. It's got to be rough losing out to a fictional character."

In spite of his exuberance, Tom stopped walking and looked at me squarely. "Fritz, if I could get one quarter of the excitement and energy I've seen the past two days, I'd be a great teacher."

"Thanks, Tom," said Ashley. "Give him a bigger head than he already has. He'll start thinking he's Harry Potter, and we'll all be taking magic lessons from him."

"Shut up!" I said. The three of us laughed. "But speaking of lessons, Tom, can you suggest any books about the physics of time travel?" He said he had a couple in mind and would check for others. When we reached the auditorium, George was waiting for me, tapping a rolled newspaper in his hand. Ashley and Tom Jaffrey went in, but I stopped, as other teachers, ending conversations as they reached us, converged on the doorways.

"You sure cooked my goose this morning, George. And from what I can tell, you got all the other teachers stuck in this all day, too."

"Well, I wanted everyone to show up. I just hadn't counted on the kids jumping on. Do you think we'll be okay?"

"Of course. Remember you're in school, George. That's when they *are* thinking. You should get back in a classroom. You'd be surprised." George grimaced. "Let's go."

"Before we go in, have you seen this?" George handed me the afternoon newspaper and showed me an article. It said the president had visited Riverboro High School.

My fists formed, and my shoulders felt book bag taut. "Let's get this over with."

As the last of the faculty took seats, George walked briskly to the lectern, which was up on the stage. The microphone squealed, but George had everyone's attention. "For the past couple of days, there have been some unusual activities in our school. Mr. Russell will explain everything." He turned, motioning me to the microphone.

Surprised at the introduction, which was nothing like the one we had discussed, I looked from George to the audience and said, "Thanks Mr. McAllister. That sure clears everything up." There were laughs from the audience, but the hall seemed like an echo chamber. The auditorium has seats for more than 800 and sophisticated sound and lighting systems. George loves to brag about his modern systems to other principals. Trying to measure the mood of the teachers, I mimicked George and said, "Good afternoon, fellow keepers of the light of knowledge. Before I go on to explain, I want to offer my apology. I know it's hard enough to keep our students focused and this, uh, this event obviously made your jobs that much harder." A low murmur came from room.

"On Friday, three of my classes were subjected to a new technology that was developed by a friend who works for a special effects company in California. He asked if I would be a guinea pig for him. He asked what subjects I would be teaching around the middle of April. I gave him a couple of options for each class and asked what he was going to do. 'You'll see,' he told me. Last week, after school, they installed a projection system in my classroom. He told me that I would be surprised and didn't tell me more." The teachers listened attentively.

"Well, surprised is hardly adequate. The system was apparently programmed for two classes, third and seventh period. The programs seemed so authentic that I kept the third-period class in the room when the fourth came in. It was Appomattox the day after Lee had surrendered." I scanned the auditorium; every eye focused on me. I'm used to being in front of an audience, but not one that wasn't talking. Not a sound, not even wiggling in the seats. "The classes met Robert E. Lee and talked to him. Seventh period, the class witnessed the Triangle Shirtwaist Company fire in New York City in 1911.

"Both programs were incredibly realistic, and for a history teacher, both exciting and troubling. But fortunately, since it was a projection, no one was in danger. But, the fire scene was alarming. It had not been on my list. I had only mentioned early twentieth-century labor history. That was unthinking of me. And my friend is in a business that makes money scaring people. I told him how traumatic it was and that without lots of discussion beforehand with the kids and planning with the company, this is not a good thing to have in classrooms. Once again, everyone, I'm sorry."

Tom Jaffrey stood up. "Fritz, like I've said to you already, I think it was fabulous. Aside from the disruption in our classes, which we all deal with anyway, I haven't seen that much animation in my students since, well, maybe never." Low-level agreement rumbled to the stage. "If we can harness this energy for our own subjects, the next few weeks could be very rewarding."

George took the microphone. "Thank you for your opinion, Tom, but I think it would be best if we don't have a repeat of Friday." Clearly wanting to get away from the teachers, George said, "If there is nothing further, I hope this will answer your questions and put an end to this unfortunate incident."

Some teachers began to get up when Liz Chambers, another history teacher, said, "George, I have a question. What was the president doing here?" The room turned quiet.

"He had to use the bathroom and then asked to see our school. So we took him around. I even asked if he would come to graduation."

Liz said, "George, I think Friday's event was a good thing. I actually talked to my kids about the Civil War. And they listened. It might only be for a couple of days, but Tom is right. I think Fritz did us all a big favor." The sounds of agreement hovered over the audience.

George said, "Well that's all. Thank you for coming." He walked off the stage and out of the auditorium. Laughter, conversations, and some smirks appeared after the door closed.

Teachers began to leave when Al Kennedy, the gym teacher and football coach, said loudly, "The president autographed one of our basketballs. Fritz, you might not have anything to do with it, but even the gym classes were talking about Friday. It must have been interesting. I sure hope George will buy a display case."

All I wanted was the nearest door. Teachers milled around, clearly waiting to say something to me, so I exited out a back door off the stage and headed for my classroom. Ashley had anticipated my escape route and was waiting at the end of the hallway. "Good show," he said as I approached.

"Let's get out of here. My place."

We gathered our things and walked quickly to the parking lot, which was filled with teachers I wanted to avoid. Sandy Horton came out behind us. She caught me at my car.

"Fritz, I know what really happened, but this could still be a good teaching tool. I agree with Tom Jaffrey. When you figure it out, would you take me with you?"

"Sandy, candidly, I'd like to avoid anything more if I can." I waved to a couple of teachers driving by. "It could be dangerous. George is a mess, and this meeting didn't really go as well as I had hoped."

She said, frowning, "Maybe we can talk about it some other time."

"Sure."

Ashley, waiting at his car and watching, caught my eye. I got the message, climbed in my car, and headed for home.

"SO HOW DID it go?" Linda asked, as we walked in the back door. Her laptop and an open marketing textbook sat on the otherwise empty table.

"This has been a very long day," I said. "George ambushed me when the day started. During morning announcements, he said I would be talking to the teachers after school about Friday. That set every kid off, in all the classes. Ask Ashley."

"Every class I had asked about Friday and did it really happen and what was Fritz going to tell the teachers? It appears to have happened in every room in the building."

"That's not the bad part," I said. "The teachers thought it was great. When we were leaving, Sandy Horton said that she wanted to go with me next time. And the president's visit is in the newspaper. This afternoon's. I'm just afraid this thing isn't going to die down."

I found the article in the newspaper quickly and showed it to Linda and Ashley. As they read, I said, "This is not going to make the president happy. I've *got* to find a way to keep it from happening again."

Linda knew my brain was in high gear. "Fritz, I know what you're thinking. I know how focused you get and how passionate you are about making things right. But, if you try to open that portal, I want to know beforehand. If you figure it out, the least you can do is tell me how to do it in case something happens."

Her knitted brow displayed her distress. Trying to relieve her concern, I said, "I love you. If we can do this together, we will."

"Me, too," said Ashley.

"I don't love you."

My phone rang. "That better not be George," I said, opening my cell phone. The screen told me it was the White House. "Hello, Mr. President."

"It's Lily Evans, Mr. Russell. Please hold for the president."

A moment later, I heard, "Hello, Mr. Russell. I'm calling to see how your meeting went."

"Mr. President, the meeting went okay. I think the teachers are convinced of the story, but they want a piece of the action, so to speak. They seem to think it's a good teaching tool."

The president said, "Well, you must have done a good job with them."

"Mr. President, if your people found anything or can come up with some idea of how to stop it, now would be a good time to tell me. I assume you know your visit here was in today's local paper."

"I didn't know. I would have found out by tomorrow no doubt. But as you know, we've changed the schedule book. Our story is set. I appreciate, though, that you let me know. Don't let it concern you. Besides, it's good PR, visiting a school."

"Mr. President, I'm doing the best I can. I just haven't had any time to work this out. Believe me, I don't like not being able to anticipate where my classroom will be. I don't want any more problems with you, or with George, and I don't want to endanger my kids most of all. It's bad enough having to lie to them."

"Fritz," said the president, calling me by my first name for the first time, "I wish I had something I could tell you to put your mind at ease. I don't yet, but let's keep in touch. If you do find something, let me know."

"Of course, Mr. President."

"Then, goodbye for now. I'm sure you know that I have a bit of a crisis, in Eledoria and in Jerusalem right now." He disconnected before I could respond.

"That was quick," said Ashley.

"I hope I made my point with him. Hopefully, he won't think I'm trying to hurt him."

"I think he expects you to try to figure this out, Fritz," said Linda. "I wonder what they found."

* * *

LILY EVANS CALLED to say Jim Koppler wanted to come up from his office. The president said to send him in when he got there.

"What's on your mind?" The president's response was crisp, not inviting.

"This." He showed the president a newspaper. "Mr. President, there is a report that you visited the school. The White House press is asking how that could have happened. There's no record of your leaving here."

"Jim, you are aware that there are other ways out of this cage, I assume? The press reports what they think they know, or what we tell them. So where I am is where they think I am, or where I want them to know I am. Do you honestly think that it makes sense to hide that I was in New Jersey when all the evidence says I was? Don't make this a public debate."

"Mr. President, I have to protest. The press has sources, you know that. You're having been in New Jersey is the least of it."

"And I have a list of people who know, Mr. Koppler." The president's responded sharply. "And I have the resources to find out where any story comes from. I want you to drop it."

"Mr. President, that's just not a good idea."

"If you'll excuse me now, Jim. I am a little busy." He was gritting his teeth again.

"Yes, sir." When his advisor left, the president took a deep breath, made a note, and returned to his report.

* * *

MY PHONE RANG AGAIN. "Hi George," I said. "What's up?"

"Fritz, Lois and I have been discussing our little problem. How about changing your classroom for now. Maybe that would help."

"I appreciate that, George. Can I make a suggestion?" I asked.

"Go ahead."

I told him that each time we traveled the door gave me a mild shock. I suggested that I could keep the kids safe if there were an empty room I could move them to. "I need my classroom to figure this out, George, and all my teaching materials and wall hangings are there. But if the buzzing opens the portal, a different room should be fine. I can just herd them down the hall."

"Well," said George, "we have some vacant rooms in the old wing. I'll fix one of them for you, or if it's a nice day, you could take your class outside."

"Thanks, George. Let me know when the room is ready. Say hi to Lois."

Nice days? "George suggested a different classroom, or going outside if it's nice out, but the portal opened when it was stormy."

Following my thoughts, Linda said, "If thunderstorms start the process and you're the connection, then any door, anywhere, could be a portal if the paperclips and books were set up. If you get a shock from a different doorknob, then what?"

"Then I'm in trouble," I said. "It could happen anytime, anywhere. But I think it has to do with my classroom."

ALTHOUGH MY CLASS routine followed my accustomed plan, my students' new attentiveness deviated from past experience. During the week, quite a few teachers expressed their interest in participating in any new traveling. They all suggested what they thought would be good subjects to cover, including Einstein, Benjamin Franklin, Harriet Tubman, Nathaniel Hawthorne, Marie Curie, F. D. R, Rosa Parks, and Jane Austen. The physics teacher, who happened to speak Italian, wanted to visit Galileo at the Leaning Tower. Each teacher I spoke with told me how exhilarated their students had become. I wondered if there was more to the electrical charge than just what I felt through my fingertips. At the end of the week, George came to me and said the alternative classroom was set up and ready to use if I needed it. I thanked him, but I wondered why he was so efficient at some times when he was often such a ditherer. By Friday afternoon, I had to remind myself it had only been a week since the adventures had occurred.

Ashley stopped by at the end of eighth period. "Want to play a round tomorrow? Supposed to rain on Sunday."

"You know, Ash, I haven't thought about exercise since we last played basketball. You know how that went. I'll talk to Linda and let you know."

"Talk to you later then," said Ashley.

Friday afternoon. Quiet. Maybe I'll have a chance to think this through. I took a deep breath, as though I was opening the valve on a pressure cooker. I looked around the room, my second home. I took the book I'd used on the Civil War from my desk and paper clipped the pages where John Wilkes Booth was described as entering the presidential box. I put it on the left side of the desk. "Left, right, center," I said to myself.

Ashley was just leaving his classroom as I reached for the doorknob. "Fritz, what are you doing?" as I grabbed the door and opened it.

"Nothing."

"Nothing?"

"Nothing," I repeated.

"You're trying to open it."

"Yeah, but nothing."

We both went into the classroom. "Nothing," I said again, running my hands through my hair.

"Where were you trying to go?" asked Ash, seeing a book on the desk.

I told him I had marked Ford's Theater. He said he was glad nothing had happened, that I could change world history if I went there. "You could end up not having been born." I told him I didn't know what I would have done, to which he said I ought to reconsider. His tone scolded.

"It's been too quiet this week. Thought I'd mix it up a little."

"You're nuts, did you know?" said Ash.

"It has occurred to me once or twice."

WHEN I ARRIVED HOME, I kissed Linda hello. "If it's okay, I'm gonna play golf with Ash tomorrow. I could use the exercise."

"Do you feel up to it?" she asked.

"Yeah, I'm fine, and maybe the quiet will help clear my head. Ash said it's supposed to rain," I hesitated, "on Sunday."

"What?" she asked. "What about Sunday?"

"Storms on Sunday. Just thinking. George has the new classroom ready to use. Do you know what the weather's supposed to be next week?"

"No, but I hope it's nice," said Linda. "It'll keep you out of trouble."

"So you don't mind if I play tomorrow?"

"I don't mind, but if you get tired, promise me you'll stop."

"And miss a hole in one? I don't know," I said. "I'll call Ash and set a time."

"Ask him if he wants food," she said.

"Ash, golf's OK. When? I'll be ready. Linda asked if you want to come for dinner tomorrow. Oh?" I winked at Linda. "Really. With whom?" I asked. "See you then," and hung up. I said, "He has a date tomorrow. Wouldn't say who."

Linda grinned. Ash's romances were a regular source of roller coaster rides for the three of us. "You're going to have to find out. We can't let Casanova off too easily."

"I'll tell him you said so. One of these days..." I held up my crossed fingers.

"Fritz, I want to talk to you." I was getting up to pour a drink but stopped and sat. "Before, when you didn't want to teach, I was concerned. But now, this portal gets you going in the morning. I think that worries me more. You're changing." I felt the chill of her eyes bore into me. "You need to be careful. For both of us."

At seven the next morning, my golf bag and I walked to the car. "Hey bud," said Ash, opening the trunk.

"Looks like a good day to play. And a good night, too." Ashley looked at me, said nothing, but wore his Cheshire-Cat grin.

After fifteen holes of idle chatter, Ashley said, "I've been thinking about Ford's Theater. I don't think you should go there. Last night, I was looking through a book about Reconstruction and thinking about how different things might be if Lincoln had lived. You could really screw things up, by making them better. Know what I mean?"

"I was thinking about that too," teeing up for the next hole. "The temptation is there, but I don't want to change history. I wonder if just going back changes anything? Linda said yesterday she thought I was changing." At that, I swung.

"Nice hit," said Ashley. "Maybe just going back improved your golf game." Ashley teed up his ball.

"So who are you going out with?" I said, just as Ash made his drive and watched it slice into the trees.

"I get a do-over," he said. "And none of your business."

"Nice retort. Do-over costs you two strokes, unless you tell me who."

"You don't know her."

"Looks like triple bogey territory to me!"

"Oh, all right," said Ash, teeing up another ball. As he was swinging again, I said, "So?" The second ball followed the first. "Will you stop that and let me shoot," Ashley groused.

"You keep shooting like that, and we're talking octuple bogey."

"Better than octogenarian bogey, like you."

"Ow, that hurts. So tell me, and I'll be quiet."

"Sandy."

"Horton?"

"Uh huh." A slight shade of pink invaded Ashley's cheeks. He said they had started talking about how cool it would be to meet Shakespeare, Austen, Whitman, Poe. "It just evolved. She's sharp."

"You need to do two things," I said.

"What?"

"Be careful what you say, and hit the damn ball." This time the ball went down the middle of the fairway. "That's five so far."

"Go to hell," Ash said.

* * *

"YOU KNOW HE'S GOING to try to find out how the portal works. Can't you help him?" she asked, looking up. The president ran his hand over the wainscoting and the First Lady faced him on a couch in the Oval Office.

"Not without being there. He's the centerpiece, the key. Whatever connects the dots starts with him. And I may have a problem with Jim Koppler. I'm trying to keep him out of this. He's seeing bogeymen while I'm still trying to see if there's really a problem. I still want Russell tested. This is as much a problem for me as it is for Jim, or for Russell."

Chapter Eighteen

ASHLEY WAS RIGHT. It rained on Sunday. A gentle spring day. Pilgrim rain. I watched the Phillies, playing in Atlanta on TV. The Weather Channel predicted the Northeast would be experiencing unseasonably warm temperatures. Monday through Thursday showed an eighty percent chance of late afternoon thunderstorms. I thought it would be best not to mention the forecast to Linda, but she knew and warned me. "If you get a shock, before you try to go into some other dimension, please call me. At least then, I'll have a concrete reason to worry. And use that other room if you have to. George took the trouble to fix it up. The least you can do is keep the kids away from another trip." It stung that she didn't think that was my greatest concern.

Puddles dotted the streets as Monday began. Just after school ended, dark clouds blew in with some rumbling but no lightning. I stayed for a few minutes to try the door, but all I got was another nothing. So I left. Ashley, sitting at his desk, saw me heading out and called. I stepped back to the doorway. "How was your date?"

"Would you believe we spent most of the evening talking about you?"

Oh boy, I thought. "And?"

"Don't worry. We talked about where we could go via the portal. But we're actually gonna try another one, date that is, next weekend."

"Do mine ears deceive me? Two dates, same woman?" I covered my mouth to show my fake surprise. "Was she bound and ear-plugged?"

"Oh stop," said Ash. "We have great conversations. I'll tell you more some other time, and not here. Maybe we can all go out for dinner."

"Well, I'll mention it to Linda." Changing the subject, I asked if he was leaving.

"Not yet. I'm waiting for…" He pointed through the wall.

"WHY DO YOU TEASE him like that? Of course we'll go out with them. It'll be nice, and he can ease into this relationship with some conversation other than one focused on you. You should have a little more compassion. He's your *friend*."

Lightning flashed, and a crack of thunder interrupted her. "I wonder what would have happened if this storm had come earlier. Linda, I've been thinking."

"Why don't I like the sound of that?"

"I think I can plan where I go. If I have paper-clipped books already set up in all three places when the doorknob gives me a shock, I can check exactly where it takes me. So I need to find places that aren't dangerous and be ready if it happens again. Then all I have to do is step in, look at where I am, and walk out again. It should be that easy."

"Why do you worry me like this? What's going to happen if you're wrong? Do you really think you can just walk back out?"

"I have before. Even took the president with me. If I can create my own itinerary, then you shouldn't be worried. Remember, I'm trying to shut this down. Lin, I may be curious and even a little adventurous, but I don't think I'm stupid or reckless." Her face said she wasn't so sure. "I know it's going to happen again.

I can feel it. I just want to be able to control the trip, know where I'm going, and keep the kids out. Lin, I have to find out how the portal opens. I don't think anyone can do this except me."

"Fritz, I don't like it. I don't want anything to happen to you." I reached out and squeezed her hand softly.

"Should I tell Ash we'll go out with him this weekend?" I asked. Changing the subject didn't change her expression.

"Why not? Let's go to a nice place, not one of his usual dives. Why don't you suggest the Old Lion Inn?"

On Tuesday, my tires were puddle magnets after the night's rain, splattering the windshield while the wipers kept time to the tunes on the radio. Classroom, doorknob, no buzz. I went to the windowsill where the books were still piled and started looking at titles. *Where can I go and be safe?* Discarding book after book, I reached for a biography of Robert E. Lee, turned to the last few chapters, and read about Lee's time as President of Washington College in Lexington, Virginia. I took out a paperclip and marked the section. The next book was the one I had looked at on Friday. *What would I do?* I put a paperclip back on the Ford's Theater pages.

Ashley walked in, stopped short. "What exactly are you doing?"

"Planning my trip.

"Have you figured it out?" he asked. His scolding voice had changed to excitement.

"No, but the weather is lousy, so I'm going to try to set up some trips. If I get a buzz during school, I'll take the kids to the room George fixed up for me."

"And if it's before or after?" he asked, worry in his voice.

"Then I can open the door, see if it takes me where I plan, and walk back out."

"How do you know you can get out?"

"I don't, except for knowing that I did before. And Ash, if I can't figure out how it works, I'll be forever at the mercy of random events. I've got to find out how to stop it."

Monday had been gloomy, but nothing abnormal occurred. Tuesday, the weather cleared a bit, so once again, it was business as usual. As classes ended, I returned to planning. On the left, Lee. On the right, Ford's Theater, although I was still unsure of the wisdom of that. *I need a third one.* Rummaging through my books, I spotted the travel brochure and was picking it up as Ashley walked in.

"What's that?" he asked.

"The White House tour brochure that got me to the Oval Office."

"Don't do that again," Ash said.

"Look, I'm trying to find safe places to go if this happens again. *When*, I should say. What could be safer? The president knows me and knows about the portal. He also knows that I'm still trying to figure out how it works."

"What if a secret service agent shoots first and asks second, or if the president just decides you're too dangerous, and oops, you disappear?"

"Good point. I should let him know I'm trying to repeat the visit. Thanks, buddy. Good idea."

"Not my idea. Don't blame me," said Ashley. "I don't think you should go at all."

A face appeared in the window of the classroom door. Short brown hair, a happy glint in her eyes. I waved Sandy in. A raincoat was draped over her left arm. I said, "I forgot to tell you. Linda suggested we all go to the Old Lion Inn. Would Saturday be okay?"

Sandy hadn't had time to say hello, but she smiled when she heard me. Ashley looked at her. "It's okay with me. Is that okay, Sandy?"

She said, "That would be great. I've only been there once. It's really good."

"I'll tell Linda. Oh, by the way, Ash, you're buying." I watched as his face turned red.

Sandy asked, "Are we driving or time traveling?"

Ashley laughed at me. "Gotcha."

On Wednesday morning, the storms were back. I ran to the door to get out of the rain and not be outside if lightning visited again. I came in early to see if I could open the portal. Nothing. No progress, no answers. I put the books and brochure away in the same order: left, middle, right. I took out my phone, paused for a moment, and punched in the number of the White House.

"Good morning, Mr. Russell," came a female voice.

"Is that you, Ms. Evans?"

"Yes it is. I'll see if the president can speak with you now." After a minute or so, the president's voice came through the phone.

"Mr. Russell, I was wondering when I'd be hearing from you. Have you figured it out?"

"Not yet, but I have some hunches, and I'm going to try to get to the Oval Office again, if I find the portal. I need to stay safe. And it's usually pretty safe at your place." His snort made me pull the phone from my ear. "But I wanted you to know. No surprises." I walked to the windows while we talked. A black Suburban slowed and stopped directly in front of me.

"Thanks for the warning," he said. "You know, my invitation stands. I would still like to do some tests." He paused for a moment. "How about this? Why don't you come down on Saturday afternoon? The tests will take less than an hour, and then we can have dinner here."

Thank you, Mr. President, but I've made plans for dinner with Ashley. He has a new, let's call it relationship. Sandy Horton, you met her, sir. Linda and I are trying to help."

The Suburban's window opened and a rifle barrel slipped out, aimed at me. Not sure what I was seeing, I ducked. I waited a few seconds and peeked over the radiator. The car was gone.

"Mr. Russell, did you hear me?"

"Mr. President, someone just drove by with a rifle aimed at the school."

"Did anything happen?"

I told him I'd ducked beneath the level of the window sill and that I had no question I was the target. After a moment of silence, he said, "That makes getting together all the more important. How about all of you coming, including George and his wife. I'll have a plane fly you down."

"Well, we're trying to get Ash to think about taking his dates to nicer places. Yours would work." I thought later that I had sounded calm. Ha!

"I think it would," the president said.

"Mr. President, I don't want to sound paranoid, but the only people who know about the portal are yours. The car was a black Suburban, like the one you rode in when you were here."

"Mr. Russell, I know you have reason to doubt me. I didn't order or send anyone. Let me check. And if you agree, I'll have some security set up for you, just in case."

"Let me think about all this, sir." Then I asked, "Mr. President, what tests do you have in mind? Frankly, I'm a little more concerned now."

"I was wondering when you would ask. Look, you know why I'm uneasy. What I want tested is basic. Do you have any physiological condition that would explain why you can open the portal? I asked my best medical guy what to do. The tests will be routine blood tests and a couple of different radiology exams—scans, X-rays, that kind of thing. Nothing unusual or sinister. If it can't be picked up routinely, then you and I can talk about what more can be done."

"I'm still anxious about it. Can I let you know later?"

"Sure, but soon. We have to arrange it," said the president. "I should be back from Brussels by then. I still have a little problem vis-à-vis Eledoria. I'll have my agents pick you up at the school at three."

"I'll try to call back later today, Mr. President. And I want to apologize again for being so ill-tempered last week."

"No problem. Talk to you later," and the president hung up.

I went to see Ashley. "We need to talk. First, about Saturday, how about dinner somewhere else?"

"Where?"

"Let's just say it's a surprise."

"OK, but the food better be good and cheap."

The bell rang, and as I turned to go, I said, "I think you'll like it. But we'll need to leave a little earlier. Then I told him about the rifle. His worry ruts and first group of students appeared together.

After the first period ended, I walked to the office and spoke to George, inviting him and Lois to join us for dinner on Saturday. George said he'd ask Lois and get back to me. "I'll need to have an answer by the end of the day, George. Reservations and arrangements, you know." I didn't tell him where we were going.

After my next class, I called Linda and told her about the president's invitation. "I'll make lasagna for them. Ash can get some wine."

The school day ended as it had begun. Thunder boomed overhead. I tried the door a couple more times and then gave up and headed for the office to find George. He was walking down the hallway toward me as I turned the corner. "Lois asked me to ask you come to our place."

"We have reservations made already George, but I have to confirm soon. Here's my phone. Call Lois and tell her."

"Where are we going?"

"It's a surprise, but it'll be worth it."

George called home and told Lois what I had said. "Okay, I'll tell him." Passing the phone back, he said, "Thanks, but we're going to pass, Fritz."

I thought about telling him where we were going. I didn't. "Some other time then," I said.

Linda met me at the back door. I put my briefcase down on the window seat and sat at the kitchen table. "George and Lois don't want to come."

"To the White House?" she asked.

"I didn't tell him. Ashley doesn't know either."

"I think you should tell them both, Fritz. George wouldn't want to miss it, and Ashley needs to dress up. You know him. He'll show up in chinos and no tie if he thinks it's the inn."

"I really wanted it to be a surprise. I don't care if George and Lois come. But I guess surprises are probably a bad idea under the circumstances." Outside, thunder rolled after a flash. "I hate having to depend on the weather," I said. Then I told her about the drive-by and my chat with the president.

"Are you scared? I am. Who could it be if it's not the government?"

"I don't know. That's why I want to cooperate. And yes, I am scared."

I called the McAllisters first. Lois answered. I told her that she and George should come on Saturday because the dinner was at the White House. She said, "Why didn't you say so. Of course we're coming. I'll tell George." Then, after a pause, she asked, "Fritz, why didn't you tell George?"

"I wanted it to be a surprise. A good surprise. I'm sorry. I should have told him."

"See you on Saturday then," she said and hung up.

Next I called Ashley. "The White House!" said Ash. He sounded like a puppy with a new bone. "I can't believe it. I told you this would happen."

"You have to wear a tie, buddy."

Finally, as I had promised, I called the president. Lily Evans told me the president was in a meeting but would call back shortly. Linda had already started making lasagna and had three large dishes she was working with.

I asked, "Are you planning to take all of them?"

She said, "No, just two. Kind of a peace offering. I figured I would make one for us. For next week."

"What? You think the president doesn't get fed. Feeling sorry for him?"

"No, but maybe he can give the chefs a night off on a couple of different days."

Moments later, the phone rang. "The president," I said. "Hello, Mr. President. Sorry to interrupt."

"No problem, Mr. Russell. Your timing is good. I was just saving the world." Thunder rumbled. "So you're coming?"

"Yes, sir. Six of us."

"Good. Then you all need to be at the school at 2:45. I'll ask James to pick you up. I've made arrangements for your testing to be done just down the street, and I'll take care of everyone until you get back. Gotta go now. I'm leaving for Europe in two hours. I've asked Tom Andrews to arrange for agents to keep an eye out but not be too visible. They'll watch your house and be near the school."

"Okay. Thanks, Mr. President. See you Saturday. Good luck in Brussels." As I hung up, I wondered what "take care of everyone" actually meant.

* * *

"What?" Koppler listened. His caller reported that they had found the school and had a picture taken through a rifle scope of Russell in his classroom window.

"He ducked, but I have a clear picture."

"Then, take care of it." Koppler pushed "end".

* * *

I wondered if the day would dawn with thunderstorms. But again, no buzz. As the day progressed, the weather got worse. I kept an eye on the traffic. By seventh period, I wanted nothing more than for the doorknob to buzz and relieve my obsession. I stood in the hallway before class began and kept grabbing the doorknob and opening the door. As my labor history class began to gather, I reached for the door once again. Nothing. "Damn," I said, louder than I wanted. I held the door open as the class entered and then followed the kids in.

"Mr. R?" said Larry. I acknowledged him. "Labor unions don't have the same clout that they used to have. I've been wondering why. It doesn't seem to make much sense to me."

I refocused on my job. "Good question, Larry. Why do you think unions have lost favor?" I asked.

"Well it seems to me that in the old days, people didn't get paid much, so the unions got pay up. But when companies moved out of the U.S., people blamed the unions. Now stuff costs as much, or more, than before, even at Wal-Mart."

"Keep going, Larry."

"Companies charge what they want, so the less they spend on production, the more they make. But couldn't they make a little less and pay the people who actually make the stuff more?"

"Would people still buy the product if it were more expensive?" I asked.

"I would. If the stuff was good, why not?"

"Good start, Larry. Class, anyone have anything to add?"

As hands went up, I felt good to be in the classroom. I wasn't bored and stale. I smiled. "Yes, Mike."

Mike Malloy said, "Big industrial unions made the middle class possible, Mr. R. Collective bargaining allowed working people to have a say in how they were compensated for their work. For years, America produced the best and most of everything. But as costs went up, companies saw that there were lots of people in other countries that could do the same work, so they moved the work to places like China and paid dirt. But the pay for the Chinese was better than they had been making. So the companies could charge the same and make more profits."

"Good, Mike."

Another hand went up. Tim Andrews said, "Unions also spent a lot of money on things they shouldn't have, like politics. I read that lots of unions were corrupt."

"Are companies corrupt if they give to political campaigns, Tim? Look back a few years. Politicians allowed the big banks on Wall Street to almost ruin the international economy. Are the banks corrupt? Or are they just doing what's best for their shareholders, you know, making profits?"

Tim replied, "But bank employees aren't underpaid; they get big bonuses."

"All of them?"

Tim paused and thought for a moment before he said, "I don't know, Mr. R."

"Class, let's look at the question from a different perspective." We discussed the nature of organizations. I told them that organizations, whether for-profit or not, want to preserve their function and that people want those organizations to preserve the personal benefits they provide, such as jobs. We agreed that a union's strength derives from improving the economic condition of its members. "Can we agree that power can be abused in any circumstance, by individuals and organizations?" More nods. "So why do workers today feel that unions are not a good thing, even if studies show there has been no significant increase in wages in years?"

Bill Robinson said, "I can think of two reasons, Mr. Russell. First, we don't make stuff here as much as we used to, so people have to compete for jobs, and for most of them, you need a more technical background. Second, PR. Lots of reports talk about how bad unions are, and there's not much advertising about what's good about them. So if all you hear is bad, why would you want to join?"

"I like that, Bill," I said. "Image is important in public discourse and certainly unions haven't done much to promote their good points for years. Also, people have become skeptical about organizations and institutions that claim to represent their best interests. But people aren't believers anymore. They simply forget that there are things that can be done better as a group than as individuals. Can you think of other factors at work here?"

The discussion continued until the bell rang. As she was leaving, Jennifer stopped at my desk. She asked, "Are you trying to time travel, Mr. Russell?"

Abrupt as it was, I was caught off guard. I looked at her, amazed. "You still don't believe me, do you, Jen?"

"No, Mr. R, I don't. I saw you opening and closing the door before. Is the doorway how you do it?"

As much as I would have liked to confide in this attentive, intelligent young woman, I said, "Jen, I can't time travel."

"Have it your way. See you, Mr. R," and she walked out as the last class of the day began to shuffle in.

When we finished our discussion of presidential succession, Franklin Roosevelt's four elections, and the Twenty-Second and Twenty-Fifth Amendments, the class exited to another round of booming thunder. The hall and classroom lights flickered, and the kids looked out the window, wondering if they should find better ways to get home. Not yet three o'clock, the hall lights were bright against the descending dark. Like my class, I walked to the exit to look.

Earlier in the day, my U.S. history classes had recited Lincoln's best speeches in the auditorium. Once each year, I devise a setting and have the kids imagine what Lincoln might have felt and envisioned with hundreds of people listening.

Returning to gather my things, I touched the doorknob, stepped through with the buzz, and I caught, cascading over the surrounding crowd, "shall not perish from the earth." Too far away for me to see, Lincoln had already taken his seat. The crowd, dozens in every direction, was quiet, stunned that the speech had ended. Next to me, an artist was sketching the scene. I turned as the wave of applause approached and walked through the rectangle directly behind me. On my desk the book of speeches lay open, a paperclip attached to a drawing of Lincoln on the stage.

I closed it, grabbed my stuff, and headed home. When I told Linda I had just witnessed the Gettysburg Address, well, the end of it, she hit my arm and asked why I hadn't called her. I told her I hadn't tried to open the portal. I was getting my stuff to come home when I felt the buzz. "I had to go in the room to get my stuff and my car keys. I only stayed a minute and walked right out." I had to think about that.

* * *

I'M BAD LUCK for women. Things happen when I date them. Worse, when I love them. Suzanne disappeared with some guy ... we never spoke again. Kathy went to California. When she came home, a driver lost control just where she waited to cross the street ... couldn't ever forget ... worst when I was still in college... Who was it who said to me the living were better company? Was I that out of it ... or just deep into my schoolwork? Was that a way of avoiding people? Saturday nights heaped the sadness higher. By senior year, I must've been a drag. Beth ... kindred spirit ... it helped to talk about our tragedies... Didn't feel better, but not so alone. Car pulled up when she was walking to meet me... asked directions ... shot her. And drove away. I'm bad luck for women. UNPREDICTABLE.

"I need to find a different book," Ashley said to himself.

Chapter Nineteen

I MET ASHLEY in the parking lot. "You weren't kidding, by any chance, were you?"

"Nope."

"Hmm, this is certainly getting interesting."

I started to tell him about Gettysburg. As we approached the door, out popped George, all a dither.

"Why didn't you tell me? Lois is so excited. We don't know what to wear. How are we getting there?"

"Slow down, George, slow down. That's more questions than I get from my ninth graders."

"OK, OK, but we just need to know. It's so exciting."

I took a deep breath. Sometimes it was hard to believe that George wasn't one of my students. I told him to be at the parking lot by 2:45, dressed like we were going to a fancy restaurant. "And you need to bring a couple of the bottles of the wine you brought to my house." I didn't mention either the tests or the president's comment about "taking care of everyone". When we reached the hallway, Ash advised that I shouldn't tell the president about Gettysburg.

It was a short time until the class day began, and the day was over almost as quickly. At least it felt that way to me. I locked my desk and looked at my empty desktop, twirling my keys on the key ring. As I headed for the door, Ashley and Sandy came in. "How about dinner. Beer and a sandwich?" Ash suggested.

"Let me call Linda." She said fine but that we should make it early. Saturday would be a long day.

As I headed to my car, a black Suburban pulled from the last parking space. If Ashley hadn't grabbed my arm and pulled me back to the sidewalk, I might have been roadkill.

"Thanks, Ash. That was close. Did you see who it was?"

"Tinted windows."

As we retraced our steps, another Suburban turned into the school lot and aimed for us. This time, we ran back to the sidewalk. The SUV stopped and the lowering window revealed James Williams.

"Are you all right? I saw what happened, but he was gone before I could catch him."

"We're fine, but why are you here?"

"The president said to look out for you. There are a few of us taking turns."

Ashley asked, "Do you know who that was?"

James shook his head and said, "tinted windows." He said he would follow me home.

We met at our favorite pub, The Mill, at six.

"Good timing, Ash. No karaoke until nine. So we won't have to listen to you."

"The good timing came in my pulling you from in front of that car."

I hadn't told Linda, so I improvised. "We don't know who it was. It could have been a kid trying to get away from school."

"Or it could have been someone who knows about the portal," said Ashley.

I didn't answer. I had other things to worry about.

A couple of hours and a couple of pitchers later, we left as the 'entertainment' was setting up.

"Won't you tell me where we're going?" Sandy tried for a last time. I looked at Linda, who nodded. "The White House."

Surprised, Ash said, "But we can't discuss it here. I'll tell you on the way home."

"Are we, I mean, you in trouble?" asked Sandy. "Why didn't you tell me before?"

"Too many ears at school," said Fritz.

It'll be nice, Sandy," Linda said. "I think we'll enjoy it. Besides, Lois McAllister will keep you occupied. She will want to make sure you get all the dirt on Ashley. See you tomorrow."

James Williams was parked in the rear of the parking lot when we left.

I took advantage of a couple of extra hours in bed. Linda had been up and about since seven. I got up and walked down to the kitchen where she was sitting at the table with her laptop, typing. I poured a cup of coffee, kissed her, and asked what she was doing.

"Typing out the lasagna recipe for James. I didn't get it for him when they were here. I figured I'd be more formal and bring the First Lady one that was printed, instead of the handwritten one I gave her. Someday she might want to play with it."

"Did you check the news, by any chance?" I asked, taking a sip. The coffee was hot. It hit me that one benefit of weekends was sitting and sipping.

"No. I've been wrapping up the lasagna and working on a project for work.

"A book?"

"Uh huh," she answered.

"Anything interesting?" This time I blew on the cup before I sipped again.

"A sci-fi story about alternate universes. I'm not far into it yet, but it has potential, I think."

Before I had a second cup, I got my laptop and returned to the kitchen. I asked Linda if she was excited. "Not really. Met one president, you've met them all. But I can't help wondering why we were invited, Fritz. What do they really want?"

"They want to test me to see if I have some weird thing that makes me able to open the portal. The rest is cover. They still think I can screw up history. Or endanger the country. And they could be right."

"Not if you don't go through," she responded, still looking at her laptop.

"Subtle," I said. I opened a screen for the news. "Nothing's been attacked or exploded yet today. There's a story about the president's meeting in Brussels." I looked up at her. "He's got to be tired. He'll be back when we get there."

A knock on the door announced Ashley and Sandy, both in jeans. As they walked in, Ashley said, "The usual suspects, complete with fresh bagels and whipped cream cheese."

Linda, a bit annoyed at not being prepared for guests (Sandy was still a guest) said, "Coffee's hot. Get your own. Morning, Sandy."

Sandy said, "I tried to talk him out of coming, that it was too early and we have a long day ahead."

"Sit," I said. "We're used to his strange, yet predictable habits."

"I'll get my coffee first. He doesn't know how I take it."

As the refrigerator closed, Ashley emerged with milk. He asked, "Anyone want a bagel?" We all said yes. "Toast mine, will you Ash?" said Linda. "Mine, too," said Sandy. Ash got to work; he knows his way around our kitchen better than his own, I think.

Conversation about the trip to the White House began with Sandy asking why Ash hadn't told her before.

"Sandy, I told him to wait. An overheard comment could become another story. You know how fast rumors fly at school." I leaned forward and met her look. I told her they wanted to do some tests to see if I had some physical reason that allowed me to open the portal.

Our trip wasn't all that was bothering me. I had taken the UAW book home to show Linda the copyright page. It had been published in 1994. "Look at this." I swiveled the book. "Twenty-one years ago. Now look at the picture again. I'm sure those are my shoes, that it's me. But how could a picture from 1937 be in a book published fifty-seven years later when I was only there two weeks ago?"

"Fritz, I don't like where you're going with this," Linda said. "You were there then and back almost immediately. Accept that it happened and find a way to end it."

She was between tears and blowing her top, and she was probably right. But I had crossed time and space and left an imprint. I might have changed what happened on the overpass. "Lin, maybe it was me that made their confrontation so brutal. Maybe they were only going to threaten, but when I was hit, they just kept going. First blood."

"Or maybe you saved them from something worse," said Ashley. "Maybe your being there and disappearing took some of the steam out. You'll never know."

"It doesn't matter," she said. "What does is that you know you can be hurt. You could have been killed. Didn't they break one man's back? That could have been you."

Exhaling, I touched my face. "I was lucky. I had an escape route. I'm glad one of them didn't follow me. Sorry, Lin. I was just thinking out loud."

With the conversation in a downward spiral, Sandy asked, "What should I wear?"

Linda said, "Sandy, it's like we were going to the Old Lion. Except we have to go farther. Wear what you were going to." Then she warned, "Ashley, wear a tie."

We ate and had more coffee refills. We talked about what living in the White House must be like. Never having a truly private moment. Always having secret service agents around. The morning sprinted away. As they were leaving, Sandy said, "I thought your projection story was pretty good, Fritz. There's so much we could do with it as teachers. This, on the other hand, is petrifying."

I agreed. "See you later."

At 2:30, Linda took two trays out of the refrigerator.

I picked up one tray, Linda took the other. When we arrived at the school, George and Lois were waiting with Ashley and Sandy. A small bus pulled up and James Williams stepped out. James looked at the trays and then at Linda.

"Lasagna," she said.

"Linda, I don't mean to be a downer, but you may not be able to bring this in. It's security protocol, but I'll call ahead and let the president decide. Sorry."

"James, it's a gift. I brought you the recipe too." Linda's disappointment resonated. "I never thought to ask."

"James," I said, "we never go anywhere without some kind of a gift for the hosts. They just live in a bigger house. Sorry."

Sandy asked Ashley, "Shouldn't we have brought something?" she said in a quiet voice.

George, carrying a couple of paper bags, started to put them down. James said, "Let me take them for you, George," and as he took them, looked inside, and said, "Same goes for the wine, George. I'll check on it too." He escorted everyone onto the bus and sat in the driver's seat.

Ash said, "Now we find out more about the secret airport."

We reached the airport in twenty minutes using main roads I had driven for years. A couple of turns and a couple of miles down a poorly maintained path, and we were there. As we approached, we saw ongoing construction. I asked James what was being built. He said he didn't know.

When we reached the plane, we boarded and took off immediately. Lois said to Sandy, "I've known these two delinquents for years. You and I should sit together. I'll educate you about your friend over there." When the plane touched down, we barely felt the bump. "You know," Lois said, "When I first heard everything, it was hard to believe, but having the president show up and then stay for dinner, well, let's just say, it's been an interesting couple of weeks."

"You should be in my shoes," I said. I touched my still-bruised cheek.

A large helicopter was sitting nearby under storm clouds. We climbed in, and James motioned the pilot to take off. Within a few minutes, after a brief glimpse of the city, we landed on the White House South Lawn.

Sandy said, "You didn't mention a helicopter."

James smiled and said, "Not *a* helicopter, *the* helicopter. If the president were aboard, this would be Marine 1." Sandy turned. "Really," she said to no one in particular.

Walking across the lawn, already a rich green, we reached a door where the president himself was waiting. He looked tired, but he greeted us with a broad smile. Sandy was mesmerized. The president said to her, "Pretty cool, isn't it?" She just nodded. "Let's go to my office," the president said and led the way to the Oval Office, through the door George and I had used. I looked at the door as the president said, "I keep expecting to see you walk through every time it opens."

The First Lady was waiting. Linda said, "I've made a couple of pans of lasagna for you, for those slow nights, you know, family dinners." James set the bag of wine on the table.

I said, "George brought more of the wine we had at our house."

"James, would you mind taking care of these?" the president asked.

"No, wait," said the First Lady, looking at the lasagna containers. "These are pretty," she said to Linda.

" 'Temp-tations Old World.' QVC."

"Really. They're charming. I'll have to check it out."

Linda said, "Oh, by the way, I've typed out the recipe," and reached into her purse. In spite of the metal detector we had passed through, and barely noticeably, James moved his hand to his belt. I assumed his reaction was reflexive. I didn't say anything, as Linda handed him a copy for himself.

"Thank you, ma'am, I mean, Linda."

James removed both the lasagna and the wine, knowing the president had said to accept them. He was headed to the kitchen when Jim Koppler appeared around a corner.

"Mr. Williams, you know the danger and the rules. Why did you let them bring this into the White House? It could be poisoned or could hide explosives."

"Sir, I was taking it to be checked. I've met these people. It's a gift. And frankly, I let the president decide what he wants to do with it."

"I'll be speaking with him later. The secret service should know better. This is a dangerous attitude to take."

"Sir, with all due respect, if they don't want it, I'll take it home," and he continued to the kitchen. Koppler returned to watch the president and his guests on his office monitor.

"Please, everyone, sit down," said the First Lady. I waited for directions. The president said they would get a private tour of the house and that he would be going with them.

He said that James would take me for the tests and bring me back. "We should still be poking around when you get here." My immediate thought was how wonderful it would be just to "poke around" the White House. As we left, the First Lady offered refreshments. I was jealous.

James and I walked through the halls to the doorway of the North Portico, where all the important visitors enter. I had to remind myself why I was standing there. James opened the back door of the Suburban for me and climbed in the passenger's seat. James said, "This is Mel Zack." I nodded.

"Where are we going?"

"G. W. Hospital. They're all set for you. No paperwork." Within ten minutes, I was in a chair with fat arms. The phlebotomist called it the bleeding chair. Next I was taken to the Radiology Department for a series of scans by different machines. "All done," the tech said to James. A doctor came in and said, "I'll have a first look done in a few minutes."

I dressed and put my tie back on. So far, James had been with me the entire time. "We'll be back at the White House in no time now," he said, trying to reassure me.

"Thanks."

When the physician returned, he said, "You're in good health, Mr. Russell. I'll send over a preliminary summary today and have a detailed report sent to the White House when all the results are back."

"Doctor? Is there anything that appears unusual to you?" I asked.

"Nothing medically," and the doctor left the room quickly. *What does that mean?*

THE PRESIDENT HAD been right. We were back at the White House about an hour after we'd left. Washington traffic moved well for a Saturday. Mel Zack had called ahead when James and I got into the car, and everyone was waiting at the entrance when the Suburban arrived.

I joined the others, who'd been enthralled by the tour. I guess the grimace on my face took some of the air out of their sails. Linda asked me what was wrong.

Looking around, I said, "Nothing. I just don't have any info."

The president said, "When the report comes in, I'll let you read whatever it says."

"Thanks." But I wasn't thankful. I was worried. The knot in my stomach felt like a basketball and bounced as much.

The First Lady led us on the rest of the tour. I couldn't help but be fascinated with the historical artifacts. My companions shared the feeling. The White House is a museum. My mood improved as my thoughts drifted to the paintings and the people who had walked those halls since 1800. I said, "It's ironic that the centerpiece of our country, our freedoms, was built by slaves."

The president said, "This place has a very humbling effect when I walk through, when I'm as alone as I can get here." Changing the subject, sounding cheerful, he said that he had asked the staff if we could eat in the Blue Room, just off the South Portico. "It has a super view, and it's a great room."

"Mr. President, did you think they would say no?" asked Sandy.

"You know, Sandy, everyone thinks the president can do what he wants. But this house has its own rules, and some of the staff has served here since before you were born. I ask, and sometimes they say yes. Let's go in, shall we?"

A spectacular view explained why the president had asked. The full expanse of the South Lawn resembled a green ocean. The National Mall and the Washington Monument were visible through the windows. "Wait until you see it when the sun goes down," said the First Lady. Her contagious excitement, even after so many years, overcame my doubts.

While we looked around the Blue Room, the Secretary of Energy, and her two assistants, Kim and Tony, walked in. "Sorry we're late, Mr. President," said the secretary.

"Shall we sit?" the president suggested. The conversation was light and congenial. George's wine was served and dinner was individual Beef Wellington with asparagus.

"This is delicious, Mr. President," said Ashley. We all agreed.

"The salad greens come from our garden," said the First Lady, pointing out the window.

"You can't imagine how hard it is to keep from gaining weight around here," said the president. "Thank goodness I have so many outside appearances that come with bad food."

For dessert, we had pastries and ice cream molded into American flags, rippling stripes of peppermint and vanilla. "We have a full-time pastry chef and staff for small gatherings like this and full state dinners," said the First Lady. "It's amazing what they come up with. And you should see this place at Christmas."

When the table had been cleared, James appeared with a folder, marked: "PRESIDENT'S EYES ONLY." The president looked over the contents and suggested we all go out on the Portico. He said, "It bothers me that not all Americans can get the thrill I get when I go out here, especially at this time of day."

After a few minutes to enjoy the view, the president asked everyone to follow him to the West Wing. We went to the Roosevelt Room, adjacent to the Oval Office. It was already set up for a presentation. While everyone found seats, the president thumbed through the folder, which he then handed to me. I was surprised at the openness.

"You're in pretty good shape," said the president. I read the report. It was one page plus the blood test results. It said simply, "There are no abnormal functions seen; there are no clinical indications for Mr. Russell's apparent conductivity of electricity. However, on a thermogram, there was an unusual activity in the thalamus area, indicating a hypersensitivity which could explain receptivity. When active, the color should be bright yellow. Mr. Russell's scan showed bright green."

I finished and handed it to Linda, who read it and looked back at me quizzically. I said, "I don't know what the color means, but the thalamus controls sensory activity. Everything else is normal.

"What I want you to see," the president said, "is what the scan of your classroom picked up. I need to apologize to you again, and you too George. Sunday morning, I sent our team back in with a better antenna, which Tony had invented the night before. I want you to see what they collected."

Disturbing as that knowledge was, no one said anything. Even George was subdued, despite the invasion of his fiefdom.

"Before we begin, I would like you all to understand that this is a secret, and needs to remain so." There was no mistaking the president's meaning, and he asked each person individually to agree. He told us that our promise was being recorded. As the images appeared, the hush was interrupted by gasps. When it was complete, the president told Kim to run it again and stop it where it was marked. None of the pictures were clear, but we could make out ghostlike images. Near the beginning, my shoes glimmered. Usual activity, kids and adults, attracted our attention. Kim stopped the projection when a clear image appeared.

I got up and walked to the screen.

"That's Lee?" asked Linda. "He has a strong face."

"Looks like him," I said.

"This is what you saw?" said Lois, amazement in her voice. I nodded.

We returned to our seats and the projection continued. There was a building on fire, but not clear enough to linger at, and then a clearer image of the president. Kim stopped again. The final image was a bright light when the desk was scanned. The president continued, "When we saw these, we knew this needed monitoring. But I know from our contact that you're as concerned as I am," he said, focused on me. "So you all understand, our ability to detect human images in blank space is a development we never saw coming. Someday, maybe, we'll announce this new find, but as I said, for now it remains secret—at the highest levels. I will hold you all to that."

The First Lady, feeling the discomfort, said, "Would anyone like some coffee?"

Ashley quipped, "I could use something stronger."

The First Lady said, "No problem." She walked to the door and asked the waiter who was standing at the door to bring in coffee and drinks. A cart was wheeled in, fully equipped.

The president said, "Normally, we would have staff here to serve, but under the circumstances, I thought better of it. Help yourselves."

As everyone rose and went to the cart, the president said to me, "We need to fix this. These images are disturbing."

I said, "Strangely enough, I can say 'you should be in my shoes.' And those were my shoes." The president smiled. "Did you find out anything about the Suburban? I can't help but think someone here is after me. Linda's worried too."

"I'm concerned about it too. I've asked Tom to see if there are any other ways we can monitor what's happening. We've been discussing what we can do. Let's get a drink." I had coffee, and the president chose sparkling water. As the seats refilled, the room was quiet, everyone lost in thought.

"Now I know how Kennedy felt during the Cuban Missile Crisis," said George.

"You know, George, this room was one of the places that meetings were held during that October. But back then, we really had an enemy. I hope you don't feel like we're enemies."

"Sorry, Mr. President, I was just thinking that being president, you have to deal with a lot. I would bet that something's going on somewhere in the world that you need to tend to right now. Not to mention Congress."

"George, you're right. You should be in my shoes." We all laughed.

What had begun as an enjoyable dinner had turned somber. Recognizing the change in atmosphere, the president said, "I wanted a nice dinner for you before we got to this. Fritz and Linda, we had more fun at your house, believe me!"

Sandy interrupted him. "Just out of curiosity, Mr. President, are we in trouble?"

"No, but you need to know the enormity of the problem," said the president. "One thing we haven't discussed is the possibility of altering history, being present when a world-altering conversation or event takes place, maybe affecting the result."

"Like being at Ford's Theater in time to stop Booth," I interrupted, glancing at Ash. Everyone looked at me, with varying expressions of surprise and shock. The president stared at me, checked his watch.

"Or what if someone forced you to do something now or in the past?" he asked. "Or you walked into a billy club? You folks have a trip to make, and I actually have a few things to do myself. I appreciate your coming, I really do." To me, he said, "Keep working at it, and if you need anything, you have my number."

"Thank you, Mr. President," I said.

As if on command, James came in. He announced that we would be driving to Andrews. Once again, everyone rose.

"Thank you for the lasagna," said the First Lady, "and the recipe."

As we left the Roosevelt Room, the president said to me, "I mean it. If I can help, let me know."

"Thanks. Talk to you soon," I said.

IT WAS ONLY a few minutes before Jim Koppler asked to come in. The First Lady excused herself, seeing her husband's piercing eyes behind lowered eyebrows, his jaw muscles rippling.

"Mr. President, I can't stand by while you take so lightly the potential threat these people pose. Food, wine. The secret service isn't doing its job. Mr. Williams said he would take it home if there was nothing wrong. He's not protecting you, and he's ignoring the rules. And who's this newcomer, Sandy Horton? Has anyone done a background check on her?"

Breathing in through flared nostrils and then blowing out through pursed lips, the president chose to remain calm. "Jim, I know you're doing what you think is necessary. I also know that the food will be checked. It was a gift. I'm trying to keep their trust, so if there is a value to the portal, we don't have self-created enemies. And I do wish you would choose to remember that I'm a pretty smart guy. I wanted Russell here. If inviting the others got him here, so be it. So far, our explanation has been accepted, and there has been no negative effect. This stays in the White House. Got me?"

Koppler left. The president knew that little would change. Furious, the national security advisor returned to his office "Let's see how smart he is." His cell was at his ear.

Chapter Twenty

BY 10:30, WE WERE BACK at school. We said goodbye to James and stood as a group in the parking lot.

"Well, we sure have a lot to talk about," said Lois.

"Not tonight. I still have some thinking to do," I said.

"Tomorrow then," said George. "We can't talk about this during school. We need to assess this."

Linda said, "Come to our house at noon. Ashley, go shopping."

"What should I get?"

"Get inspired."

Watching the verbal volleying, Sandy said, "I'll help. See you tomorrow."

"We'll see you at noon then." Linda said.

When we arrived home, I almost fell into an armchair in the family room. "Nice dinner," I said.

But Linda wasn't in the mood for small talk. She said, "Fritz, they're not fooling around. Now I'm more afraid of *not* finding the portal again." She sat across from me.

"I know. Those images alarm me. They didn't even notice all the things I did. I could make out the kids' faces. The fire was there; we were there. And they pulled it out of thin air. That's actually pretty impressive, but it's scary." The reality finally slid into my head. *What if someone else finds out? I could be kidnapped or killed.* I didn't mention that to Linda.

"Fritz, what are we going to do?" She was sitting on the edge of the couch.

"Exactly what we've been doing. I'll have to ask George if I can come in after hours, so no one will disturb me."

"Us, you mean. I'm coming with you."

"Okay," I said, surprising her. "I'm strangely tired. Let's go to bed."

Sunday started later than usual. Neither of us had slept well, and we moved slowly. Linda spent a bit longer than usual in the bathroom.

"Are you okay?" I asked.

"Nerves. Dinner was great going down but didn't sit well. I'll be fine."

At 11:30, Ashley showed up in his Sunday best—torn jeans and what appeared to be a new flannel shirt. He carried a bag of groceries, and Sandy had a twelve pack of beer that she put in the refrigerator. She seemed to feel at home.

"New shirt?" I asked, while Ashley emptied the groceries. I had seen almost all of his wardrobe at one time or another.

"Yeah. *L.L. Bean.* Bought a couple. I put my elbow through one last week, and these were on sale."

"You shopping? That's something new." The portal? Sandy? I wondered.

At noon, the McAllisters arrived. A black Suburban drove by as I opened the door. We had set the table in the dining room, and the food was ready.

Lois took the lead. "So now we know what the government is thinking. What else do we know?"

I had the answer, the list I had been developing in my mind. I went through all I knew about the weather, lightning, the door-knob buzzing, the paperclips. "What's new is the brain activity. I looked up thermograms earlier. The bright green thalamus in-dicates hyperactivity, not something abnormal, but it might explain my susceptibility to electrical charges. We also know they broke into the school."

George said, "I'll have to check the tape storage and see if it tells us anything."

"It probably won't, George. They know how to erase it."

"I'll check it anyway. Can't hurt," George replied.

I continued, "We also know that the president considers this a priority. As friendly and cool as he tries to be, there's no doubt he will act to eliminate the threat if I can't. We took an oath of silence." They all stared at me. "That probably wouldn't hold up in court, but it would be a nice final reminder just before a gun goes off in your face or you get pushed out of a plane at 30,000 feet over the ocean."

"Oh, come on, Fritz," said George.

I raised my hand to stop him and then said slowly, for emphasis, "George, every one of us is going to be watched. We already know they bugged us here." I suddenly worried whom else they might have bugged. "You all need to stay tight-lipped. I need to solve this, because I think we're on a timetable, and we don't know how much time we have. The president has too much to do to worry about us. Like you said, George, something is going on somewhere that demands his attention." Hesitating, I looked around the table. "They have the problem solved if I am permanently gone, but that leaves you all as accessories. With me gone, you're not direct problems because I think I'm the only one who can open the portal. But even a suggestion that time travel is real, or that the government can detect those images puts us all at risk. And what you know puts you at risk."

"How much time do you think we have?" Ashley asked, his fork poised to dive into the potato salad.

"I don't know, but he might let us keep trying until we run out of ideas. You heard him offer help. If they do try to help, without our asking, that's when I think time will be running out."

Lois, having listened to all this calmly, said, "Then you need *us* to help. Like you've said before, Fritz, we have some pretty smart people here. What do you want us to do?"

"I started writing what we know at school. I haven't actually written down anything since. Let's put a list together, with dates, so we can follow our progress."

"There's one thing that I don't understand from the projection," said Sandy. "What was that bright light at the end?"

"My desk," I said. "Hold on. What about my desk?"

We discussed all we already knew once again. Then I remembered that my cell phone was in the desk drawer when they scanned the room. It was turned on, and the lights were turned off. I said I didn't remember their being near any electric sockets. "If that antenna thing was so sensitive, the phone battery could have been enough to make that image. But we're already pretty sure the desk has some role in this."

* * *

AT HIS DESK early Sunday morning, the president scanned the *Washington Post* absorbing reactions to his speech in Brussels. He lifted his coffee cup as Tom Andrews knocked and entered.

"Good morning, sir."

"How did it go?"

"I got all of them sir. Houses, cars, classrooms, the school office. This time, no one will find them. Each one has its own receiver. We'll know anything and everything. I was listening to what we picked up in the parking lot last night. They're meeting at Russell's at noon."

"I really hate doing this." For a moment, the president hesitated. "Has Mr. Koppler said anything to you?

"Sir, he thinks there's some kind of conspiracy. I don't think he trusts teachers, which is strange. Did you know both his parents were teachers?"

"I did, but I'm not going to say anything. I hope they figure this out soon. Without us. And Tom, see if you can find out why he doesn't trust teachers."

The door opened and the First Lady entered, looked at her husband, and then at Tom before she said, "I'm interrupting, sorry."

As she turned, Tom said, "I was just leaving, ma'am." When he left, she saw the look on her husband's face, and said, "You didn't!"

"Tom took care of it last night, while they were here. They are all a problem now. I want to monitor what they're doing. And I want to know if they find anything. Plus, they could be in danger. They're getting together at noon."

* * *

"HERE ASHLEY. Take this home," said Linda, handing him the remainder of his shopping. Most of lunch was uneaten. As everyone prepared to leave, I said, "I want to get into the school at off-hours, George, so I can work this out without interruption."

"Well that's kind of irregular, Fritz."

Lois said, "George, don't be stupid. He's not going to raid the soda machine. This is important."

Stunned by her outburst, George said, "Well, all right. You'll need to let me know when, so I can give you the keys."

Lois exclaimed, "Jee-zus, George, make him a set! If he needs us, he'll let us know. Won't you, Fritz?"

"Of course." I was as surprised by Lois as George was.

Lois finished, "You'll get the keys made by tomorrow, George."

Ashley and Sandy left next. "You two need to think about the desk," I said. "Ash, I may need to take it apart to see if there's anything unusual there. Will you help?"

"Sorry, I'm busy." I gave him a dirty look.

Linda shook her head and said to Sandy, whose look of bemusement was almost comical, "This is what you've gotten yourself into. It's amazing they haven't gotten into more trouble."

"We're making up for it now."

Ashley went out, but Sandy turned to Linda and me. All she could say was "unbelievable," and then she left, too.

A black Suburban passed the door. I watched it disappear around the corner.

* * *

THE RESIDENCE PHONE rang. "Yes," said the president, after he listened to the latest report. He hung up, and then picked up the phone again. "Would you get me the Secretary of Energy please? No, I'll hold on. Thanks."

The White House operator came back on. "I'll connect you now, sir."

The president asked the secretary to provide a copy of the image scans. "Tomorrow will be fine," he said. "Thanks, Brenda." and he hung up.

The First Lady waited for an explanation. "Tom called. They think the desk is somehow involved, more than we suspected. That's where the bright flash was. I just want to look at it and see if I can see anything myself."

* * *

"FRITZ, I NEED to talk. I know you want to find out more, and I understand why, I think. History and you are inseparable, and the portal gives you access to people and events you want to see. So far you've been lucky. But what if you go through and can't get back. You keep asking about the portal changing things. It's changing you. You've always been careful, cautious, and considerate. This is like some kind of, I don't know, temptation. Almost an obsession. Like Gettysburg."

"Lin, I want to know more because frankly I'm afraid of the government. It used to bother me when a cop car pulled up behind me. This is way worse. I will be careful if I do find it again. If I know how it works, I'll know we're safe, because it won't be random."

"For the past week, I feel like you're somewhere else. I know the president scares you. Not him directly, maybe. But I wish you would talk to me about what you're thinking. Maybe I can help. I'm not just your wife. And I love you more than Ashley does."

I laughed at that, but I knew she was right. She had put my feelings into words. That didn't surprise me. I told her that I really didn't know what to do, that I was guessing at every step. "I can't help but feel we don't have a lot of time. So timing is going to matter. But I can't promise absolutely because I really have no idea when or even if it will happen again. And Gettysburg wasn't my fault."

"Then promise me this. If it happens and you can call me, you will. I can be there in no time. Maybe we can go together. Fritz, we're partners, for better or worse. Remember."

"I promise." I meant it.

Leaning against the red brick wall, cooling in the late fall shade, Tom Sawyer *his companion. A girl named Kathy sat down on the cement pad next to him and asked what he was reading. Freckles. Three boys came up, taunting. The book lowered with a cement book mark. Anger glaring. They continued so he stood. The challenge had been made. Suspended for a week; Dad's strap. She kissed his cheek. The three boys left her alone, avoided another fight.*

"Shit," Ashley said. He slammed the book shut and went to bed.

* * *

FRESHLY MOWN LAWNS owned the morning air as I headed for work. *Smells like Monday,* I thought. *Sunny blue sky. I never thought I would complain about good weather.* When I arrived at school, George was waiting.

"Fritz, I color-coded the keys so you would know what went to which door. This one is for the first front door; this one is for the second door; and this one is for the side doors. Remember, the camera will turn on when you unlock the second door."

"Thanks, George."

"Fritz, I really hope you have some luck with this."

"Me too. It's tough having it hanging over my head."

"*Our* heads," added George. He was right.

"See you later. Thanks again."

I removed the books from my briefcase and the brochure from the lower desk drawer. On a whim, I changed the position of the books. Ready for another week, I walked out of the room, as Ashley walked out of his.

"Hey," said Ashley.

"You look awful." Staring at me, undisguised by a grin, were dark circles. "You look like a raccoon."

"Didn't sleep much. Reading late. Interesting weekend, huh?"

"You could say that."

"Imagine how much we could brag. Or the tales we could tell the classes. We'd be the most interesting teachers in New Jersey."

"I already am." He laughed.

Sandy walked in from the parking lot. "What's so funny?" she asked.

"We're going to be Teachers of the Year," said Ashley.

"Except nobody will know," I said. "See you later." As they headed for their classrooms, I reached for the doorknob, and ... a buzz. "Hey guys, a shock."

"No lightning," said Ash. He and Sandy walked back.

"Stay here." I opened the door and took a step in. It was my classroom, the same as always. Sandy and Ashley watched me, both faces grim. "Now I'm really confused. How did this happen?" Neither of them had an answer as the hall began to fill with students.

"We can't talk now," said Sandy.

"After school," said Ashley.

I agreed. Steven Chew walked by, said "Hi, Mr. R," and entered the classroom.

"Hi Steven," I said, nonplussed.

I decided to move my classes. I put a note on the door, and the kids, with their overloaded book bags, all that knowledge that I hoped would make it to their brains, followed me. I took them to the room that George had prepared and explained that mine might get painted that day, if we were lucky. They were appropriately dubious. For the entire day, I taught in a classroom foreign to me. I had much more on my mind now than teaching. Each class seemed twice as long as usual. Finally, eighth period ended after a rousing game of government-baseball won by Mary Anne Leslie's team on a home run by Dennis Rogers. The question, which had been a trick, was which state was the last to ratify the end of slavery, and when?

Dennis' answer, "Mississippi, in 1995."

"Going, going, gone," I said, wondering what bowl of historical Wheaties had energized Dennis. "That's correct, Dennis, the state legislature passed it in 1995. But the ratification was never filed with the National Archives. The actual ratification was completed in 2013. Class, remember this. You might find it on a test."

As Dennis finished his home run trot from desk to desk, the bell rang, ending the day. When the students left, so did I. As I grabbed my classroom doorknob, I got another shock. I slowly opened the door and again walked into the classroom. It was unchanged. I walked to the desk and again reversed the books. I walked out, opened the door again, and got shocked again. Still nothing. I slapped the wall next to the door, went back in and sat. Ashley and Sandy came in. I said to them, "It happened again.

What am I missing?" I tapped my fingers on the desk. I felt like frustration was fencing me in.

"Did anything happen in the other room?" asked Sandy.

"Nothing." But I had to think about it for a moment. "Except one of my kids had the answer to a very obscure question. I wonder if all this portal business is changing the kids. I gotta get out of here. Why don't you come over?"

I told Linda that Ash and Sandy were coming, and she asked, "What happened? I can see it on your face."

I put my briefcase down and tossed my keys on the counter. Ashley and Sandy came in, and we all sat at the kitchen table. Linda asked if I had heard about the plane crash in Philadelphia. The pilot hit the front of the runway, so no planes could land.

Planes were backed up for miles.

* * *

"SORRY TO INTERRUPT, Mr. President," said Tom. The president looked up from his desk. "His fingers got a shock. But no portal opening. It happened at the beginning of the day and then again after school."

The president looked behind him. "It's a nice day," he said. "Thanks, Tom."

The president pondered—*a nice day. None of this is making any sense.* He returned to the papers on his desk. He was still searching for a way through the crisis in Middle East. Jim Koppler listened to the president's conversation. He said to himself, "So he's got the classroom bugged. It's time to up the pressure." He picked up his phone, dialed, did not bother to introduce himself, and said, "I need something."

* * *

"THAT'S THE FIRST TIME it's happened on a sunny day," I continued. "I'm missing something, and I can't see it."

"Well, it feels like we're closer," said Sandy.

"But to what?" said Ashley. "Maybe the weather really does make the difference."

The remainder of the week was ideal, sunny and just warm enough and the kind of days that Ash and I could choose a basketball workout or a round of golf. But I wasn't ready for basketball. There was no recurrence of Monday's shocks, and classes settled down as soon as I started talking about final exams. Like many other teachers, I pick up the pace to make sure we covered all the course material by end of term. During the next weekend, I began to prepare the finals, knowing I had only a few weeks left. Classes seemed to return to their norms. But my students' spring fever had no antidote, and keeping their attention was more difficult. I also had the feeling that my time was running out; black Suburbans appeared everywhere I went.

By the second week of May, news reports were starting to mention the lack of rain, and there was discussion of a drought come summer. "Are there any predictions for rain this century?" I complained to Linda. "If we don't get some bad weather, I'll never be able to solve this."

"At least, you haven't had any shocks again," Linda said, trying to find something positive.

"Lin, I've said this before. Can you imagine me, or anyone, being upset about the weather we've been having? But that has to be it."

"I hope you're right, Fritz. I know it's wearing on you, and I think about it all the time."

* * *

"TOM, DO YOU HAVE a minute?" asked Mel Zack.

"Sure, Mel, what do you need?"

"I got a call. From a friend, I can't tell you his name. He asked me what's going on with the service. When I asked what he was talking about, he said a rumor was floating that the secret service was involved in a conspiracy to drop the level of the president's protection. "Tom, it's a black bag job. He told me that within the next month, either the service is going to be exposed, or the teacher will be, well, you know. Are we talking about that guy in New Jersey?"

"Mel, I don't want a name, but can you tell me the agency?" He ran his tongue over his teeth.

"I'd rather not, but you can be sure no one will find out. Accidents happen."

Tom leaned back in his desk chair. He could feel a knot growing in his shoulders. He thought he knew which agency, and he knew Mel was telling the truth. Mel was one of the best.

"I need to think about how to handle this, Mel. Slandering the service is serious. But, don't tell anyone you told me. It could put you in the crosshairs. Literally."

* * *

THE PRESIDENT AND First Lady were sitting in the private sitting room off their bedroom. She walked to the door of the Truman Balcony and watching the traffic pass the Washington Monument, said, "You can't expect him to have an answer if he needs bad weather to complete the connection. He can't do anything, good or bad, if the weather isn't cooperating. Besides, you really do have more things to worry about."

"I know, but it still makes me nervous. At least, so far, none of them have been talking, as far as we can monitor. I think our boy Fritz has scared the bejesus out of them."

"He's a smart guy. He has you figured out, and he's willing to trust you, but not too far. He knows you only trust him so far. If we get the weather, I bet he'll be calling you."

The president didn't have long to wait. Each spring, for as long as he could remember, Tornado Alley became active. Some years, there were a lot of storms but few twisters. The year had been quiet so far, but in mid-May, the warm weather across the southern tier of the U.S. had begun to produce tornadoes in clusters. Mornings were clear and warm, but as the days heated up, storm clouds and strong winds blew in. From the Gulf of Mexico to Pennsylvania, through the heartland, east to the Atlantic, storms appeared. Even early tropical storms had begun off the coast of Africa. Half the country was under cloud cover, tornadoes playing hide and seek with the stormchasers. Reports of damage came daily to the president's desk, and he knew he would need to tour the areas most severely affected when the storms subsided.

* * *

I WATCHED THE weather reports, and Linda watched me. "Be prepared for strong winds and late afternoon thunderstorms into the evening for the next few days," said the local news. Relieved, I said, "It's about time." On Wednesday, I went to school in a better mood than I had known for weeks. On the way in, I met Ashley and Sandy.

"Looks like the weather is finally ready to help," I said. My life wouldn't be back to normal until I found the portal's secret.

Ashley asked, "Are you sure you want to do this alone?" Ash was laser-focused on me. "I'll go with you if you want."

"Thanks Ash, but I need you here to report if I don't get back." He and Sandy looked at me, signs of worry on their faces. "If this goes as I planned it, I'll go in and come right back. The problem is still the connections. I don't know the trigger."

As we approached our classrooms, Ashley and Sandy watched as I walked into mine. Sandy looked at Ashley and raised her hands with fingers crossed. When I came out, I could hear them exhale from down the hall. "Nothing yet," I said.

As the day passed, all three of us went through the motions, class after class. I was continually staring out the window. I wondered if there had been a local sale on Suburbans. When seventh period ended, Jennifer Bennett asked me if I was planning a trip. As she was leaving, she said, "Come back safely, Mr. R."

By the end of the eighth period, the sky blackened and the storm arrived in force. I was prepared, books and brochure in place. Ashley and Sandy stood at their doors. The kids hurried out, and the wind picked up. A flickering flash, a loud thunderclap. I went to the door. I looked at Sandy and gave Ash a salute. As I reached for the doorknob, another flash lit the hallway. I grabbed it. Nothing. I grabbed the doorknob again. I threw my hands up, and said, "WTF!" Only letters. I knew better than to swear in school. The storm flashed again. I grabbed. Nothing. I was defeated for the moment.

"I don't get it. I thought that would be it," I said. "Everything is where it's supposed to be. What am I missing? I'm going home." I scratched my head, gently, behind my left ear. "Linda will be worried. See you later." I put the books and brochure away, locked the desk and left. Sandy and Ashley watched me go.

I called home on the way to the car. "Are you okay?" Linda answered.

"Fine, nothing happened. I'm on my way home. I'm really puzzled by this. I tried three times, including after one of those big flashes. Nothing. Just nothing."

"I'll see you in a minute then," she said.

* * *

THE PRESIDENT PICKED up his phone. "Yeah, Tom?"

"Sorry to disturb you, sir. Russell tried again during the storm in New Jersey. To quote him, 'Nothing'."

"Really?" said a surprised president. "I'll be going west to the tornado sites tomorrow. If anything happens, you know how to reach me."

"Yes, sir. Mr. President, do you have a moment to talk."

"GOOD. HE'LL BE GONE. Tomorrow." He hung up the phone. Koppler sat, looking grim.

* * *

LATER, THE FIRST LADY asked, "Can't you think of a way to help him?" The president complained that he had too much to do given the storms in the Midwest and the continuing problems in the Middle East to spend more time worrying about the portal. She said he should give Mr. Russell more time, that the weather had just begun to cooperate. He asked her to consider what would happen if Russell found the portal again and changed history so they had never met.

"Listen to yourself," said the First Lady. "That should be enough for you to want to help. Isn't there a way to use the portal to do good?"

"I've thought of that. But all he could do would be to become some kind of spy." He paused. "Hmm, I wonder if he would agree to something like that?" Then he said, dismissing what he knew was pointless, "Even if he would agree, he's a teacher, not a field operative."

"Now you sound like Koppler. What if someone went with him, like Tom? Or some CIA person?"

"That just means more people know."

"But they all have top clearances."

"Maybe I should let Jim Koppler have some time with him."

Just then the phone rang. Another problem in Eledoria, this time a hostage-taking. He called Tom.

* * *

WHEN I WALKED IN, Linda had already poured me a soda. Lightning flashed just as the door clicked shut. "Hi," I said and kissed her on the cheek. I took the glass, looked at the bubbles, and exhaled. "I can't believe this. Not even the buzz."

"Fritz, you've considered all the variables. Maybe it's just the order of things, or maybe it really is random."

"Lin, if it is random, we're in trouble. That means we'll never figure it out. Then I disappear."

"Don't say that!"

"If the storms continue, we're going back tonight to try again." It didn't sound like it, but I was really asking her.

"Okay," she said, sadly.

The storms did continue. At about 7:30, Linda and I went to the school. Linda brought a flashlight, but with all the flashes and the street lights, we didn't need it. I set up everything, went to the hall, and tried the door. Nothing.

"I'm missing something. I just don't know what," I said.

"Let's go home, Fritz."

* * *

"MR. PRESIDENT, just to let you know. Russell was at the school just now. Still nothing."

"Thanks, Tom. You know," he continued, "I've been considering this whole portal situation. I think we need to do something. Let's step outside. This is what I want you to do."

Tom listened carefully to the president's idea. "Yes, sir. I'll take care of it," he said.

"Tom, take someone with you," said the president.

* * *

THURSDAY'S FORECAST was more of the same. Linda was in the bathroom when I was ready to go.

"Is your stomach still bothering you?" I asked. "Why don't you go to the doctor?"

"Fritz, it's just nerves. This situation is starting to take a toll on me, too."

"I wish you would make an appointment and get it checked."

About three blocks from school, I noticed a black Suburban pull into traffic behind me. When I pulled into the school parking lot, the Suburban kept on going. *Am I being paranoid?*

George was waiting for me at my classroom with pursed lips and something to say. He asked if I had been in the school the previous night. When I told him I had, he reminded me I was supposed to call him. George being irritated was not how I wanted to start the day. It must have shown on my face. He asserted that he was responsible for insurance issues along with everything else, and that I needed to remember that. Then he asked if I had discovered anything new.

"Unfortunately, no."

"Well, maybe you'll have some stormy weather for a few days."

I laughed. "For me, it's been stormy for a while."

"You know what I mean," he snapped.

I reached into my pocket for my keys and pulled out some cash that had gotten caught in the key chain. I put the cash on the desk and unlocked the drawers. I reached for the books and brochure, my new daily routine.

Ashley walked in, and said, "You're early. What's up?"

"Just got up early. Linda and I came in last night during the storm and tried again. No luck."

"What's with the cash?" Ash asked.

"It got tangled up in my keys."

"You carry that much?"

"Not usually. I got it before we went to D.C. Just in case. I haven't put it back yet."

Ashley picked up the $100 bill and looked at the picture. I looked at it too. "I think I like these new engravings." I rubbed the bill between my fingers. "I didn't at first."

"Why not?"

"I think historians just like some things to be traditional." I slid the money into my pocket.

"Are you going to try again today?" Ashley asked.

"If the weather cooperates. You were right from the beginning, Ash. I think it's the lightning, but there's another link. I just don't know what yet."

As I was talking, I was also watching the cars drive by. "What's wrong?" asked Ash. I pointed to the passing Suburban and told him I had been seeing them constantly, that one had followed me to school. I said that either I was getting paranoid, or my time was running out.

"Fritz, they've been everywhere for years. You are paranoid," said Ash, who looked out the window again. "See, there's another one."

"Or the same one."

Chapter Twenty One

I STEELED MYSELF for the teaching I had no interest in right then. The students noticed, and more than once during the day asked if I was okay. I lost my train of thought with each crack of thunder. Something was roaming just beyond my reach. It bugged me. I popped an essay test on the kids during seventh period. It gave me some quiet time, a trick I'd learned early in my career. Another black Suburban went by. Scanning its details, I wondered if it was the same one. I walked around the perimeter of the class with my hands in my pockets, and it clicked. By the end of eighth period, I couldn't wait for the kids to leave.

I took out the books, checked the paperclips, and placed one on the left, one on the right, and the White House tour brochure at the center. I walked into the hallway. Lightning flashed. I touched the doorknob. BUZZ. I walked in and found myself on the top step of a brick building in an alley. A young man with a mustache brushed by and said, "Pardon me," with a southern accent as the door closed. Another man was holding a horse. Seeing the door outlined, I walked through, back to the hallway. I grabbed the doorknob again, no buzz. I walked into my classroom.

"My God, that was John Wilkes Booth," I said aloud. I grabbed the Civil War book, thumbed to Lincoln's assassination, and looked at Booth's picture. "I've got it."

I paused for a moment, my pulse pounding like a jackhammer, and walked out into the hall. I grabbed the doorknob again. I walked through and into the office of Robert E. Lee at Washington College. Lee, sitting at the table he used as his desk, looked up, not startled, almost as if he had expected me. He said, "Why, Mr. Russell. I wondered if I might ever see you again."

Taken by surprise that the general would remember me, I said, "General, this is an experiment. I can't stay, but may I visit again?"

"Of course, but before you go, you should know that after your last, uh, visit, I sent some men to try to stop Mr. Lincoln's killer. They were unsuccessful."

"General, I think history doesn't want to be changed. The past fights back. I don't mean to be rude, but I must go." I turned to leave, but a thought hit me. "General, what year is it now?"

"1868. What year is it where you come from?"

"General, in my calendar it's about a month since we first met."

"Mr. Russell, since our first meeting, I have had an abundance of time to consider our conversation. I hope we will have time to discuss this further."

"General, I would enjoy that. Perhaps it will be soon. But I really must go now."

"Of course."

Once again, I walked through the door and back into the hallway. I reached for the doorknob. Nothing. I opened it and walked into my classroom.

"I think I've got it. This has to be it." I returned to the hallway, and tried again. *I ought to call him first.* I didn't. I opened the door and stepped through. The Oval Office. Empty. I stepped back into my world.

* * *

JIM KOPPLER JUMPED in his chair. There was Fritz Russell, standing in the doorway of the Oval Office. He put out the alarm. And then watched Russell disappear. "I've got to put an end to this." He picked up his phone.

* * *

I LET THE DOOR shut completely to break the connection and went in. I took the Ford's Theater book and the White House brochure and put them on the windowsill as a black Suburban pulled into the parking lot. I walked into the hallway, quickly grabbed the doorknob again, and returned through the portal to Robert E. Lee.

Ashley told me later what happened while I was gone. Tom had hurried directly to my classroom. He peered in the window and noting my absence and my personal items still there, he headed back to the Suburban. Mel Zack was in the passenger's seat, ready for any action Tom directed. They had been called by the national security advisor, Tom told Ash later. The car windows were tinted and opaque, so no one could see in, but Mel saw Tom coming back empty-handed.

Ashley left his classroom, intending to go to my room. As he looked down the hall, he saw the Suburban parked ten feet from the door and Tom heading around the front of the car. At that point, a flash silhouetted the passenger in the car. He took a couple of steps down the hall, but the Suburban pulled away in haste, not wanting interference. Ashley said he thought, *like a getaway*, and ran to my classroom. As Tom had done, he looked in the window, then opened the door. He saw my stuff and knew I wouldn't leave without it. Leaving the room, he went across the hall to Sandy's classroom. "Have you seen, Fritz," he asked. His forehead had more wrinkles than his shirt, Sandy told me later.

"What's wrong?"

"I just saw Tom," he said, and paused at her questioning look. "You know, the secret service agent. He pulled out of the parking lot very fast, and there was someone in there with him, and Fritz isn't in his room."

"Did you go to the office? Maybe George knows why Tom was here or where Fritz is."

Ashley turned for the door. Sandy said, "Wait for me."

Together, they ran to the office, footfalls heavy on the granite floor. Ashley knew that time was critical, and he was panicky. George stood in his office doorway, getting ready to leave. He saw them running down the hall and asked, "Is something wrong?"

Leaning in the door frame, Ashley asked, "Have you seen Fritz?"

"No. Why?"

"Did you know that Tom Andrews was in the school?"

"Who?" asked George.

"The secret service agent." Ashley was losing his composure, and George wasn't helping.

"No. Why was he here?"

"I was hoping you could tell me that," said Ashley, who headed back down the hallway, with Sandy a few steps behind. Thinking he should investigate, George followed them.

"Wait for me," he hollered down the hall. Ashley glanced back but kept running. Sandy slowed to allow him to catch up.

"What's going on?" George asked, gasping.

"I'm not sure. Ashley saw Tom drive away fast. Fritz is nowhere to be found. Ash said there was someone in the car with Tom."

"Why is Ashley so upset?" asked George.

"Honestly, George, don't you see what's happened? If Ashley's right, Fritz has been kidnapped. And you know that Fritz has been worried about the president doing something just like this." She shook her head and resumed running, leaving George to catch up.

Another burst lit the hallway when Ashley reached my door. Then an immediate crack of thunder. He yanked the door open and looked around, hoping to find me in a corner or hiding under my desk or something. My briefcase was on the floor next to the desk, and my raincoat was draped over the back of the chair. But I was very definitely not there. Sandy opened the door and before it could close, George walked in. Both looked around.

"Is there anything that looks out of place?" asked George.

"No, nothing. Except that Fritz isn't here," replied Ashley. Ashley had no patience for George being obtuse at this point. He picked up the one book sitting on the desk, opened to the paperclip, and read.

Sandy asked, "Ashley, what are you reading? Does it tell you anything?"

"This was the book Fritz was marking in case he got through the portal. Back to see Lee. He marked the time where Lee was head of the college."

"Maybe he went home," offered George.

"Without his stuff? Not likely," Ashley roared. "Besides, he left his keys in the desk lock. So his car is in the lot."

"Maybe Linda picked him up?" George was reaching for straws; he disliked disorder. Fritz's being kidnapped more than met that definition.

"Ashley, why don't you call her and ask?" said Sandy, trying to stop more inane questions.

"Not yet. No reason to worry her. He could be anywhere in the school. But I doubt it. What I'd like to do is call the president, but I don't have his number."

"You could call the White House and ask for Lily Evans," said Sandy. "That would get you through, I think. She may not know you, but she'll know about Fritz. Tell her you're calling the president because Fritz disappeared."

Ashley thought a moment and agreed. "My phone is in my room." Replacing the book, he walked out.

Sandy said sharply to George, "Are you coming?" as she started to follow.

"Of course. I'll just take Fritz's things with me." He picked up the briefcase and the coat, locked Fritz's desk, removed the keys, and followed Sandy out.

As they were leaving my classroom, Tom was running back down the hallway. He yelled, "Don't let the door shut. Hold it open! Mr. Russell went through the portal. He's still there."

Ashley came out of his classroom, phone to his ear, and followed Tom back to my room. Sandy and George were dumbstruck, but at least George had held the door.

"What's going on?" George barked. Ignoring George, Tom went past him and into the room, straight to the desk.

"Where are the desk keys?" Tom shouted. "Quickly! That's what opens the portal!"

George resisted. He said, "How do you know that?"

His toughness uncloaked in his deep voice, Tom said, "The president figured it out. And the room is bugged. Mel heard Mr. Russell go through just now on the monitor. GIVE ME THE KEYS!!"

"Who's Mel?" hollered George.

Sandy, realizing what was happening, said, "George, give him the keys, or Fritz will be trapped."

At last, Lily Evans answered. Ashley told her that Fritz had found the portal, that one of them would call her back, that Tom was with them, and cut the signal. "Of course," Ashley said, "the key. Ben Franklin, the key, electricity. I've had that bouncing around in my head all day. And we have a thunderstorm."

Tom put the key back in the desk's lock. He turned to the others and said, "I hope that he can come back. If the key is the trigger," his gaze turned to George, "you may have cut him off."

Returning to his status as principal, George turned an angry shade of red, and said, "What do you mean, bugging my classroom! You had no right!"

Tom said, "If we hadn't, Mr. Russell would be gone forever. We still don't know if he can get back. We need to leave the classroom and wait in the hallway."

As the four of them left the room, Ashley asked Tom, "What are you doing here in the first place? Fritz has been watching black Suburbans drive by all day, and he's been worried. I thought he was getting crazy, but obviously, he was right. So, why are you here?"

Tom simply said, "The president sent me."

Ashley drew a long, deep breath to calm himself. Taking a step closer, eye to eye, he strained to remain calm but pointed. "That may be, but for what purpose? You may be a government agent, Tom, but Fritz is my best friend, and I want to know what you were planning. Because you aren't leaving here without an answer."

"Are you nuts? Are you threatening me?" asked Tom, pulling his suit jacket open and showing Ashley his pistol.

* * *

"THANK YOU, GENERAL, tea would be nice," said Fritz.

"As I said to you yesterday, Mr. Russell, I was in a position to try to stop Mr. Booth."

"Excuse me, General, 'yesterday'? I was just here."

"It was yesterday when you asked if you could visit again. What day is it in your time?"

"General, you may not believe this, but it's about five minutes since I saw you."

"I'm not sure how all this works, Mr. Russell, but it certainly raises a myriad of questions. But as I was saying, I asked two of my best officers to go up to Washington City and warn them of the attempt on Mr. Lincoln's life. Since the war was not yet completed, there were guards on all the roads entering the city. It seems Confederate officers in uniform, even with a white flag and a letter from me, were not yet welcome. Though I am not surprised, I was hoping that there might at least be an officer who would recognize the danger. I was wrong."

Lee sipped his tea and continued. "I told my men not to approach the city armed but to leave their weapons where they could retrieve them. That probably saved their lives." He sighed. "They told me they tried three different roads to get into Washington but were resisted each time. No Union officer was willing to listen. At the second entry point, my men had to escape before they were arrested. Fortunately, the Union troops were not prepared to fight. Fast horses were a value."

I listened intently and when the general finished, I said, "I have a couple of questions I would like to ask, if I may?"

"Of course," said Lee.

"After our first meeting, did anything happen that seemed unusual or unlikely to you when we left?"

Lee thought for a bit. "There were two things that struck me as most surprising. The first was on April 12, as my men surrendered their arms and our battle flags. General Grant had ordered that General Joshua Chamberlain of Maine command the surrender of arms, and when the parade of our boys began, Chamberlain ordered a salute to the surrendering army, a gesture that will remain in my heart as most noble."

I interjected, "General, do you know that Chamberlain is Governor of Maine?"

"I am aware of that and wish him the best. That reception did a great deal to lessen the hurt of defeat. The second event that surprised me concerned President Davis. I fully expected him to be shot or hanged. Although he spent two years in prison, and at first in a squalid place, public protests up north got him removed to a real prison. I think people of the North wanted the war to end, and President Davis was a continuing reminder. He was never tried for treason. You know, of course, he was a West Point graduate, and served as Senator from Mississippi. But, I..."

At that moment, there was a pop that startled us both. The portal had vanished. I went to the office door and opened it. It led to a hallway outside the General's office, not the one at school.

I turned to Lee. "General, I'm afraid that my return to my time has just disappeared. I'm not sure I'll be able to go home."

"Young man, please sit. In my years of command, I learned one thing above all. Patience. Not everything is as good or bad as it seems. If you are in fact forced to remain here, we will find a way for you to live on as best we can. But let us not be too hasty. Perhaps your portal is just taking a rest." His face crinkled. Lines abundant, eyes reassuring, Lee smiled at me.

* * *

"IT'S NOT A THREAT. The government can't just kidnap people or shoot them or whatever you were going to do," Ashley shouted, nose-to-nose with the agent.

At that, Tom smiled. "Ashley, the president figured out that the desk key was what opened the portal. He's out touring tornado country but asked me to bring Fritz to the White House to discuss a matter of urgency. I can't tell you what. But we aren't going to harm him. The president wants to ask a favor. Not something he wanted to do on the phone."

At that moment, Ashley's phone rang. He looked at the screen. It was the president. "Hello?"

"Mr. Gilbert, this is the president. I know you're concerned, but Tom is there at my request. I need very badly to speak to Mr. Russell. I know he's found the portal trigger, but I had figured out how it worked yesterday as I watched the tapes."

"Tom's here now, Mr. President, but Fritz has gone through, and we don't know if we can get him back."

"Why? What's happened?"

"George took the keys out of the desk."

"Put them back. The key opens the portal," said the president, agitated, just short of shouting.

"Tom put them back already, but nothing has happened yet. That was just a couple of minutes ago." He thought a moment. "Maybe the portal doesn't open immediately. Maybe it takes time for the different times to match up." He was talking more to himself than the president. "Mr. President, what do you want with Fritz?"

"Mr. Gilbert, I really didn't want to do this over the phone. I can't tell you the specifics, but I need to use the portal, and if he will help, it may save several lives."

"Wow," said Ashley. He and I later decided that the president had chosen to trust him with that much to show how serious he was about protecting us and about getting me back.

* * *

"GENERAL, PLEASE excuse me, but right now, I'm a bit distraught. No one but me knows how the portal works, and no one knows that I have come here." Standing up, I scanned the room. I was struck at how bare his office was. A large credenza behind him, a closed cabinet and papers spread on the table. No decorations, no memorabilia.

"Mr. Russell, if the portal returns, then you must leave immediately, but perhaps you might visit again, and maybe," Lee hesitated and finished with a tone of hopeful anticipation, "take me back with you. I would so like to see one of your automobiles."

I smiled at him. "General, I don't know if that's possible. But if it is, I would be most happy to show you whatever you would like to see." We both sat quietly, nervously waiting for something, anything, to happen. Before I could take another sip of tea, the portal reappeared.

"Goodbye, General, until we meet again," I said, reaching to shake Lee's hand.

The general took my hand and said, "Godspeed, young man" as I returned through the portal.

* * *

WHILE ASHLEY WAS SPEAKING to the president, I returned through the classroom door.

"He just came back, Mr. President."

"Would you put him on, please, Mr. Gilbert?"

"Welcome back, dude," said Ashley, exhaling heavily. "The president wants to speak to you."

I was trying to get my bearings. I was back, but I didn't know why they were all in the hall, why Tom was there, why the president was on the phone. I took the phone from Ashley, and said, "Hello, Mr. President." I was still a bit disoriented as I looked at the others, wondering what was happening.

The president said, "Fritz, I didn't want this to be this way. I'd hoped to explain in person. But I need to ask a favor. It might be dangerous, but you could perhaps save several lives. Last night, our ambassador in Eledoria was captured and taken to a house as a prisoner. His family is in their own residence, but also under guard by kidnappers. We know where they are, but we can't get to them. If we could use your portal…" He hesitated, I think to let me absorb what he was asking. "We have maps in detail, and Tom has the best shot in the service with him. If we could use the portal, we can rescue them without anyone knowing how we did it. Will you help?"

"Mr. President, what makes you think it will work?"

"I don't know that it will, but we do know that they will kill him and his family, as a political statement. His children are eight and ten. I have to try." Thunder rumbled.

"This is all so confusing, but, yes, of course. What do you want me to do?"

"Tom has the maps. Would you put him on, and I'll tell him what to do?" I handed the phone to Tom, who walked down the hall listening to the president's instructions. He told the president he had received a distressed message from Mr. Koppler. "Mr. President, I'll tell you about it later. You won't be happy." He handed the phone back to me, headed to the Suburban, and motioned to his companion to come in.

The president said, "All you need to do is set up the paperclips on the maps. First, get the family. Then, get the ambassador. Once they are safely in the school, Tom will bring them back to Washington. You know that trip already."

I shook my head, not believing what was going on around me. "Mr. President, no promises, but I'll try. This is all new to me. Do you want to hold on?"

"I do, but it's better if you call me back when you've tried it. Okay?"

"Okay. Talk to you shortly." I handed the phone back to Ashley, as Tom and Mel joined us.

"Good to go?" asked Tom. I nodded and led them into the classroom. Tom handed me the maps. Moving the book off the desk, I looked closely at the locations for the extractions. I took out a paperclip, fit it so it touched the room they were trying to reach, and set the map on the desk. "What now?"

"OK. We all need to leave the classroom," Tom said. "It would be best if you three," speaking to Ashley, Sandy, and George, "were hidden somewhere. If this goes well, we'll be back in a matter of seconds. If not, there could be some shooting. I have no idea what will happen. I just don't want you in the line of fire."

Sandy understood, grabbed George's arm, took hold of Ashley's shirt, and pulled them to her classroom. With everyone out, I grabbed the doorknob, nodded affirmatively to Tom, and opened the door. Tom entered first, with Mel right behind. I held the door open for a second as the scene changed. Tom motioned to close the door. I couldn't see anything through the window. After only a couple of minutes, just as I was stepping back down the hall, the door opened quickly. Two barefooted children, a boy and a girl, both in pajamas, and a dark-haired woman walked into the hall, followed by Tom. Mel arrived moments later with a duffel bag.

"It worked," said Tom. He told the ambassador's confused family that they were safe and that he would explain everything shortly. Speaking in staccato, he quickly introduced me and walked them to Sandy's classroom. Returning to my classroom, he placed the map of the ambassador's location on my desk.

"Do you know where he is?" I asked.

"We think he's here," he pointed. "The upper rooms. But we're not positive." I placed the paperclip. "Mr. Russell, this may take a little longer. And it might get hot. So stay away from the door." Both agents removed pistols with silencers attached. "Ready, let's go."

I got my friendly shock and opened the door. Across the hall, voices came from Sandy's class. I walked to the entry, and Ashley came over. The ambassador's wife was holding her children. Sandy and George were kneeling with them.

"What's happening?" he asked.

"They're in the portal," With a lowered voice, I said, "they think this will be harder, maybe gunfire." Pointing to the family, I asked, "How are they taking this?" Lightning flashed again.

"Not sure. They're confused; who could blame them. But they'll be all right. They don't know they're in New Jersey yet."

Suddenly, three bent figures ran from my classroom. Gunfire exploded behind them. Tom turned and pushed the door closed. I noticed blood on Tom's pants leg.

"Are you hit?" I asked.

"Yes, but it's not bad, I don't think. I need to call the president."

The president answered instantly. Tom told him they had been successful. He handed the phone to me, as the ambassador looked at his surroundings, confused.

"Yes, Mr. President."

"Fritz, I can't thank you enough. This is significant, but we can't let anyone know. We have to keep the ambassador hidden for a couple of days to keep you safe. No one can know. I'm not even sure we should tell them they just walked into New Jersey. You'll tell the others?"

"Sure, Mr. President. Will you tell me how this all happened?"

"I will, but not now. We need to get everything settled first. Thank you again."

"Mr. President, Tom's been shot. Should I take him to a hospital?"

"Let me speak to him." I handed the phone back to Tom.

"Yes, sir. It's not bad, sir," he said in response to the president's question. "I'll dress it here and get it looked at when we get back. Yes, sir. I will. Talk to you in a couple of hours." Tom put the phone back in his pocket.

"We need to leave quickly, Mr. Russell. I'm sure the president will be in touch soon." The two agents and the ambassador walked across the hall, gathered the family, and hurried to the Suburban.

Back in my classroom, Ashley hugged me. No one really knew what to say.

"Are you all okay?" I asked. "I need a drink."

Ashley, Sandy, and George all said they were fine. Ashley explained what had happened when he thought I had been kidnapped. Then he asked, "Where did you go?"

"I had tea with Robert E. Lee."

Epilogue

WITH A PHONE to his ear, he said, "I don't care what it costs. The result will be worth it many times over. We need to mix in the Arabs, so try the Eledorians. They're already suspects. You know the rest. Get them ready. We'll know when the time is right. And this time, get it done."

* * *

I WAS HAPPY to get home that day with more stories for Linda. Ashley and Sandy came for dinner. The president had called to thank me again, and explained how he had figured out the puzzle of the portal. He had played the tapes of my desk a dozen times, he said. Frame by frame, he finally saw the lock on the drawer. The key. Ben Franklin. He said the realization was so clear to him, such an obvious clue, he wasn't surprised we'd found it ourselves so soon after he had. "Fritz, between us, I'd love to talk to you about places we could go together."

* * *

THE BOOK, COFFEE table-sized, sat on his lap. Sandy had gone home after their long day. In gold embossed letters, *UNPRE-DICTABLE* blazed at him. His hands covering his face, his shoulders shuddering in secret wracking anguish that no one shared, Ashley again closed his high school yearbook.

* * *

THE SCHOOL YEAR ended, and the seniors heard a commencement address by the president of the United States. The McAllisters, Sandy and Ashley, and Linda and I were all guests of the president for a weekend at Camp David, where we met and spoke with the ambassador and his wife. During the summer, the president announced the retirement of Jim Koppler after a long and illustrious career in service to our country.

Summer vacation kept us busy. We went to the ballpark and "down the shore." Linda watched the Tour de France in July, her All-Star game.

As the riders sped downhill, I remembered our first meeting, accidental. And almost an accident. Standing on Fifth Avenue, all I saw were two wheels aimed straight for me. She swerved and missed. Not enough time for more than a quick glance at her face. She smiled and kept pedaling.

When we met at a party later, she said she remembered my face. I had a different look on it then, she said. Panic, she recalled, chuckling.

I asked her if she wanted to grab a cup of coffee. She smiled again. And said yes. She told me about her love of bike racing and that she worked as an editor and also part-time at *Bicycle Habitat* in SoHo. She wanted to own a bike shop business, a chain or a franchise. But before she did, she wanted to get her MBA. Now, I don't really believe in this stuff, but by the time the evening ended, I felt like I'd known her forever. I'd never enjoyed coffee more.

"Fritz, I need to get riding again. I miss it so much."

Before the summer ended, we spent one weekend on Long Beach Island with Ashley. At dinner, we discussed the role the portal played at the end of the year. In the sun, with the waves providing sound effects, I listed what we had discovered. The portal opened with a combination of thunderstorm, my desk key in the lock, paperclips pointing to a location, and a shock on the doorknob. We found that time traveled at different speeds. I still wondered if we were going back or if the portal transported the past to the present? And more than anything, we needed to determine if we were affecting the future by using the portal. My bruised face had finally returned to normal. I joined Linda and Ashley with a scar of my own. Not as long as Linda's, nor as dramatic as Ashley's, I bragged that mine was much older. We had learned that the portal was dangerous, and we all had questions as yet unanswered. I couldn't get over an eighty-year-old photo of my feet.

"Do you think the kids were changed because we went through?" asked Ash.

"I don't know, but maybe we'll know more in the fall."

Linda said, "Then I hope we have perfect weather, every day for the next ten years."

ONE AUGUST AFTERNOON, past the heat of the day, I went to the backyard. Linda was harvesting tomatoes. I took two from her, intending to slice them and with a little salt and pepper, cure my rumbling stomach until dinner. I showed her the file folder I had brought out.

"What is it?"

"My book. Well, a couple of chapters anyway."

"That's great. Let me pick some peppers, and I'll read it."

We were again invited to the White House for dinner, this time as special guests, but none of the other guests knew why. And to add to the summer's events, I got the scare of my life.

"Fritz, I spoke to Dr. Rosenblatt a few minutes ago."

"Is everything okay?"

"Fritz, he said he found something growing." Her not looking me in the eye sent a shiver through me.

"Lin, I'm here no matter, I promise. Did he say what he thought it was?"

"He did." She hesitated. I held my breath. "Fritz, you're going to be a father." Then, her eyes sought mine, and I realized they put the sky to shame.

That summer ended, as all summers do. Vacation was over, and another school year was about to begin. On the night before classes started, Linda and I sat together on the sofa in our family room, watching the local news and weather. As the local weatherman was predicting a 70% chance of thunderstorms, my phone rang.

Looking at Linda, I answered. "Hello, Mr. President."

A Last Request

Dear Reader,

If you have finished this book, and enjoyed the story, I have a request. Each writer wants, perhaps needs, to know that their effort has been worthwhile. Only you, the reader, can decide that. So, I'm asking you to tell the world what you think. Please leave a review, on Amazon, on Goodreads, or any social media site you choose. All writers will thank you. Certainly, I will and do.

Michael R. Stern

Sneak Peek

Continue reading an excerpt from **SAND STORM,**
  book two of the Quantum Touch series.

Chapter One

"**YOU'RE TELLING ME** the world is a dangerous place? Me?" The man's patrician arrogance stormed the phone. "You've continued to do what you want because the world remains a dangerous place." Standing at his window, the Washington Monument as a backdrop, he scoffed at the little people below, scurrying from place to place. *As if they were important.* "We need to proceed carefully," he said in a calmer tone. "Not knowing what they know, we can't allow what *we* know to make us careless."

The man sat down behind the mahogany desk in his elegantly decorated office. Photographs of himself with the power elite of a generation covered the walls. Gray-haired, immaculately attired in a Savile Row gray pinstripe, he kicked off his shoes. The calfskin loafers breathed while his toes caressed the plush carpet.

He switched the phone to his other ear. "I don't care what it costs. The result will be worth it many times over. We need to mix in the Arabs, so try the Eledorians. They're already suspects. You know the rest. Get them ready. We'll know when the time is right."

AT FOUR THIRTY, two black Suburbans pulled up in front of the Russell house. Fritz had been watching and walked outside to meet the president. More people than he had expected climbed from the cars. The First Lady had come along, as she had in the spring. The president introduced the others. Fritz said hello to Tom Andrews, head of the president's Secret Service detail and agent James Williams and then spotted Mel Zack, still in the driver's seat of the second Suburban.

The president said, "Tom is taking the team to The Mill to get security set up for when we go to dinner. They'll be back later." Overwhelmed in more than numbers alone, Fritz refused to let the intimidating company dictate whatever his decision needed to be.

An attractive young woman with a mischievous look examined Ashley's car. "Nice ride," said the president. "Ash's baby?" Fritz nodded.

Fritz's wife, Linda, and his friend and fellow teacher, Ashley Gilbert, stepped out on the landing. Ashley stared, then coughed and cleared his throat when introduced to Dr. Jane Barclay from the Department of Homeland Security.

"Uh oh," Fritz whispered to Linda.

"Yup," she whispered back.

FRITZ INVITED his visitors into the family room. Late afternoon sun reflected off the flat screen TV on the wall. Ashley brought extra chairs from the dining room and claimed a seat where he would be able to keep an eye on Jane Barclay. His place secure, he went to help Linda bring in the food.

While the others found seats, Fritz and the president pulled two of the dining room chairs to the middle of the room, facing each other. "Fritz, I've brought some of the people who are most involved in protecting the country," the president said. "They know what you did last spring. They also know about the portal. This meeting is top secret, of course."

Fritz nodded to each of the president's advisers. "What is it that you have in mind?"

The president said, "You mean, what do I want?"

"I was trying to be polite, but yeah, what do you want from me this time?"

"Fritz, the Narians have completed their nuclear project. Forget what they say, it's a weapons program. I'm talking about an imminent nuclear threat, and they're in the starting gate. Israel is weighing its options. We're doing everything we can to hold the Israelis back, but I don't know how much longer."

"What do you want me to do?"

"Fritz, we," he swept his hand toward his advisers, "have discussed possible scenarios where your help might be, well, helpful. I know you're hesitant, but no one else can unlock travel across time and space. No one else can open the portal. I want to fill you in on our analysis and to talk with you about how much and what kinds of things you would be willing to do."

"Mr. President, as I said last night, I'm a teacher. I love what I do, and I like working with the kids." With an abrupt jolt, he absorbed a new reality: his boredom with teaching had evaporated. "If I can help, you know I will. But I still don't know all the things about the portal that might make a difference. We both know how it opens, but beyond that, I don't know what the consequences of using it might be."

Linda spoke up. "Mr. President, I'm afraid that using the portal might have a negative effect on all of us. It's not that I don't want Fritz to help, but I don't want him in danger. Or changing history. Or the future." She placed a hand on her growing belly.

"Linda, that's why we came. We think it's important, but we still want your input, and we wanted to meet in a less intimidating place than the White House."

"Mr. President," said Fritz. "Tell us what you think you'll need."

"We've been considering some of the world's hot spots. I'm sure you know that the situation in Eledoria is still unresolved. It's quiet right now, but..." Fritz nodded.

The CIA director said, "Mr. Russell, we have people on the ground who have infiltrated Narian research centers and given us key locations. In addition to our not wanting the Narians to get the bomb, we are concerned that nuclear material will find its way to market. We need to stop them before it does. If the Israelis move soon, we may lose the ability to control this thing."

"In other words," said the president, "we can't openly attack, and we don't want Israel to do it. That could mean warfare throughout the Middle East, or worse. No one will win that fight."

"So let me get this straight," said Fritz. "You need the portal so you can blow up the Narian bomb program?"

The secretary of defense said, "It's more than that. Before we can destroy the facilities, we need to extract computers and confiscate the research they've completed. We want the program crippled well into the future."

Fritz looked at the president. "At least you have something easy for me." He sighed and looked at his wife.

Linda asked, "Are you bringing any radioactive material into the school?"

"No," said the president. "There's far too much. We'll leave it. We want to incapacitate the facilities, make them toxic, unable to be rebuilt."

Fritz asked, "And you know exactly where? I assume it's underground."

"We hope we have all the locations."

"You want me to help you do all this. Are you nuts?" Around him, his visitors sounded like a chorus of straws at the bottom of a finished milkshake, shocked he would speak like that to the president. As he scanned their faces, he questioned if any of them had ever been asked to do anything as difficult.

The president ignored the gasps, and rather than anger him, Fritz's comment amused him. He said, "I've been called worse. Yes, Fritz, not only do I want your help, but I think we need it. And obviously we're going to need the school. There's an eight-and-a-half-hour time difference, so we should be able to accomplish everything while school is out."

"When are you thinking of doing this?" Linda asked.

"Within the next couple of weeks. We don't have much of a window."

"So all I need to do is put the paperclips in place or take your already paper-clipped papers and open the door?" Fritz asked.

"That's it," said the president. "If this works, I don't think I need to tell you how much trouble you will have prevented."

"And lives I can save. Yeah, I think I've heard that before," said Fritz. "What else do you want me to do?"

Dr. Barclay said, "If I may, Mr. President—Mr. Russell, there's nothing specific at this point. But you know what kinds of things might crop up. In addition to the nuclear issue, for example, we've detected an increase in internet noise. If we obtain actionable intelligence in places we can't easily reach, you could help us."

Fritz looked at Linda and then at Ashley. Ashley looked attentive, but Fritz had seen that look before. Ashley had a new woman on his radar. "It seems you've spent some time thinking about this, Mr. President."

"We have. Once you stumbled into my office, it didn't take long for any of us to understand where things might go. In the past few months, the portal has excited and scared me. I'm sure you know what I mean. Time travel, immediate access to the past and more valuable, the present, has created an opportunity. Fritz, I've hoped you'd accept this chance to do good. I made a pledge to make the world a safer place when I first took office. I may have nothing to do with it directly, and we can never say anything about how things get done, but who gets the credit doesn't matter if the result is a good one, does it?" A tight jaw and deepened crevices across his forehead replaced his calm demeanor. "Fritz, this isn't about my legacy or politics. But it is about my family and yours. Lots of families."

Fritz said, "It's a good thing this isn't our first date. You sure ask a lot. Well, at least I get dinner." Everyone laughed, but the only real ones came from the president and Fritz. Still, Fritz's insides were doing jumping jacks.

The president turned to Linda, whose scowl told him just how much she disliked the direction of the conversation. "Linda, I wouldn't ask if we didn't think we faced an emergency. All I need is for Fritz to open it and then stand back. I suppose George could end up being the biggest problem, but I will deal with that. We could commandeer the school, but that would be a tad too public. So I just have to sell him on the importance. I'm sure he will agree."

"Mr. President, pardon me, but who's George?" asked Dr. Barclay.

Ashley responded quickly. "He's the principal at Riverboro High School. Our commander-in-chief." His eyes twinkled.

Fritz said, "He'll do it for some kind of quid pro quo. That's how George operates. So, have you got any *other* surprises?"

The president said, "We've discussed a possible intervention in a hijacking or even a problem on the space station. We would have to be exact with the coordinates or the portal would open in thin air, literally. Or no air. But we don't need to talk about that now." The president paused. "Fritz, none of this conversation matters unless you're willing to be part of the team." Fritz sat up and took a deep breath, tilted his head, and met the president's eyes. "Sorry," said the president. "Sometimes I get too rah-rah. I know I don't need to do that with you. I'll save it for George."

Linda said, "And you only want him to open the portal?"

"Linda, the only other thing we would ask is that Fritz works with the commanders or leaders of the projects so we can co-ordinate details. If the paperclips are in the wrong places, we could have a mess on our hands. And our guys have to know how to get out."

"So you need a dry run into a safe area first?" Linda asked, hoping they had thought of it.

"If we use the portal, we'll be going into harm's way, no matter where. It has to be done right. But I'm not asking Fritz to go in. Just to help set it up."

"Mr. President, I think you know that you've made a compelling case. My concern is how the portal gets used, because we will be changing the future's history. So far, the portal reaches backward in time and to other places at the same moment as when I walk through the portal, but who knows what damage we would do to events, or people, fifty or a hundred years from now."

The president rested his chin on his left hand, brushed his lips with his index finger, and considered the serious man watching him. He had spent countless hours analyzing this concept. Does time travel change the future? Neither quick to answer nor glib in his chosen words, his answer would affect more than just his present audience. "Fritz, I've thought about that too. But consider this. What if, instead of damage, we improve the lives, the possibilities for people fifty or a hundred years from now? For those children you teach, for your new child? We can't guess which will happen, bad or good."

Fritz listened with an ear tuned to politician-speak, processed the thoughtful answer, and glanced at Linda. Her almost imperceptible nod told him to keep going. "Mr. President, you mentioned guidelines last night. As you know, school began today. I haven't had a lot of time to think about this. I want to talk this over with Linda before I give you an answer. But you need to know that under no circumstances will I participate in activities that are obviously partisan or that are intended to kill people. I'll want a full briefing on any mission you want me to be involved in. And I am really worried about how many people will have to know. When we got involved, when you first came here, you said national security concerned you, not just the dangers to you and to me. The numbers are growing." He waved both hands toward the other people in the room.

"Fritz, we came to address any questions or objections you might have," said the president. "I expected you to speak to Linda privately, and I don't want you to make a decision right now if you feel pressured. But I do need to know soon. I've told you what our situation is. And it *is* important. You need to decide for yourselves if it's important enough." He looked at Linda and back to Fritz.

"About your guidelines, you haven't asked anything unreasonable. As far as other people being involved, the portal has the highest level of security clearance. You'd be stunned at how seriously even the ambassador's children have been about keeping quiet. They tell their friends how cool the rescue helicopter ride was. Everyone will be sworn to secrecy. No written documents and no digital accounts of the portal's existence are permitted. I don't think there will be any leaks as long as we use it properly, but even if there are, who would believe it? It would just sound like a headline from the gutter press. You have a code name, by the way."

"Can you tell me what it is?"

"Sure." The president offered a gentle smile. "Friend."

"Mr. President, thank you for respecting my position and our," he glanced at Linda and Ashley, "intelligence. I want my help to mean something more than an easy way to make war. I'm a teacher, I study history, and I've seen politics too often erase the good that government is supposed to do." He met the president eye to eye. "I'll have an answer for you soon."

The president leaned forward, and Fritz could almost feel his brain signaling. "Fritz, we both know the portal is important. We've had this conversation before. So, thanks. How about we go have dinner?"

A RIVERBORO police cruiser stopped at the sight of the Suburbans and the group of agents milling around. The officer got out and opened his mouth wide when he recognized the man walking toward him. The president offered his hand. "Officer, this is a matter of security. You cannot mention this. If you need to report something, just say you checked and everything was fine. That way, it won't be necessary for us to be involved. Can you do that?"

"Yes, sir. No problem, sir. Sorry, sir."

"Thank you. Perhaps you might do one more thing for me." The president didn't wait for a response. "We will load up now and proceed to a pub called The Mill. Are you familiar with it?"

"Yes, sir."

"Do you think you could lead us there, take the point? No siren, no lights?"

"Sure, it's only about five minutes from here, Mr. President. No problem."

"What's your name, officer?"

"Jim Shaw, sir."

"Good. Mr. Williams will give you more details. Thank you."

While the president finished his conversation, Fritz and Tom Andrews stood by the waiting Suburbans. "Mr. President, Linda, Ashley and I will take my car and follow you. We'll have a chance to talk en route. You've put me in a difficult position."

The president said, "You should be in my shoes." They happily shared the joke, each knowing the other used the phrase often. The others left the house, and when Linda saw James, she greeted him with a hug.

"James! It's nice to see you again. Has your wife tried the lasagna recipe?"

"Hi, ma'am, sorry I mean Linda. Yes, we've had it a couple of times. She knows how much I like it."

The Suburbans' doors were open and waiting. Officer Shaw stood at the driver's side of the police cruiser. Fritz signaled Ashley, took Linda's arm, and headed to his car. He backed out of the driveway, and the procession pulled away.

Fritz said, "What do you think?"

Ashley spoke first. "I'd rather go see Robert E. Lee."

Linda said, "Fritz, I already know you're going to say it's okay. And you already know how I feel." She glared at him. "I hope he keeps his promise, and your part will be really limited."

"We needed to hear him out. He knows that I'll stop him if he goes too far," Fritz said. "But unless you say absolutely not, I'll tell him I'm in. His real problem will be George. If the school is the staging point for this stuff, George could be a pain."

Ashley leaned forward and asked, "Can I say something? When you told me the president would be coming tonight, I wondered what he would say. I didn't think he'd be so blunt. But they haven't figured it all out yet."

"Speaking of figuring things out, how did things go with Sandy today?" Linda asked.

Fritz said, "He's burning bridges faster than the Germans blew up the ones crossing the Rhine."

"Shut up. Let me tell it. Before we broke up, I told her I didn't think it was time yet to meet her parents. They're here this weekend. She's ignoring me."

"And if you've broken up, what difference does that make? It sounds to me like you don't see this relationship as completely over." Linda's hands rested on her hips, even as she sat. "Ashley, *you are too old* to play games, and Sandy isn't going to let you. You're not serious and never saw her as long term."

"At least I was up front with her."

"Ash, she's twenty-five years old and she wants to get married and have a family. She's attractive. She's smart, and she's not going to waste her time. So if you want her to stick around, it's up to you to decide what *you* want. I guess I'll have to get used to cooking for you again." Then she told him their welcome sign always applied to him.

"We can't think about that now. I want to know if you've figured out what this Narian business is going to mean. I haven't got much of a clue."

"Neither have I, Ash," said Fritz. "Underground? Nuclear facilities? What else do we need to worry about?"

"What about the weather?" Ashley asked.

"We'll have to ask at dinner. If they want to do this soon, we better hope we have some thunderstorms soon."

"Maybe they've figured something out. Tell you what. I'll sit with Dr. Barclay and talk with her about the weather." Fritz saw the Cheshire Cat in the rearview.

"Lively dinner conversation, Ash. You'll thrill her, I'm sure," Fritz said.

Linda said, "Weather, huh. Somehow, I'm not surprised. Hot air is your field of expertise."

"That's a different story," said Ashley.

Lightning Source UK Ltd.
Milton Keynes UK
UKHW011315260221
379413UK00010B/580/J